MW00528706

THE COMPANY SHE KEEPS

JAMES WOOLF

Copyright © 2024 James Woolf

The right of James Woolf to be identified as the Author of the Work has been
asserted by him in accordance with the Copyright, Designs and Patents Act 1988.

First published in 2024 by Bloodhound Books.

Apart from any use permitted under UK copyright law, this publication may only
be reproduced, stored, or transmitted, in any form, or by any means, with prior
permission in writing of the publisher or, in the case of reprographic production,
in accordance with the terms of licences issued by the Copyright Licensing
Agency.
All characters in this publication are fictitious and any resemblance to real
persons, living or dead, is purely coincidental.

www.bloodhoundbooks.com

Print ISBN: 978-1-917214-03-2

For Zara and Ruby

PROLOGUE
13 JULY 1961

Rebecca is unsure whether to tell her father about the boy on the bus who just asked her out. She's so excited, she'll surely have to tell someone. But she doesn't want to jinx it, or for her father to puncture the moment. Not that he'd do that deliberately. He might tell her not to count her chickens or say these things have a habit of not working out. On the other hand, she so loves chatting to him these days.

The house is silent when she unlocks the door. Rebecca knows her mother will be working at the furniture store and Eileen and Roland still at school. She goes straight into the front room where her father often sits reading. It is empty. She calls out to him. She definitely needs to tell him about the advert for the government trainee hairdressing scheme. He cuts all three of their hair so neatly, this is surely the course for him. Though to be fair, Roland's complaints of looking like a pudding basin are usually justified. Her father could be out shopping, though he hates shopping. Or maybe he's visiting his father.

She looks into the dining room, then shouts up the stairs. There is no answer. He's not having a nap in bed and there's no one in the bathroom. He is a habitual mender of broken objects, and it occurs to Rebecca that he must be in the garage engaged in some tedious task. She goes back downstairs and through to the tiny back garden and, sure enough, the garage door is unlocked. There's a bulb switched on somewhere, but it is still murky inside. He must be on the stepladder, as he's pretty high up when he turns towards her to say hello. A shaft of light from the door catches his face and she begins to tell him what a great day she's had, but he keeps turning until she sees the back of his head which is balding, and, very slowly, he comes round a second time and, as her eyes adjust to the light, only now does she see the rope, thick, sturdy – probably brand new.

CHAPTER ONE

6 APRIL 1979

It is a Friday morning and Rebecca is driving north to Harrogate. Despite being fairly close to Leeds, it's not a journey she makes often. But Pamela has been trying to arrange this weekend away since she telephoned Rebecca out of the blue, and Rebecca's looking forward to some decent food, a bit of banter, and plenty of wine, of course.

There is a delay caused by roadworks. A man in overalls comes right up to the driver's side window and peers inside, grinning inanely through his beard at Rebecca before moving on to chat to a fellow workman. Rebecca watches the way they effortlessly joke with each other, then she switches on the radio, thinking she might catch *The Golden Hour*. She is quickly drawn into a local news report about a bus driver, Ronald Marwood. Yesterday morning, he was driving the first service of the day in Halifax and saw what he thought was a bundle of rags in the park.

"And now we've got Jean Markham on the line," the presenter says. "Tell us what you saw, Jean."

"Well, I was waiting for the bus–"

"This was on Savile Park Road, yes?"

"Yes, Savile Park Road, it was early–"

"Six thirty, wasn't it?"

"About then, and I looked across the road and I thought it was a bundle of rags too. But then I saw a shoe nearby."

"A shoe, did you say? And what happened next?" the presenter asks.

"Well, I went across the road. And I was about to pick up the shoe, you see, but then I saw the rags weren't rags at all, but a person. It was a young lady. I went up to her and, well, she was clearly dead..." The voice of Jean Markham has started to tremble.

"Go on, Jean."

"Well, I ran back home to call the police."

The traffic is moving again though Rebecca barely registers this fact. She is finishing the news story in her head. It's leading to the inevitable outcome that she doesn't wish to hear, but she also finds herself unable to switch the radio off.

It hadn't taken long to identify the victim of the crime, the presenter continues. A thirteen-year-old paperboy was crossing the playing fields, saw the police activity and recognised the same shoe seen earlier by Jean Markham as one belonging to his sister. He'd sprinted home to his mother and stepfather and after checking her bedroom and finding it empty, they'd informed the police.

"And last night we had confirmation of the distressing news," the presenter says, although he himself doesn't sound distressed at all. "After lying low for three hundred and twenty-two days, the Yorkshire Ripper has struck again." The latest victim, the police had notified the public, was Josephine Whitaker, "An innocent nineteen-year-old building society clerk."

Rebecca switches off the radio. This one was Halifax, but most of the murders have been in Leeds. She thinks about her sister Eileen, walking back to her flat late at night. Rebecca knows Eileen does this, whereas she travels almost everywhere by car. Perhaps she should offer Eileen lifts home wherever and whenever she needs them, or even buy her a car. She certainly can't count on Dan to look out for her. She'd met her sister's latest layabout when she babysat a few nights ago. She didn't like the lewd jokes Dan made in front of the twins, before he and Eileen set off to get hammered in the pub. They weren't appropriate for kids who'd barely turned ten. It was sweet how Archie and Lindsay later lined up their dolls, puppets and other figures for "an identity parade". Where did they learn about that?

Rebecca approaches the Majestic hotel on the Ripon Road. What makes the police so sure that the same man has struck again? There is information being withheld. She knows this is standard procedure in murder cases. Censuring herself for the thought even as it occurs, Rebecca realises that she'd like to know the details of whatever they're holding back.

CHAPTER TWO

6 APRIL 1979

Rebecca and Pamela had first met soon after Pamela's family moved to Leeds in 1961. On Pamela's first morning at Roundhay High School, the sixth form were informed that something terrible had happened in the Ferguson family during the summer and that they were not to ask Rebecca about it. Later, another girl told Pamela precisely how Rebecca's dad had "topped himself" in their garage. Within weeks, Pamela and Rebecca had become firm friends.

The two women embrace in front of the Majestic Hotel reception desk. Although Rebecca is still thinking about the news on the radio, she tells Pamela that they're going to have a ball. One or two minutes are spent cooing over the opulence of the grand lobby before they check into their rooms. Later that afternoon, they're sitting in Bettys Tea Rooms. They admire the rows of delicious-looking jam on the dark panelled shelving and agree how terrific it is to be in contact once again.

"It was nobody's fault we lost touch when you moved to Nottingham," Rebecca says, looking through the huge window into a small park over the road. "Except you never did give me your new phone number," she adds, raising her eyebrows quizzically.

"I know. And I kept meaning to, so I was to blame."

"Maybe..."

"But Davina wouldn't have welcomed another woman ringing me at home."

"Like that, was it?"

Pamela nods, smiles grimly. A young man with a military haircut delivers teas and cakes to their table, bowing slightly before departing. Rebecca looks back across the road to the park.

"Awful news this morning, wasn't it?"

"Terrible – absolutely terrible," Pamela agrees, eyeing her cake. "And just nineteen."

"This time a building society clerk. A bit of variety," Rebecca continues.

"I'm not used to this," Pamela says. "We didn't have mass murderers rampaging in Nottingham. This date and walnut cake looks very good."

"I wouldn't say anyone is exactly used to it."

"You know what I mean. This is the first since I've been back here. I seriously considered whether I should take this job. But I thought, 'You can't let that put you off, Pamela'. Don't you worry about that maniac on the loose?"

"You have to have that attitude," Rebecca says. "But we're all a lot more wary. If I'm meeting someone, I'll make sure it's somewhere busy."

"Me too, damn sure." Pamela finally takes a huge bite from her slab of cake. A full thirty seconds later, "And I'm really careful around my car. Before I left this morning, you'd have thought I was checking for an IRA bomb or something."

They laugh, drink tea.

"He tends to strike in the dead of night, not first thing in the morning," Rebecca points out. "I do worry about Eileen though.

I even wonder what will happen when Lindsay grows up and starts seeing her first boyfriend."

"Oh come on, they've got hundreds working on this. Surely it's only a matter of time before they catch him."

"The police aren't exactly covering themselves in glory. There are some serious management failures if you ask me."

"Talking of the police, how's Simon?"

"Simon? He's fine, I would say."

Pamela is checking her face with a small hand mirror. "You would say?"

"I don't see that much of him. For various reasons."

"And what might they be?"

Rebecca had always enjoyed her friend's bluntness. Similar to her in that respect. "Well, I'm obviously very busy. And he's obviously very married."

"I didn't know that."

"We meet for rather short periods of time that consist of rather extended sessions of you-know-what. It's very problematic."

"So, to sum up," Pamela laughs, "you're probably the most successful businesswoman in Leeds. You have an amazing house, just off Roundhay Park. You've got a no-commitment relationship with a super handsome copper that consists of sex and little else. I think you might just have the perfect life."

CHAPTER THREE

6 APRIL 1979

"In actual fact," Rebecca says at dinner that evening in the hotel (after a bottle and three-quarters of a very decent Chablis), "I don't have a perfect life at all. And what you said earlier shows you don't know me as well as you think."

Pamela waits for their dessert plates and cutlery to be cleared before replying. "So, tell me more."

"When you were trying to contact me in January, or maybe February, you didn't hear back because I was depressed. I'm being serious. Depressed."

"That doesn't sound much like you."

"Perhaps not."

Pamela drains her glass, narrows her eyes, clearly hoping for elucidation.

Rebecca says that she'll explain as best she can, although even now it doesn't make that much sense. At the end of January, she won a business award, an industry thing, not for the first time, as it happens. And remember what the weather was like at that time? The same night she'd been presented her award, she'd arrived home but instead of going inside to make a hot drink, she remained outside.

"There's something about the beauty of a thick late-night snow fall, isn't there? But as I watched it, I experienced a crippling sense of helplessness. Which turned into a proper episode of depression."

"That sounds really bad," Pamela says vaguely.

Yes, Rebecca replies, the next day she couldn't get out of bed until midday, and then when she did, she walked compulsively to a bridge overlooking a busy road. She'd obviously looked in a state as a woman with a dog had asked if she was okay and had then accompanied her off the bridge. After this episode, she saw her GP who referred her to a psychoanalyst.

"I'm very cut off from my feelings, apparently. I tend to intellectualise everything and am not developing intimate bonds with those around me."

"Uh-huh," Pamela says, nodding.

"You're meant to disagree! In fact, I used you as an example. 'What about Pamela?' I said. 'We've been friends since we were sixteen'."

"Except we haven't, technically."

"I glossed over the nine-year break. And by the way, an on-off fling with a married policeman is typical of relationships people with my 'attachment patterns' form. It's getting rather hot in here. Do you fancy a walk?"

Pamela looks hesitant.

"For Christ's sake," Rebecca says. "There are two of us and it's a Friday night."

They go as they are, without coats, noticing immediately the drop in temperature. It will be okay, Pamela says. The alcohol they've consumed will provide extra insulation.

Rebecca talks about her father's funeral, how as a teenager she'd resolved not to let his death destroy her. And generally, she'd been doing pretty well. Until January.

"I suppose, because I wasn't at the school at that time," Pamela says, "I never really knew much about that. About your father, I mean."

"There isn't much to know. He didn't have a job. It became too much for him."

"He once worked for Tetley's, didn't he?"

An imposing three-storey mansion, with bay windows and a traverse arch above its doorway, looms on their left-hand side.

"Tetley's, yes. I must have spent two sessions talking about Tetley's, so I'd rather not get into that right now."

"What's it like being in therapy?" Pamela asks.

"So, everything has meaning." They continue walking for a while without speaking. "You see, notice that silence? Silence has all sorts of meaning."

A few moments later, Rebecca's shoe comes off on the corner of Cheltenham Road; she sits on a bench, laughing as she puts it back on.

"Even this has meaning. Me losing my shoe."

"I agree," Pamela says. "Had you been wearing a sensible pair, it wouldn't have happened."

"Excuse me, these shoes are perfectly sensible."

"They're too high. And you're always in trouser suits too. You need to learn to relax, woman!"

Rebecca only half hears this last riposte. Her mind has lurched back to Josephine Whitaker losing her shoe a couple of nights before in Halifax under very different circumstances.

"I'm not saying you're uptight, because you're certainly not that," Pamela continues. "But you could do with dressing down a bit. If you want to find a decent guy to commit to, that is. From what you were saying earlier, I think you do."

"Is that a fact?" Rebecca pretends to sound really irritated, before realising that she *is* actually irritated.

"It is a fact. And you could devote more time to your social life and less to your work. And try to be less vocally opinionated."

"Okay, putting that piece of advice into practice," Rebecca says, "why don't you just fuck off?" And they both scream with laughter.

They are approaching Harrogate's tall red-brick theatre. A group of youths begin singing drunkenly.

"One Yorkshire Ripper. There's only one Yorkshire RIPPER. There's only one Yorkshire Ripper."

"How utterly charming," Rebecca says, loud enough for the youths to hear.

The three youths are barring their way. Pumping their fists in the air, they've moved on to a different song. "He's back! He's back! He's back and on the attack – ha-ha!"

Rebecca holds her ground and speaks directly to the boys. "Look, could I suggest you three roll a little further into the gutter, so we can walk past?"

The tallest, wearing a stained white T-shirt, puckers his face in disgust. "What did you slags just say?"

The other two stand by, awaiting his instructions.

"I know a song too," Rebecca says, removing both shoes and holding the right one aloft, stiletto out, like a dagger, then sings a line from *Psycho Killer*.

Pamela knows this one too and joins in heartily, including the suggestion that the boys run away.

As they sing, Rebecca moves slowly towards the boys, her eyes steely. Unnerved by the display of solidarity, the youths back off, grumbling about aggressive drunken women.

"You won't get away so lightly next time," Rebecca calls after them as they retreat.

For a minute or two, neither Rebecca nor Pamela speak. The wind has picked up and both are feeling the chill. Without agreeing to do so, they're heading back towards the hotel.

"That was very appropriate," Pamela says. "*Psycho Killer*."

"Well, I thought if they can sing about serial killers, so can I."

"You were fearless, Rebecca. That's what I admired about you at school. It's what made you attractive to me."

"It was?" Rebecca says.

"Yes, absolutely. I never told you, did I? – but I had a massive crush on you."

Rebecca laughs loudly for a few seconds, but it sounds slightly strained. "Well, you learn something every day."

CHAPTER FOUR

9 APRIL 1979

Three days later, Rebecca is getting dressed for work. Checking herself in the mirror, she puts on her new black and white houndstooth jacket. Pamela's comments about her fashion sense have been on her mind, and now the jacket seems overly formal and fussy. With the palm of her hand, she smooths her somewhat wayward ginger hair with little effect.

On the radio, two women are arguing.

"I didn't say you've got it wrong. But by marching with placards saying, 'No curfew on women – curfew on men', don't you think you're encouraging women to put their lives in danger?"

"Encouraging men to murder us, you mean?"

"That isn't my point, of course."

"What we're saying is that women should be able to walk anywhere at any time."

"But there's a deranged killer out there!"

Rebecca checks her watch, switches off the radio, heads downstairs.

Three-quarters of an hour later, she arrives at Ingrow Bridge and manoeuvres into the car park. Even in April, her breath is freezing in clouds in front of her. She unlocks the door to her premises. Unsure if she is alone, she calls out to her long-standing PA. Sally comes down the hallway and joins her in the small office, her short black hair gleaming and immaculate. Sally's eyes linger a little too long on Rebecca's jacket, and Rebecca mouths, "Is it too much?"

"How was your weekend?" Sally says, avoiding answering the question.

"Fine, thanks. We went to Harrogate."

Sally is now sitting down at the desk opening a pile of post with the wooden elephant letter opener.

"Leave those for Debbie, if you like."

"It's all right," Sally says. "Was that with Pamela? In Harrogate?"

"Well remembered. Apparently, she used to fancy me at school. How strange is that?"

Sally shrugs. "Not particularly."

Rebecca smiles, glad that Sally feels comfortable enough to contradict her.

Rebecca goes down to the basement into a windowless room where a dozen people can, if necessary, squeeze round two tables joined together. Now certain that it doesn't look right, she removes her jacket and hangs it on a hook. As she switches on a small electric fire, she sees Roland, tall wiry body, black glasses, the family's signature flamed hair currently in need of a cut.

"Morning, sis – guess who I had a drink with this weekend? Simon!"

"How come?" Rebecca tries to sound as neutral as possible. She hasn't seen Simon in two months.

"We ran into each other at the Emmotts. He said having a drink with me was a way of staying close to you. Without the worry of being spotted. You're the love of his life, apparently."

"Was he drunk by any chance?"

"Yeah, but he meant it."

"He's got a funny way of showing it."

Roland changes the subject. The Local Gold report. It won't go down well with a certain person. Rebecca says not to worry. Just mention the relevant figures and she'll handle the difficult stuff.

They fall silent as Brian Sheridan and Dave Townley come in. Roland looks up at Sally, who's followed by Debbie with a tray of teas, coffees and Garibaldis.

"Morning," Brian says gruffly, tossing his dank bomber jacket over Rebecca's.

"Ey up," Dave says.

"Morning, everybody," Rebecca says. "Just a few things today, so hopefully we won't keep you long."

"Local Gold's on your list, yeah?"

"It's on the agenda, yes, Brian."

First, Rebecca asks Roland to report back on off-trade promotions. It's all looking very positive, he says. "Morrisons are really keen to stock our five best-selling lines."

"That's great," Dave their engineer says, then lowers his eyes to his lap.

"It doesn't mean they'll sell any of the buggers," Brian says. "Sales of bottled beer have always been about to go through the bloody roof – except they never did."

"I'm not sure I agree," Rebecca says. "Our sales of bottled beer have risen steadily."

"Against my better advice that we ever went there in the first place," Brian mumbles.

"Yes, totally against your advice," Rebecca agrees.

There is silence. Debbie, who's making notes, takes the opportunity to grab a biscuit.

"You can't argue with the stats, Brian," Roland says. "I'll show you some graphs, if you like."

"Oh, you people love your graphs, don't you? I expect Maggie Thatcher loves graphs too."

Rebecca considers reminding him that when she took over the business it had ground to a halt, but why waste her breath?

"Shall we move on to the next item. Roland? How's Local Gold been received in our selected pubs?"

"Really disappointing, to be honest. The market test has not been a success. I've got return figures from the five landlords."

"What are you saying?" Brian is outraged. "I went to the Ferrands Arms in Bingley – it was going down a bomb. My mates all loved it."

"Who was buying the rounds?" Dave quips.

Roland pushes photocopied figures across the table. Dave and Sally scrutinise their papers, Brian leaves his in front of him.

"I'm not convinced that launching it now is the best thing," Rebecca says. "We can maybe try again in a few months."

"You've no guts, woman. You need to learn to take a risk. Wouldn't you say, Dave?"

"I'd say we're doing okay," Dave mutters.

"I put my heart and soul into that ale," Brian says. "It's got orange rind in."

Rebecca closes down the conversation. She tells Brian that she's sorry, but for whatever reason the market isn't ready. Instead of financing a risky launch, she's decided to re-advertise Wilberforce.

Brian affects disbelief. "Wilberforce! That's a dead duck. We should concentrate on new products."

It's a fantastic ale, Rebecca says, and they just need to reconnect with the people who used to love it. She's thinking about a campaign on local TV.

"What about Saatchi & Saatchi? Thatcher loves them and all."

"Brilliant idea," Rebecca says. "I'll take you up on that."

The only *any other business* is raised by Roland. He's set up a meeting between Rebecca and Mervyn Harris, an industry journalist for the following week. To discuss the launch of the new product.

"You'd better cancel that then," Brian says.

"No," Rebecca says. "Leave it in the diary, there'll be plenty to talk about."

Chairs scrape as everyone gets up to leave.

"Would you mind staying behind for a moment, Brian?"

Brian rolls his eyes towards Dave but Dave's already heading into the corridor. Debbie closes the door as she leaves. Rebecca and Brian are alone.

"So, what gives?" Brian asks.

"I do, Brian. A hell of a lot of my time and energy keeping you in a job and making this business profitable. Which it now is by the way. And all I get in return from you is bellyache. I was as patient as anything in the development phase of Local Gold, but I underplayed how bad the feedback actually was. The trial confirmed all that."

"Oh, the trial confirmed it," he says, steeping the words in sarcasm.

"Want to see the feedback forms? 'Fizzy marmalade' – that's how somebody described it."

"So, what are you going to do? Fire me?"

"Getting a job isn't easy for a man of your age."

"So, are you, or not?"

"I'm thinking about it."

"Okay, so if you're not going to fire me, stop wasting my bloody time!"

And with that, Brian retrieves his jacket and leaves the room.

CHAPTER FIVE

9 APRIL 1979

That evening Pamela telephones, and Rebecca tells her about the awkward encounter with Brian Sheridan, the most senior survivor from Ingrow Ales – the original name before she changed it to Keighley Beers.

"And he kept going on about Margaret Thatcher. I think he'll have a breakdown if she becomes prime minister."

"So, he's from the company you bought?"

"Yes, a couple of years back."

Rebecca had read that the failing brewery would be closing, with up to a dozen local redundancies. She was familiar with their most successful ale, Sailor's Watch, but it was a snap decision to buy the company, based on emotion rather than business sense.

"So, what do you think I should do about Brian?" Rebecca says.

"If you're asking for advice, I'd give him the heave-ho. He won't change. Certainly not overnight."

"I know I should. It's just he's the same age as my father when he died."

"You can't make business decisions based on that, surely," Pamela says.

The doorbell rings. Rebecca walks towards it with the handset, the cord stretching like a ringlet of hair pulled taut from the scalp.

"Have you got a visitor?" Pamela asks.

Rebecca is looking through the distorting glass panel on the left of her front door at a tall blue blur on the other side. "It's a policeman."

"At this time?"

"Yes. I'd better go."

They send a policeman round when one of your relatives has died in tragic circumstances. She knows they're not brilliant at breaking the news. Sometimes they give you a lift to identify the body. Unless they're doing house-to-house enquiries about something else. She releases the gold catch and opens the door.

"Good evening, madam, I've come to speak to you about an extremely serious matter."

He's looking her straight in the eye, not smiling.

"What are you doing here?" She tries not to sound too irritated.

"Hoping that you'll invite me in. I'm on a shift, you know."

"I'm not brilliant with surprises, Simon."

"Yes, you once told me your least favourite word is *impromptu*."

He follows her inside, through to the living room, pleased with himself.

"At least take that stupid hat off, or you'll damage my chandelier."

He does so, resting it on the back of the sofa with the zigzag pattern in seven shades of brown.

"Now it looks like I've got a policeman hiding behind my settee. You don't normally do this. What's going on?"

"This is…" He smiles.

Simon comes up to her and slides his hand underneath the front of her skirt, but she pushes him away, tells him to stop, offers instead to make him a cup of tea. The stress of the last few days must be coming out. She's irritated too that she hasn't seen him in months.

He stands at a respectful distance as she fills the silver kettle, unembarrassed by what's just happened. She's aware that he's watching her closely in the way that he does. Tonight, this feels stifling, although usually she likes it, that sense of being protected, that he's interested in every small detail of her life.

"What is it, Simon? Why are you looking at me like that?"

Nothing, he says, then tells her that he finally saw *The First Great Train Robbery*. It had this fantastic action sequence with Sean Connery standing on top of a train. He had to keep ducking under bridges to avoid being decapitated – it was very funny, he tells her.

"So, I heard you saw my brother."

"Yes, we went for a drink. He looks like you, doesn't he? And I don't think I knew he works for your company."

"He's our marketing manager."

"He seems so young."

They go back into the living room with their teas. Rebecca has become self-conscious about the décor which, ever since her most recent visit to Eileen, feels crass and blundering. Although permanently on the breadline and too proud to accept handouts from Rebecca, Eileen throws second-hand furniture and furnishings together with effortless urban chic.

"I have a meeting with Saatchi & Saatchi next week," Rebecca says.

"Ha-ha, very funny."

"I do. I'm going to get them to produce an advert for Yorkshire Television."

"You'll be going to London for that, I expect. No doubt you'll seal the deal over margaritas in their swanky offices."

Rebecca laughs. "Actually, they're sending two executives up by train and I'm meeting them at the station. They want to see the Keighley Beers office. It's not like you to play the chippy Yorkshire man," she adds.

He apologises. She's always admired his ability to admit when he's wrong, or stepped too far, a quality she associates with his unshakeable sense of self.

She asks about his work, and he tells her that he's moving across to work on the Yorkshire Ripper case. "Just me and three hundred others."

"So, you should be doing that rather than coming here and shoving your hand into my knickers."

"Theoretically," he says, a smile surfacing again. "Although the investigation won't collapse because I've sloped off for a few minutes. I'll make up the time if you like."

"Maybe you can tell me this. How do they know it's the same man? Like on Friday. How did they know?"

"He tends to batter his victims on the head with a hammer from behind when they're least expecting it. And that causes terrible damage to the skull, of course, and would probably be enough to kill them on its own. But he finishes them off with a frenzy of stabbing, often revealing their torso by pulling up their clothes–"

"All right, Simon–"

"And the last one, he penetrated her with a screwdriver, but I don't think that's typical."

"That's enough, for goodness' sake. I don't need all the details."

"Well, you did ask."

"But you didn't have to answer with so much enthusiasm."

He looks slightly hurt and she regrets saying it almost immediately.

"Is there anything wrong?" he asks. "You don't seem yourself."

"I've been thinking very seriously about our relationship," Rebecca says. "I'm not finishing things now. But it's only right to let you know that I'm looking for something more suitable."

CHAPTER SIX

18 APRIL 1979

"So that's the fermenter," Rebecca says to the journalist. "We're doing this slightly out of order for some reason. I'll show you the coppers next. What were you saying just now?"

"That we're not having the best season ever. But I've got faith in Manny Cussins."

"Manny Cussins?"

"Yes, the chairman," Mervyn Harris says. His is an ageless face, narrow eyes and a mass of curly brown hair; she's guessing that he's a few years younger than her.

"I met him once," Rebecca remembers. "He seemed very kind."

"You met Manny Cussins? I'm impressed."

"When I was a teenager, my mother worked in his furniture store. It's a long story."

"Yes, but I'm interested."

"He came to my father's funeral, if you must know."

"Oh. I see."

There is a moment's awkwardness.

"Which publication were you thinking of by the way?" Rebecca asks.

"*Off-Licence News* or perhaps *The Publican.*"

"Do you have any cuttings of things you've written?"

"I've got some in the boot of my car. I'll show you later."

"That would be good. This is our mash tin," Rebecca says.

"Quite a bit smaller than the brew kettle."

"These stacks carry the steam out of the building, releasing it outside."

"That explains the fantastic malty smell on the bridge. Beer in the making!"

Rebecca nods enthusiastically. It's going better than she'd expected. Mervyn is affable, if slightly odd, taking much more of an interest than the men from Saatchi & Saatchi had.

"I remember that from my childhood," she says. "People said they could always tell the brewing days at Tetley's. My father worked there for years."

"It's in the blood then." Mervyn smiles, his overcrowded mouth like a badly constructed Lego model. "But what a fantastic gift Tetley's has given to Leeds over the years. I'm researching a book on Tetley's."

"Really?" Rebecca says, her expression darkening.

"All right, I know they're your rivals now."

She'd asked Debbie to stay late to bring them a cup of tea, which appears ten minutes later in Rebecca's office. She and Mervyn are sitting at the small round table and Rebecca is noticing that his questions are becoming less about Keighley Beers and more about her.

"Perhaps we could have a few biscuits too," she says to Debbie. Debbie sighs and tells Rebecca she'll have a look in the biscuit tin and heads back out.

"Getting motivated staff is always the challenge," Rebecca says, laughing.

"Speaking of that, I read you also own a recruitment consultancy."

"Yes, but I'm a back-seat driver in that business. I go to the odd board meeting."

He narrows his eyes, flipping his hand over back and forth a couple of times, as if weighing up the value of two competing propositions. "Recruitment, then beer. That's quite a leap."

"Well, Just the Job began as a support service, helping local men back into work if they found themselves unemployed unexpectedly," she feels she's suddenly jabbering, "but it kind of took off."

Mervyn smiles again, patiently, as if this doesn't explain everything. "So, what's all this about Saatchi & Saatchi? I've never heard of a brewer using them."

Rebecca tells him that they're relaunching Wilberforce, which ten years ago was a steady performer throughout Yorkshire. They need to remind people how much they used to like it, and get new drinkers enthused about the ale too.

"Well, they're world famous. They must be able to do that for you."

"You'd have thought so. They sent a couple of directors up last week. Chris Flowerday was one."

"Typical name for an ad man. Young guy, is he?"

"Forties. He told me I was scarier than Margaret Thatcher. Apart from that, he did little else but boast how brilliant they are."

"Did they have any ideas for the adverts?"

"Yes, one, and it was terrible! He talked about an ad with women dressed in boiler suits, men in dresses, a grandmother in an astronaut suit, all enjoying pints of Wilberforce, with the strap-line, 'You'll love Wilberforce, whoever you are'. I told them I wanted something simpler, like a Leeds footballer drinking Wilberforce instead. The sort of thing local people will relate to."

"Actually, I'm a mate of William Byron Stevenson."

"Is that the romantic poet who invented the steam train before he wrote *Treasure Island*?" Rebecca laughs, and Mervyn laughs too.

"He's a soccer player, a Welsh international," he tells her. "I'm sure he could be persuaded. And he's handsome too."

"Yes, but will people have heard of him, because I certainly haven't?"

Later, when they go out to the car park, so he can show her some of his articles, she says that she would like him to ask his friend about being in the commercial.

He smiles as he reaches into his untidy boot, feeling amongst the empty cans of Coca-Cola, sandwich wrappers, screwdrivers and other tools before producing a small folder.

"Maybe we can have a pint when you've read these?" he says.

"That would be nice," Rebecca responds vaguely, whilst surveying the debris in his boot. He closes the boot sharply and hands her the folder.

CHAPTER SEVEN

27 APRIL 1979

Rebecca had been handed a leaflet saying: "If you wear a short skirt, people say you've asked for it. If you've walked down the street, you've asked for it". The flyer is for a Reclaim the Night march, which aims to demonstrate that women should, like men, be able to walk anywhere late at night on their own, without the threat of sexual attacks. Rebecca has persuaded Debbie, Pamela and Sally to go with her. And Dan is looking after the twins so Eileen has also joined them.

In Whitelock's beforehand, a woman in simple jeans and a yellow top addresses the forty or so women. "This is a celebration, sisters. It's a celebration of being women and, yes, of being alive. And of course, we're angry too, but I've never let that stop me having a good time. We're angry that the papers only get interested in certain murders around here, depending on who you are. And that being attacked on the streets is our problem apparently, not everyone's. 'If you don't want to be raped, dear, then perhaps it's best if you avoid going out at night'. Well, I'm sorry. That's not actually terribly helpful if you're a shift worker or are told to work late by your boss."

Rebecca realises she's asked Debbie to stay late quite a bit recently. She catches Debbie's eyes and mouths, "Sorry."

"Or if you like going to movies or clubs or you're involved in prostitution," the woman continues. "You don't have to have been attacked or raped to come on these marches. All women are welcome – tell your friends about it. We're not all Marxists or man-hating viragos. I hope some of our menfolk will feel brave enough to join us later."

The evening hadn't begun well for Rebecca. When they first arrived, she'd been asked by a woman in a tie-dyed T-shirt if she was a member of the Leeds Revolutionary Feminist Group. Eileen had been quick to respond on her behalf.

"My sister wouldn't join an organisation with a name like that! It would offend her sensibilities, wouldn't it, Becky?"

"I don't know..." Rebecca was trying to remain light-hearted despite her annoyance that Eileen was seeking to put the boot in in front of her friends. "I might become a member if I had the time."

"Or if you could be in charge," Eileen said. "I was surprised you were coming on this march. I didn't think it would be your cup of tea."

"We're all women and we can all take an interest." For once Rebecca had managed to get the last word.

The woman in the yellow top is now on to the practicalities. "So, we're going to cut across to the Parade and head north. Plenty of noise when we go past the town hall please – let's make those columns shake, and beep your beepers at the museum, us women can have fun getting our horns out too!"

This gets a good laugh.

"Then we'll be heading right towards Chapeltown Road. And depending on how far we get, we'll turn round about ten and will hopefully be back for last orders. So, plenty of noise and have lots of fun."

The march certainly is making plenty of noise when Simon is delayed by it on Calverley Street. He can't help peering through the back windscreen to see which colleagues are accompanying the ladies. The man in the car behind leans on his hooter, but the sound is lost in the general cacophony. Simon drives slowly on, past the group with Rebecca. Neither see each other.

Five minutes later, after having parked his vehicle, he tries the first house. There is no answer. He waits half a minute, rings again; there's no one home. Allowing his hand to glide along the boundary hedge, he approaches the next one along. A woman in her late thirties answers, wearing a dressing gown. Before he can begin his pre-prepared speech, she calls out, "Look who we've got here!" and they're joined by a woman with suspiciously blonde hair, sucking at the remnants of a cigarette. "I think we must be in luck," the woman in the dressing gown says.

"Good evening, ladies. I'm making some enquiries in relation to a murder in Halifax. You've probably heard about it. Is your husband at home by any chance?" Simon says to the woman who opened the door.

"Husband! I don't have a husband!"

"Nor me."

"Chance would be a fine thing."

"She'd like one, that's for sure."

"So would you."

"Are you two sisters?" Simon asks.

"We can be sisters if you want," the one with peroxide hair answers, making them both laugh.

"We can be anything you want us to be."

"I can be a nun and she can be Cleopatra if you like." And they laugh so hard it sounds like their chests will explode.

"Look, do you mind if I come in for a moment?" Simon cuts through the laughter.

"Of course not!"

"We'd love you to come in. Put your feet up, have a cuppa."

"Trish does a lovely massage too. All part of the service."

Five minutes later, having found no hint of a male living in the premises, Simon makes a hasty retreat.

"You will visit us again?"

"When you're off duty!"

"Though some men do like to mix their business with a little pleasure."

They're still calling after him as he rings the doorbell of number 77.

The women are in good spirits as they continue down Calverley Street. Some carry flaming torches, many have placards. A grey-haired trumpeter toots periodically into the dark sky. There's plenty of banter with the locals, most of it good-humoured, although an overweight man in a suit calls across the road, "Could I respectfully suggest that you all get a fucking job?" This provokes a barrage of honks and feisty responses.

On her left Rebecca hears Eileen asking Debbie if she gets proper breaks in her job, adding that she must need them working with a load of oiks in a brewery.

"It's busy, but I do get breaks," Debbie says. "Rebecca's very focused, but she's also extremely fair."

"Thank you," Rebecca chips in. "And by the way, I don't employ oiks."

"We're having a private conversation," Eileen says.

Feeling her hackles rising, Rebecca turns away, towards Pamela and Sally, but they're locked in an intense conversation.

A woman in a straw hat is walking alone in front of them. Rebecca quickens her pace, catching her up.

"So," Rebecca says, "do you come here often? On these marches, I mean."

The woman, who's about her age, laughs. "It's my second. My friend's not well but I came anyway. Apart from anything, it's a chance to look around and see what a great city Leeds is."

"I'm guessing you've always lived here," Rebecca says.

"Only since studying art here. I fell in love with the place. And you?"

Rebecca says she grew up in Armley. Apart from university, she's always lived around and about. "Where did you study art?" she asks.

"Jacob Kramer, although I spent as much time in the Pig and Whistle as I did the college."

"I drank a lot too as a student. My way of coping with the death of my parents."

The woman nods in understanding. "Drink can help with that. It sounds like a rough period."

"You get through it," Rebecca says. "You have to, don't you?"

CHAPTER EIGHT

27 APRIL 1979

"Good evening," Simon begins. "I'm making some enquiries in relation to a murder committed in Halifax. You've probably read about it in the newspapers."

The man is leaning on the door-frame, clearly not in good health.

"Do you have any other males living in this house with you?"

The man shakes his head, seemingly unwilling to say a single word.

"Would you mind if I come in for a minute? I won't keep you long. I can see you're busy."

"I'm not busy." The man finally says, slowly, deliberately, as if each word is costing him money. He doesn't budge and Simon would have to push past him to get inside.

"We're doing house-to-house enquiries about the killing of Josephine Anne Whitaker. She was found three weeks ago near a bus stop."

"I know all about it," the man says, anger rising in his voice.

"What do you do for a living, sir, if you don't mind me asking?"

"The railways. I used to be a railwayman." There's breathlessness when he speaks. Surely there can be nothing suspicious about someone so infirm, clearly old before his time.

"I would like to come in for a chat, sir. If you don't mind?"

"I'd rather not talk about it. I know you're doing what you have to. It's just our Jayne, he killed her two years ago. This brought it all back."

Simon looks into the man's bloodshot eyes and remembers. Jayne MacDonald, the sixteen-year-old victim. Hadn't she lived at 77 Scott Hall Avenue? Why on earth hadn't he remembered instead of blundering in?

"I'm very sorry, sir, I do recall now."

"She were just an assistant at Grandways. She weren't no prostitute!" He spits out every last word.

Simon reaches out and places a hand on his shoulder.

"I'm very sorry about your daughter."

Just as the sentence finishes, the man pulls the door tightly shut.

***

Rebecca is pleased she made the effort to talk to the woman in the straw hat. She has a maturity about her, and Rebecca feels she can cope with anything she chooses to tell her.

"My mother never recovered. She died within a couple of years. Me and Roland, and Eileen, of course," she looks behind her as she says it, but sees only Pamela and Sally, "we had to deal with all that, her dying too..." – were Pamela and Sally holding hands? – "all that in the space of a couple of years."

"How old were you at the time?" the woman asks.

"Sixteen when Dad died, eighteen when Mum died."

"And you're the oldest?"

"Yes," Rebecca confirms. "We moved in with our uncle and aunt before I went to Sheffield."

"That's a lot for three young kids to deal with."

"You say that, but I can only imagine what it's like to have a loved one taken from you. Deliberately. In an act of violence. How do you begin to cope with that?"

They continue walking, without speaking for a while. Then the woman says that her husband is part of the team trying to catch the Yorkshire Ripper. "He's obsessed with it right now. It's difficult for him to just switch off and be a normal husband."

"I see," Rebecca says.

"I've noticed how he spends more time alone, brooding, and then he'll disappear for hours unexpectedly."

There is laughter to Rebecca's left, she instinctively turns and sees a man urinating in the street for the benefit of his cheering friends, making no attempt to even cover his genitals let alone the thin arc of liquid falling onto a lamp-post. Her companion has seen this too and rolls her eyes at Rebecca. They walk quickly on.

"And he doesn't feel that George Oldfield is on top of the job. The man in charge?"

"Yes, I've seen his name in the papers," Rebecca says.

"Simon doesn't rate him at all. Apparently, he's been receiving letters from the killer and he still can't catch him. How ridiculous is that?"

"Did you say Simon?" Rebecca can almost feel the blood draining out of her.

"My husband, yes. He says Oldfield botched the investigation of the IRA M62 coach bombing too. The woman they put behind bars is innocent." Rebecca is no longer focusing on the words, feeling short of breath. "The IRA even issued a statement saying she wasn't involved. Why would they say that? They never normally issue statements like that."

"I'm sorry, I think I should find my friends." Rebecca turns and abruptly disappears. She realises that the woman must be wondering if she'd said anything wrong.

"Good evening," Simon says. "I'm making some enquiries in relation to a murder committed in Halifax. You've probably read about it in the newspapers."

This time a more friendly face, a man with a beard, a finely manicured grey beard. He's well turned out too.

"Sure, I've read about it. You want to come in?" His is an American accent.

As he goes through the doorway, Simon recognises the familiar scent of Brut. "I hope I'm not disturbing you, sir."

"Not at all. Have a seat."

Simon sits on a leather armchair. Everything is tasteful, immaculate – there are several oil paintings, some landscapes and a still life. This man takes real pride in where he lives.

"Nice place," Simon says. "Have you been in England for long?"

"Not so long," the man says. "I moved to the UK in March 1978." This would put him in the clear; he is completely innocent if this date is right. "I have the papers if you'd like to see them?"

"No, no, of course not. Are you living alone?"

The man nods. "Yeah, just me. I have family here though."

He talks about his brother who's been settled in Newark for some time, married and working successfully as a builder specialising in loft conversions.

"And what do you do?" Simon asks.

"Okay, so I'm a financial consultant. I run my own business."

"Well, it looks like you're doing very nicely for yourself." Simon rises from his chair. "I'm sorry for wasting your time."

The man gets up too. "You do know that two of his victims lived on this street? Wilma McCann and–"

"Yes, Wilma McCann, I did know that."

"She was the first one, lived at number sixty-five. Then there was Jayne MacDonald, of course."

"I just met her father unfortunately."

"Oh, I know Wilf. He's a broken man," the American says matter of factly. "Yeah, two women, both living within a stone's throw of each other, both victims of the same murderer. What are the chances of moving into a street like that?"

"Pretty slim," Simon agrees. He thanks him for his time and heads back outside. The man smiles and waves from his doorstep. Simon is always impressed how friendly Americans are.

As he walks back to his car, Simon recalls that Jayne often used to babysit Wilma's children. Wilma was a feisty woman, a mother of four young children, with a habit of choosing violent partners. Jayne was a sixteen-year-old who loved going out roller skating; truly the favourite with her father, she'd recently left school and was working locally. He can't think that they found much to talk about when Jayne came over, but they must have had something in common. Perhaps they discovered they both loved a Flake chocolate bar and shared a moment, comparing when they'd eat them and how long they could make each one last. If he were making a film about this sorry episode, Simon would have that conversation as the opening scene. An innocuous exchange between a mother and babysitter who'd both become victims of the same deranged killer.

He unlocks his car and climbs inside. He's feeling low, in fact, has been for some time, ever since Rebecca told him that she was looking for someone more suitable.

CHAPTER NINE

MAY AND JUNE 1979

R ebecca finds Chris Flowerday preoccupied whenever she speaks to him, in the months leading up to shooting the Wilberforce advert. She puts this down to Saatchi's preoccupation with keeping their more famous clients, the Conservative Party, happy. Those who will eventually watch the advert, with its iconic image of William Byron Stevenson in front of the Bluebell pub drinking from a glass tankard of Wilberforce, could not begin to imagine the tense conversations that preceded its making. The advert's message not to delay if you fancy a Wilberforce is emphasised by Stevenson still wearing his full Leeds United kit, the match ball resting on the table in front of him. It was Saatchi's idea, suggested late in the day, for the advert to show Stevenson in the match at the stadium, and this was the principal cause of the arguments.

Rebecca and Roland recognised the brilliance of the Saatchi twist to their original concept of the footballer simply drinking in front of a pub, but when Rebecca received a revised schedule of costs including hefty additional items for shooting at Elland Road, she called the agency and asked to speak to Charles Saatchi. Instead, she was connected to Flowerday, who told her,

"Charles doesn't speak to clients; he doesn't even speak with the prime minister." By the time the conversation had finished, Flowerday had promised that the additional charges would either be scrapped or drastically reduced. These concessions helped their relationship return to a friendlier footing.

At the final shoot in Kettlewell, Rebecca finds herself chatting to William Stevenson as he sits in his football shorts and jersey under a blue umbrella in front of the Bluebell Pub. It's the first time Rebecca has met him and he's telling her about his dream to run a pub when he retires from football.

"As long as you stock Wilberforce," Rebecca says with a smile.

"How could I not?" Stevenson replies in his Welsh accent. "By the way, I'm in awe of everything you've achieved."

"You don't have to say that. You're being employed to look like you enjoy drinking the ale, not to lick my boots."

"I'm not just saying it," Stevenson says. "Just the Job helped a good friend when he was sacked as a hotel porter. They got him to retrain and he's deputy manager in a shoe shop now."

Rebecca nods, now feeling bad about her outburst. "My father lost his job when I was a teenager. To be honest, he could have done with an agency like mine too."

The film crew are continuing to set up the shot when Mervyn Harris arrives. Stevenson gets up and he and William hug each other. Then Mervyn turns towards Rebecca. He doesn't smile.

"Thanks so much for that piece in *The Publican*." Rebecca remembers that they left it that she would contact him when she'd read the articles he gave her in the car park. "It was great," she adds.

"No problem. It's my job," Mervyn says.

"And for introducing us to William. Saatchi says he's a natural in front of camera."

Stevenson laughs but Mervyn's still looking frosty. "Can we speak for a moment?" he says.

They move away on to the grass on the other side of the road.

"Did you read my articles?" he asks.

"I haven't had time. I'm really sorry."

"It was just an excuse for me to see you again," he says.

"Oh! We can make an arrangement now," Rebecca says. He seems nice enough, certainly intelligent, and it's so long since she had a date with anyone remotely available. "We can meet here, if you like."

"Next Saturday? The thirtieth."

"Perfect," she says. "Oh look, they've started filming William."

As they watch the footballer sipping from his frothy pint in the blaze of the film set lighting, Rebecca tries to picture the advert with its story elements seamlessly knitted together. The muddy footballers playing before a packed crowd in Elland Road, interrupted by William picking the ball up in his hands and running off in front of bamboozled fans towards the stadium exit. And then cutting to this shot of him, in front of the Bluebell, with a reassuring, gravelly, Yorkshire voice speaking the line which Rebecca is proud to have come up with: "So don't delay, it's a Wilberforce day!"

CHAPTER TEN

26 JUNE 1979

The day Rebecca turns thirty-four, she is sitting with Sally, Debbie, Roland and Dave in Wild's coffee bar, where they sometimes go after work. The conversation turns to the police announcement in which the head of the Ripper investigation, George Oldfield, had played a tape of a man with a Wearside accent claiming to be the Yorkshire Ripper. Oldfield said that the same man had also sent him letters, the most recent just days before the death of Josephine Whitaker. And that both letters and tapes could only have come from the murderer because they contained information that wasn't known by the public.

"What if it's all a mistake?" Debbie says. "What if this Wearside Jack isn't the man? Where would that leave us all?"

"But it sounds like it's him, to me, doesn't it?" Dave says, and a look passes between the women, as if to check they understand his question. Does it sound like they have the right man, or does it sound like they have the right man according to Dave? Either way, no one answers.

Sally says that when they were on the march, she and Pamela agreed that it's all being approached from a very male perspective. "I mean, have you seen those police press conferences? There's not a woman in sight."

"That's true," Roland agrees.

"It might help if we had the view of a woman or two from time to time," Sally continues. "Even better, why can't we have a woman leading the investigation?"

"We've got a woman prime minister now," Debbie says.

"Exactly," Sally says. "If it were up to me, I'd put Rebecca in charge."

Rebecca opens her eyes wide in surprise. "Why me?" she says.

"I've worked for you for years," Sally says. "Barring the odd little one, you don't make mistakes."

"I agree," Roland says. "Put Rebecca in charge. In any case, George Oldfield looks like Brian Sheridan's older brother."

Sally makes retching noises and there is laughter.

"You're a good judge of people, Rebecca," Sally says.

"I do have a degree in psychology," Rebecca concedes.

"Think of it as a promotion on your birthday!" Sally gives Rebecca a rebellious look.

Debbie and Dave simultaneously check that it is actually her birthday. Rebecca says she didn't want to make a big thing of it, in fact had asked Sally not to say anything.

Following a brief discussion about not looking her age, Rebecca says, "I've noticed that lorry drivers don't honk their horns at me when they drive past as much as they once did. I used to find that insulting when it happened. But somehow, it's more insulting when it stops."

"What are you doing to celebrate your birthday?" Dave asks.

"No particular plans," Rebecca tells him.

"Let's all go into town for something a bit stronger," Roland suggests, always keen to spend more time with Sally.

They agree on The Cobourg at the junction of Woodhouse Lane and Clay Pit Lane.

"I'll stop by the office and give Pamela a ring," Sally says.

Rebecca gives Roland a lift as his car is being serviced. She mentions her forthcoming date with Mervyn Harris which she's now unsure about.

"What's wrong with him? He seemed nice enough."

"I just don't feel comfortable about it anymore. He looked me up in the telephone directory. And he's called twice to check that I'm still okay for Saturday."

"A bit over the top," Roland agrees.

"He said how much he was looking forward to it, then added, 'I want to keep you safe'. Don't you think that's peculiar?"

"Maybe that's his idea of being chivalrous."

"Well, I'm a big girl and I can look after myself."

There are mirrors on the wall of the pub advertising Tetley's beers; they occupy a corner. It is crowded and the oxygen is fighting a losing battle with cigarette smoke. The conversation turns back to the announcement earlier that day. There is disagreement about whether the letters and tape are genuine. When put to a vote, opinion divides along gender lines: Sally, Pamela and Rebecca think they're the work of a con artist. Dave, Roland and Debbie's fiancé Kelvin believe it's the Ripper taunting the police.

"I don't get why anyone would do that, unless it was real," Dave says.

"I could understand it if it was funny," Roland agrees.

"Yeah, if it were really funny, I'd say it were probably a joke," Kelvin says.

"It can't be a joke, because people's lives are at stake," Sally says.

Rebecca tells Debbie that she now has the casting vote as to whether the tapes and letters are genuine. Debbie dislikes being put on the spot and abstains, to the annoyance of everybody.

The discussion moves on to lesbians. Rebecca is not sure how the bridge was made from the Yorkshire Ripper to this subject, but no doubt fuelled by alcohol, Sally has just declared herself to be a lesbian and in a relationship with Pamela, who she met at the march.

"You're joking, aren't you?" Roland smiles glassily.

"I had no idea," Rebecca says, embarrassed that in all the time she's employed Sally, they've not had a sufficiently personal conversation for this to have surfaced.

"I kind of kept it from you," Sally says. "I didn't know how you'd react."

"It needn't be such a surprise," Pamela says. "There are plenty of us in the public eye these days."

Rebecca's surprise about this revelation does not compare with the one she's about to get on her way to the toilet. As she turns into a different section of the pub, she sees Simon sitting at a table with a significantly younger woman. He is leaning over her shoulder as she rifles through the contents of her handbag; both are laughing flirtatiously, and Simon does not see Rebecca. Rebecca quickly turns around, remembering that Simon had rung her to ask whether he might see her on her birthday. She'd told him that she was too busy, suggesting he might take his wife out instead. Apparently, he'd since got a better offer.

Rebecca returns to the table and tells the others that she's feeling unwell and is going home. Roland follows her to the door and she explains that she's just seen Simon with another girlfriend. She is incandescent.

"It might be his wife," Roland points out.

"It's not his wife, because I met his wife on the march! This is some blonde floozy."

Roland admits that whether it's his wife or another woman,

THE COMPANY SHE KEEPS

it would be embarrassing for Simon to bump into Rebecca right now. But they could simply find another pub. He can tell the others that they fancy a change of scene.

"They were going through her handbag," Rebecca says indignantly. "God knows what they were looking for."

"Look, do you want to go to another pub or not?"

"No, I don't," Rebecca says. "My evening has been completely ruined by that serial adulterer." And with that she leaves the pub, still needing to pee. In fact, she immediately finds another pub in order to do so.

45

CHAPTER ELEVEN

29 JULY 1979

The houses on Lidgett Park Road are well spaced apart, though not so far to prevent two next-door neighbours washing their cars from having a conversation. One Sunday morning in late July, Rebecca and her neighbour Ken Tobias are doing just this. His is a black Pontiac Firebird, which she's heard teenagers describing as the coolest car on the market. Rebecca has a peppermint-green Opel Kadett. For Rebecca, their vehicles encapsulate something of their attitudes to life, or at least how they're perceived by others.

Ken is a successful actor living with a girlfriend and young child. He isn't unfriendly, the opposite in fact, but tends to avoid talking about himself or his work.

"It's a lovely morning for it," Ken says.

"Absolutely." Rebecca wonders whether "it" refers to cleaning cars, or some big community event that she knows nothing about. "How's everything?"

"Everything's great," Ken says. "Or as they'd say in the twenties, it's all tickety-boo." He ducks out of view to give his hubcaps some special attention.

Rebecca only recently started washing her car on a regular

basis following comments by a used car salesman, known in the Keighley Beers office as "Mr Misery". She could use the local car wash but resents the expense, so has diarised one weekend in four instead.

"How's tricks?" Ken is stretching over his car to sponge the centre of the roof, looking for all the world like he's appearing in a glossy commercial. He's attractive but definitely not her type.

Rebecca's not sure what he's asking about so mentions the relaunch event for Wilberforce coming up next week, which William Byron Stevenson will attend.

"That sounds kind of cool," Ken says. "But should I know this William Stevenson fellow?"

"Only if you like football. He plays for Leeds."

"That explains why I didn't recognise the name," he says, laughing. "Where's it being held?"

"In the pub where we filmed it. They've got a nice dining room. And our staff are inviting two friends each to give it a bit of a buzz."

She suddenly thinks about Simon, who she briefly toyed with inviting before dismissing it as a thoroughly bad idea. The fact she'd considered it demonstrates why she needs to put down this limping dog of a relationship. If she could just meet someone else, someone available and suitable, she could free herself from his clutches once and for all.

At the same time Rebecca and Ken are washing their cars, Simon, recently promoted to detective, arrives at an address in Bradford with Andrew Laptew to conduct an interview. They'll be speaking with a man whose black Sunbeam Rapier car has been recorded thirty times in various red-light districts. The interview has been outstanding since February, such is the overburdened and chaotic state of the investigation. Andrew has done hundreds of these interviews; this will be just one more to the list.

They're shown into the living room by Sonia Sutcliffe, and Simon can't help but notice the resemblance of the man sitting by the window to the photofit of Marilyn Moore's attacker in 1977, although he's aware that facial images based on the memories of witnesses can be hopelessly inaccurate.

Andrew begins the conversation, as he often does, with a joke to break the ice. "Now's the time to get rid of your husband if you want to," he says to Sonia Sutcliffe.

Usually this line provokes a laugh, or elicits some other response, but neither husband nor wife crack a smile. Andrew and Simon catch each other's eyes, then Andrew continues with the questions proper.

"What do you do for a living, sir?"

"I'm a driver," the man replies.

Simon studies the man, his well-kempt, nicely trimmed beard. He's quite good-looking, but there's something weedy and annoying about him too.

"And who do you work for?" Andrew continues.

"Clark's," the man says. "Clark's at Shipley, that is."

Simon has the impression that he's being defensive, but also that he's not wanting to arouse suspicion.

"You seem to do a lot of driving in your own time too," Andrew says.

The man looks up with curiosity.

"I mean by that, your car has been seen many times in red-light districts in Manchester, Leeds as well as Bradford."

The man shakes his head. "That wouldn't be me," he says. "I'm not a visitor to those places."

"Are you quite sure about that?" Andrew says. "It would be

strange if the same registration number had been noted down, incorrectly, thirty times."

Mr Sutcliffe seems slightly thrown by this and glances briefly towards his wife before saying, "I'm very sure, thank you for asking."

It's clear he won't be drawn further on the subject, and after a few more questions they terminate the interview.

As soon as they get into the car, Simon asks Andrew, "What did you think?"

"They were a right funny couple. And I don't have a good feeling about him."

"Me neither," Simon agrees.

"Just too many links. Too many coincidences."

"Like the Marilyn Moore photofit?"

"Yeah, but not just that," Andrew says, as he turns the ignition over. "He even has the gap between the front teeth. Did you notice? You know, the bite marks left on Josephine Whitaker's breasts?"

Simon feels himself shudder, then looks at his colleague as their car pulls away from the house. "Maybe we should go back and arrest him?"

"No, we can't do that. Not on a hunch. But we'll do a report – and I mean a comprehensive report, yeah?"

"We can get a secretary to type it up," Simon suggests.

"Good idea. Hopefully that'll get it read faster."

The following week, at Andrew Laptew's suggestion, he and Simon are in the incident room, waiting to speak to Dick Holland, the man at the helm of the Ripper investigation. But there are around sixty others in the same room, and when they locate Holland, he is mid-discussion about a humiliating defeat for Yorkshire in the county championship. Eventually, Andrew senses his moment.

"Sir, we wanted to let you know that we paid a visit to this couple in Bradford. And neither of us was happy about this bloke. In fact, they were a right funny couple."

"A right funny couple?" Holland scoffs. "I may need a little more to go by than that."

"We've written a report, sir," Simon says, trying to help out. "He's a lorry driver and his car has been picked out numerous times in red-light districts. He was clearly lying when we questioned him about that."

"I'm not surprised," Holland says. "I don't like my wife knowing about these things either." This generates a significant guffaw from the men standing around.

"And he has the gap in the teeth," Andrew says.

"And his shoe size fits too," Simon adds.

"Is he a Geordie?" Holland asks.

"No, but he is a dead ringer for the Marilyn Moore photofit," Simon replies.

There is a pause and it seems that everyone in the room is waiting for Holland's response. "If anyone else mentions another fucking photofit to me, they'll be in uniform till the end of their service. Or till they drop dead, whichever comes first! Now piss off and find a suspect with a Geordie accent."

As they try to make themselves invisible in the crowd, Simon can't but help feeling a little annoyed with Andrew for suggesting that they speak to Dick Holland.

CHAPTER TWELVE

26 AUGUST 1979

Soon after the relaunch of Wilberforce, Rebecca invites Eileen, her boyfriend Dan and the twins over for Sunday lunch, confident she now has the emotional energy the occasion will demand. Dan's brooding silences are difficult to deal with, but Rebecca couldn't not invite him. And as Eileen thinks her work life is terribly boring, Rebecca plans on telling them about the advertisement, dropping copious references to Saatchi & Saatchi. She imagines boasting (particularly to Archie) about how she's now friendly with Byron Stevenson, and explaining how she came up with the idea for the advert herself. Hopefully Eileen will have seen it on television, but she'd settle for the twins or even Dan being familiar with it, providing they fill her sister in on the details.

The idea is to go to the park straight after lunch, and in order that they can get there quickly, Rebecca puts all the food on the table at once and they dig in. The mushroom vol-au-vents look particularly good. Rebecca cautions the twins that the filling is hot and is told by Archie that they're no longer babies. Eileen says that the quiche Lorraine could have come out the oven earlier.

"Well, I think it's all great," Dan says. It is pretty much the first time he's spoken since arriving, and he goes up in Rebecca's estimation a notch or two.

"I don't know whether you've seen any TV adverts lately," Rebecca starts to say, but Eileen cuts her off.

"Instead of you monopolising the conversation with all your business stuff, which to be honest we're not always terribly interested in, how about you listen to some of our news? Because we also have news, you know."

It is one of those classic pre-emptive strikes. No matter how prepared Rebecca thinks she is, her sister is always capable of landing the verbal equivalent of a hefty punch to the head in the first round. Had it been anyone else, Rebecca would be quick to respond, no doubt putting them in their place. With Eileen, she avoids confrontation at any cost, especially in the presence of the twins.

"So, what is your news?" Rebecca says brightly, helping herself to salad and sliding the vol-au-vents towards Dan.

"Tell Aunty Becky about your prize," Eileen says to Lindsay.

"What prize?" Lindsay says.

"The prize you just won!"

"Oh, not that."

"Yes, it's brilliant, and we all want to hear it."

"You want me to say it out loud?"

"You know it off by heart, don't you?"

"Oh, all right then," Lindsay says, overplaying the reluctance.

Like her mother as a child, Lindsay is quite the performer. She stands up and recites her poem with a dash of sugary menace.

Evenings after school
You're perfectly safe in the evenings

He's not interested in children your age
Why not run out and play, my darling?
That's right, put a bookmark in that page
Go to the park or just outside on the street
There's plenty of people around at this hour
They'll make sure you're all right
So please, Lindsay, don't sit there and cower
You can bring a sandwich, some biscuits
And a beaker of orange squash
Go out and have some fun, my darling
Then come home and have a good wash
Like I say, he never hurts children
And it's always late at night
It's us women that need to watch our backs
Or else he might just give us a fright

Eileen explains that Lindsay was the winner of the school's annual poetry prize. Rebecca says she's not surprised, the poem is amazing, especially considering Lindsay's age. And so topical too.

"I love your dining room," Archie says, although he's seen it many times before.

"She did have a bit of help from me," Eileen says.

"Even so, it's brilliant," Rebecca says.

"It's so cosy," Archie continues.

"What do you think of it, the poem?" Rebecca asks Dan.

"How do you mean?" Dan says.

"What do you think of Lindsay's poem about the Yorkshire Ripper?"

"I think it's absolutely lovely," Dan says. And that ends the conversation.

CHAPTER THIRTEEN

26 AUGUST 1979

They get their things together and set off for Roundhay Park, Rebecca bringing the black Wham-O Frisbee she bought specially for the occasion. As they come out of her house, Rebecca sees a Hillman Imp parked a little further down the street, curly brown hair poking above the driver's seat. She immediately thinks of Mervyn Harris, remembering their awkward encounter at the relaunch party. They didn't speak but he was clearly furious about their cancelled date, his anger compressing his lips into a single mean brushstroke. What's he doing sitting in his car on her road with the engine turned off? Does he even know where she lives? She is tempted to check who's inside and challenge him, but the park is in the opposite direction, and the others are already heading enthusiastically up the road. Rebecca follows them, now wondering if it really is Mervyn's car. He'd given her his articles in the car park, taking them from his boot, but now she can't remember the make or colour.

They reach the park and position themselves on a large grassy space just off the path. Dan tries to demonstrate how to throw the Frisbee, although he's far from impressive himself as

Eileen points out. Lindsay soon gets the knack, and Archie finds intermittent success, but Rebecca's throws keep swerving drastically to one side and then rolling down the hill. Each time this happens, Archie chases after the Frisbee and returns it to his aunt.

A man with silver hair and a neat beard walks towards them. He has a young face, is perhaps in his late thirties, smartly dressed in a grey blazer checked with thin red lines. He stops and in an American accent politely asks if he might have a go. Eileen, smiling coquettishly, hands him the Frisbee. Stepping back a few feet, the man sends it humming towards Rebecca, a venomous insect flying low and straight in the direction of its prey. Rebecca stretches out her hand, fumbling at first, but then she recovers and catches the disc just before it hits the ground.

Archie cheers Rebecca, and the man says, "Bravo."

Lindsay is desperate for the man to throw it again and snatches the Frisbee from Rebecca, hand-delivering it back to him. This time the man steps further away, over the other side of the path, and skims another perfect flying saucer towards Rebecca.

"That is a thing of beauty," Rebecca says.

"My thoughts exactly," the man says, as Rebecca cleanly catches the Frisbee.

Dan wants a go now, but his attempt is wildly inaccurate and crashes into a tree. They continue playing, taking turns to emulate the man's immaculate deliveries.

"It's all the product of a misspent youth in Volunteer Park, Seattle," he says.

"Are you on holiday?" Rebecca asks.

"Actually, no. I moved here last year. Look," he says, throwing it again, "it's all in the wrist action." The game goes on for another twenty minutes or so.

The man is making his goodbyes when Rebecca says they're

going to get a cup of tea. "The café's only fifteen minutes away and you'd be welcome to join us."

Eileen gives Rebecca a meaningful look.

"That's a fine idea," the man says. "You English and your cups of tea."

As they walk, he and Rebecca lag behind. He introduces himself as Larry, a financial consultant who has a brother in Newark in the building trade. Rebecca says she's a local businesswoman, adding that she won't bore him with the details.

"I'm sure it would be anything but boring."

"Well, I bought a brewery in Keighley two years ago. That's what I'm concentrating on right now."

"So, you're the boss, yeah?"

"Well, I own the business."

"I'm going to call you 'The Boss'."

CHAPTER FOURTEEN

26 AUGUST 1979

The Lakeside Café is doing steady business, but they find a large table outside overlooking the lake itself and Rebecca orders teas and coffees for the adults, strawberry-flavoured Cresta for the twins, and some pastries. The food and drinks arrive minutes later and Archie and Lindsay are soon competing to do the best imitation of the cartoon polar bear with his familiar catch phrase, "It's frothy, man."

"We sometimes get Cresta on the way back from school," Archie explains.

"I love that drink too," Larry says, "but I wasn't sure I'd be allowed one." He smiles at Rebecca.

"Lindsay and Archie are very independent these days," Eileen says to Rebecca.

"We get buses in and out of town," Lindsay says.

"When they're together, they're allowed to get buses," Eileen clarifies.

"Tell them about that man," Lindsay says. "The man on the telephone."

"Oh yes!" Archie is clearly delighted with this story. "Well, we sometimes catch the bus from Horsforth to the city centre.

57

You know, up the ring road to West Park and down through Headingley? And that's a red bus."

"There are only red buses and green buses," Eileen explains to Larry.

"Let me tell this story," Archie says. "So, the green one is the number thirty-two, and that one goes into Leeds from Kirkstall Road."

"It's really confusing," Lindsay says.

"It is," Archie agrees. "And a couple of weeks ago I telephoned the bus station – I wanted to know the times, but I didn't know whether it was the red bus station or the green bus station – so I asked the man, 'What colour buses do you have?' And he says in his thick Yorkshire accent, 'I don't know, love. What colour buses do you want?'."

Archie goes into fits of giggles and bangs his fists on the table and Larry catches his Cresta bottle, dislodged in the commotion.

"Thank you," Rebecca mouths.

"What colour buses do you want?" Archie cries out. "I'll always remember that."

"It's a very Yorkshire story," Larry says. "But I couldn't tell you why."

"Yorkshire folk are helpful," Dan says, staking his claim to rejoin the conversation.

"Yes, Yorkshire people will do anything for you," Eileen says.

"They'll do anything for you," Rebecca says, "but they'll resent it afterwards."

They laugh, and Rebecca and Larry begin chatting again. She notices how easy it is, how little he projects himself to the forefront of their conversation, how quickly a casual exchange can feel intimate. Today he just wants to hear about the boss, he says. Well, at least he can tell her something about his interests, she replies.

"Lazing around," he says, smiling. "But otherwise, I'm getting into the local history of the area."

"I'm interested in that too," Rebecca says. "Did you know that thousands of years ago we had a much warmer climate? We had hippopotamuses wallowing in the River Aire, and wild oxen on the hillsides."

"You don't say."

"I think it's time for another game of Frisbee," Archie says, affecting a yawn, heading off with Lindsay and Dan. Eileen pointedly picks up a newspaper and goes to find "a sunny spot", leaving Rebecca and Larry alone at the table.

"So, is the boss married?" he asks.

"No, the boss has never been married." Rebecca colours slightly.

"Maybe the boss doesn't have time, brewing all that beer?"

"I don't actually brew it myself. We have a team."

"I'll bet you do. And I'm guessing your folks were professional types. Or teachers maybe?"

"My mother worked in a furniture shop. And my father was employed by Tetley's."

"Ah. Beer again."

"I never thought that was significant. But I realised recently it must be."

"You're being very mysterious," Larry says.

"It's a long story."

"I'm an American in Leeds with too much time on his hands. Tell me the story."

"So, when I was thirteen, my father was sacked from his job. He was accused of stealing at a charity event. A hundred pounds or so went missing, and his boss blamed him. He would never have done that. But Tetley's believed Terry Martin, and because of the scandal – it got into the local papers – Dad could never find proper work again."

"Didn't he contest it – the stealing thing?"

"People used to just accept things."

"But it was a miscarriage of justice."

"It was, absolutely. And we carried that with us, in our daily lives. Does that make sense?"

He nods.

"Sometimes I'd go with him on a Saturday. He'd pop into shops and ask if they needed help. My mother would be waiting at home – she'd pounce as soon as we set foot in the door. 'Well?' she would say. 'Nothing doing', my father would answer. He'd always use that phrase. 'Nothing doing'."

"Very hard for a young girl to deal with."

"We managed as best we could. Eileen and I have a brother too."

"And you said it was significant. Tetley's?"

"My father took his own life. I found him after school in our garage." She looks at him, gauging his reaction. He holds her gaze. "Well, that was because of Tetley's – or Terry Martin, the man who framed him. He was notoriously aggressive, but good at his job, Dad always said. We all thought Terry Martin stole the money and later we discovered he was an alcoholic and had left Tetley's under a cloud himself."

"And you bought your own brewery. Interesting."

"Only after I'd run another business helping unemployed men back to work. That became a recruitment agency."

"I'm starting to see a picture here."

"Yes, it all stems back to my father. I didn't realise that until this year if I'm honest."

Rebecca notices a row of birds, one each on a line of wooden beams projecting upwards from the lake.

"I saw those little fellows too," Larry says. "They're separate – but they're together, right?"

"I'm sorry to have gone on about my father like that. I feel rather embarrassed. You're a total stranger after all."

"No worries, really." He hesitates for a moment. "I'll tell you something that I haven't talked about in ages. My wife also took her life. Coming up to four years now. I'm not looking for sympathy. Just floating it out there."

"Is that why you left the States?"

"Too many painful associations. I was seeking a fresh start."

CHAPTER FIFTEEN

26 AUGUST 1979

S oon afterwards, Rebecca and Larry are rejoined by the twins, followed by Eileen and Dan.

"Is he Aunty Becky's boyfriend now?" Archie asks.

"Of course not," Eileen says. "He's just a man we all met in the park."

"I'd like him to be her boyfriend," Archie says.

There is silence and Rebecca tries counting the birds balanced on the beams.

"Maybe I should ask your aunt for her phone number before we pay the bill?" Larry says.

"I know it off by heart," Archie says and proudly reels it off, loud enough for any of the people at surrounding tables to hear. "Aren't you going to write it down?"

Larry looks to Rebecca for instructions.

"It's fine," she says, blushing.

Larry gets out a small red notebook from his shoulder bag.

THE COMPANY SHE KEEPS

On the walk home Eileen is irritable, perhaps because she's so used to Rebecca being single that the thought of any change is unsettling. Rebecca makes a big effort to talk to Dan. He's recently started working on an occasional basis for a family dealing in scrap metal, a subject Rebecca knows next to nothing about.

"What will you say to that man when he calls?" Archie asks his aunt.

Rebecca laughs. "That would be telling."

Archie is not so easily put off. "I mean, if he asks you out. Are you going to say yes?"

"I might do, yes."

"But what if he wants you to marry him?"

As so often happens when Rebecca faces an embarrassing question, everything goes quiet around her.

"He wouldn't do that on the first phone call," she says.

"But in a few months' time," Archie persists. "What will you say?"

"What do you think I should say?"

"I reckon you should go out with him but not get married. Because you never know, do you? Mummy got married and we all know what happened to that."

Thinking that now would be a good time to change the subject, Rebecca tells Lindsay how well she recited her poem earlier. "The writing is fantastic, of course, but the way you delivered it was so professional."

"I want to be an actress," Lindsay says.

"Do you? I live next door to an actor."

"Do you think they'll ever catch him?" Lindsay asks. "The man who kills all the ladies?"

Rebecca hesitates for a moment. "Yes, of course they will. And hopefully very soon." She reflects for a moment on the inadequacy of her response. "Is it something that you worry about?"

"Not really," Lindsay says brightly.

"But it's obviously something you chat about at school."

"We used to a bit," Lindsay admits. "But now everyone's talking about the Boomtown Rats instead."

CHAPTER SIXTEEN

"I love the way they bang into each other and still keep going," Rebecca says. "And even the battered-up ones that look like they're about to explode, they keep going too."

There is a roar as loud as an aeroplane as a dozen or so engines stream past. The woman next to Rebecca resumes waving her yellow flag right in front of their faces, and more people are leaning on the metal rail in front of them, which also impedes their view.

"It's a metaphor for all human life," Larry says. "Even the ones about to explode keep going. But listen – stock car racing. How come I'd never even heard of this sport?"

"I hadn't either," Rebecca says. "One of my suppliers told me about it."

"And it's so lucky that we have a track in Bradford."

"They do it all over the country, apparently."

"I have to say, in the USA, we might, possibly, make it look a little more... polished?"

"You mean you wouldn't handwrite the numbers on top of the cars with felt-tip pens?"

"We call those 'markers'. But that's totally the beauty of this thing."

"Never underestimate how professional we Brits are at appearing amateur."

"Ha-ha, you guys have it down to a fine art."

Another race ends and the man with the chequered flag leaps onto the back of the winning car and is driven slowly around the track. He waves to a man in a yellow boiler suit standing on the roof of another car. Two cars lie on their sides nearby. Everywhere there is hubbub and activity, except the grassy area in the centre of the track where a single white van is parked with several men idling around it.

"This is awesome," Larry says. "When I called you up, I never thought we'd be doing anything like this."

"You assumed I'd take you for tea at the Griffin Hotel?"

"Something similar. But the boss has surprised me."

"It's great fun, isn't it?" Rebecca says. "And driving like that could certainly speed up my journey into work."

"Kind of dangerous too," Larry says. "Do you think people get killed in this sport?"

"Probably all the time. I'd love to have a go though. Sadly, all the drivers seem to be men. How come us women don't get to join in the fun?" Rebecca makes a mental note to look into this at some point.

"Well, you won't catch me doing it," Larry says with a loud laugh. "It's scary enough driving on the left-hand side."

"Poor you. So hard being an innocent American in wild and dangerous Yorkshire!"

They walk around the track, thinking they may get ice creams; it still feels like a perfect summer afternoon. Larry is fascinated by a row of men wearing a variety of coloured tracksuits, sitting in their cars, legs poking out of open doors, drinking tea from thermoses.

"Look at those guys. I mean, they're total celebrities for a day, right? And tomorrow, they'll be back in their jobs, delivering mail, or whatever."

"That's pretty much the idea," Rebecca agrees.

"But even today, in their moment of glory, they can't resist putting their feet up and having a cup of tea!"

"And why would they resist it?"

"Did you see that? The car that just went past had 'Stock Car' written on it. That's like a footballer in a match with a label saying: 'footballer', isn't it?"

Rebecca squints as the car takes another bend.

"It says 'Stock Car Racing'."

"Oh, so it's telling us where we are. I love this place so much."

"So, you'd come back?"

"Absolutely. But only with the boss. It wouldn't be the same without you."

Rebecca smiles. She says they could bring Archie and Lindsay next time. Who, by the way, were straight away two of his biggest fans.

"Maybe so," Larry says. "But not your sister, I'm guessing."

"She just got annoyed because you didn't pay her much attention."

"That was her boyfriend there, wasn't it?"

"It doesn't matter. She's used to being the pretty one of the two of us."

"She is?" Larry is incredulous.

"Oh yes, it was always eye-catching Eileen, and reliable Rebecca."

"That's not how I saw it. Are you telling me I'm chasing after the wrong one?"

"I'm telling you you're definitely chasing after the right one."

"Now that's a relief," Larry says, and without awkwardness turns and kisses her squarely on the lips, then carries on walking.

"Did you say we're getting ice creams?" Rebecca manages to blurt out. She would have kissed him back had she had a moment to do so.

They don't speak until they reach the pink van screaming *YIPPEE! It's Mr Whippy*. She buys a 99 Flake, and he chooses a Lord Toffingham as it sounds so British.

"It would appear the boss likes dicing with death."

Rebecca stops, decides to treat this as a joke. "Because I bought a 99 Flake?"

"No. You want to take part in these crazy races."

"Oh! That was just a fleeting fantasy. And to be honest, I'm probably busy enough anyway."

"If I'm honest," Larry says, "isn't there enough danger for ladies in Yorkshire right now without deliberately adding more?"

There's a pause before she replies. "What struck me after this latest one was that no one talked about it at work."

"You mean that student from Bradford?"

"Yes, Barbara Leach. Unless they discussed it when I wasn't there, everyone was avoiding the subject."

"I avoid talking about it myself, though by chance I moved into a street where two of his other victims lived. I can't wait to move somewhere else."

"It's as if we think that by not talking about it, it's not happening. And several friends and myself went on a Reclaim the Night march too."

"I can't imagine what it's like for you women."

"Do you know what, Larry? We can discuss this anytime we want. But let's not do so this afternoon."

"Agreed, we won't let him interfere with our outing to the races. I'm going to look back on today with such happiness. I don't want those memories tainted in any way."

As always, he has said exactly the right thing.

CHAPTER SEVENTEEN

16 SEPTEMBER 1979

There is shouting, excitement, somewhere near the stand selling hot dogs and sandwiches. A policeman runs clumsily towards the commotion. Rebecca and Larry are drawn towards it too; the crowd have edged back, forming a crescent around two grown men squaring up to each other. The younger, beefier, with tumbling strawberry-blond hair is snarling at his older adversary, egged on by a woman, his girlfriend presumably – "Smack him one, Andy – go on, smack him!" and also by the older man himself, "Come on, son, if you want it, you can have it, you fucking toerag!" The older man's voice is familiar.

"All right, folks," the breathless policeman intervenes. "This isn't *The Streets of San Francisco.*"

The girlfriend who has been circling the action suddenly turns to Rebecca, as if confiding in a friend. "He came up to me from behind, cupped my boobs, he did! – while we was waiting for our hot dogs."

"Would I be right in saying that you're with drink, sir?" the policeman asks the older man.

"He groped my missus," the strawberry-blond man says.

"Come on, sir," the policeman says. "Best come with me. You reek of alcohol."

Rebecca suddenly steps forward, placing herself in the thick of the action.

"Don't arrest him. I know this man to be a person of good character."

Brian Sheridan looks at Rebecca and rolls his eyes.

"He's one of my employees," Rebecca continues. "I own Keighley Beers."

The policeman looks impressed. "Don't delay – it's a Wilberforce day!" This gets a sizeable chuckle from the crowd and a smattering of applause.

"If he's been drinking, it's because his wife has been seriously ill," Rebecca says. "We know all about it in the office."

"Well, if I'm not arresting him, you'd better take him home, love," the policemen says. "But please don't give him any more Wilberforce."

They drop Brian Sheridan off in front of his terraced house in Bradford. He has been silent the whole journey, other than admonishing Rebecca for lying on his behalf. "The wife's absolutely fine," he said. "There was no bloody need to say that."

Larry, seated in the back, watches as Brian steps out of Rebecca's car without saying another word. After tripping slightly on the pavement, he charts an unsteady path to the front door, then turns around, as if he's forgotten something.

"I guess I'll see you in the morning," Brian says and goes inside.

There is a moment of silence in the car.

"Is that as good as it gets?" Larry asks. "'I guess I'll see you in the morning'?" And suddenly he and Rebecca are howling with laughter, it could be the funniest thing they've ever heard. Larry goes round to the front seat and they're still laughing as Rebecca turns left out of the street.

"Could he have been any less grateful?" Larry gasps. "I mean you just saved the guy from a night in a cell."

Rebecca admits he'd have been hard pushed to be less grateful.

"And you're his boss, right? You're literally his boss. This is like a comedy sketch."

"I'm glad you're finding it so amusing," Rebecca says.

"There was something Shakespearean about it," Larry says. "When you stepped forward from the crowd. 'This thing of darkness I acknowledge mine'."

"I don't know that one." Rebecca is impressed.

"Prospero admitting that Caliban belongs to him. I once wrote an essay about it – he's owning up to all the dark stuff in his unconscious, recognising his own humanity. All very Jungian."

"My God," Rebecca cries. "I'm the one who studied psychology and you know more than me."

"It was just a subsidiary course. That line stuck in my mind."

"Shall we have tea at my place?" Rebecca asks. "I can drop you back later."

"Sure," Larry says.

"I'm sorry we had to leave the racing early."

"It's fine."

In Rebecca's kitchen, Larry tells her to be wary of Brian Sheridan. There is something not right about the man.

Rebecca has hastily made Sandwich Spread sandwiches, another peculiarly British innovation that Larry has never encountered before. They're enjoying them with a pot of English Breakfast tea.

"Yeah, I didn't get a good feeling," Larry continues. "And I didn't like the sound of what he did to that lady either."

"Brian's harmless, all mouth and no trousers. There's someone else I'm much more worried about."

She tells him about Mervyn Harris, his persistent attempts to make a date with her, and then the probable sighting on her road.

"That's a little strange," Larry says. "But you're not completely sure it was him?"

"I'm not, and I guess I may never know. Look, Larry, I'm sorry to bother you with all of this nonsense. You probably just want me to give you a ride home soon."

It is four thirty in the afternoon. In the event, Rebecca does not take Larry home for another fifteen hours, dropping him off on her way to work.

CHAPTER EIGHTEEN

19 SEPTEMBER 1979

R ebecca and Larry have agreed to meet at the Brownlee Arms in the evening. The pub is roughly halfway between her work and his house, and she has been there several times with Roland. Their second official date is very much on Rebecca's mind throughout the morning. She wonders whether it will culminate in another marathon session in bed, and whether, indeed, she should cut to the chase by heading straight over to his home. She smiles as she recalls the bumper bag of underwear she'd bought in Marks & Spencer during her lunch hour, the day after their first date.

That Sunday, three days earlier, she'd been perfectly honest with Larry as they lay beneath the sheets. Other than occasional trysts with an over-friendly policeman, this was the first sex she'd had with anybody for seven or eight years. Her last proper relationship, now she'd come to think about it, had been an intense fling with a much younger man who, lovely as he'd been, was at a completely different stage of his life.

"What about the policeman?" Larry had asked.

"What about him?"

"Should I be worried?"

"He's married and I recently discovered that I'm not the only distraction from his vow of fidelity."

"A woman in every port."

"It would seem so."

At this point Rebecca asked Larry whether there'd been others since his wife died.

"None," Larry said. "It's as if I've been wandering in a desert, without even admitting to myself my own raging thirst."

"Well, you're certainly drinking deeply from the spring tonight!" Rebecca had responded.

Now at her desk, and theoretically reviewing the rejuvenated sales of Wilberforce since the campaign began, it occurs to Rebecca that Larry was uncomfortable saying anything much about his history, although she'd been frank about her past relationships. He clearly finds it difficult to "open up", and certainly, if this very male tendency existed before his wife's suicide, it could only have been exaggerated since. In any case, Larry has many other good qualities, so she's prepared to accommodate, and perhaps work on, his reticence to disclose.

Brian Sheridan has requested a meeting, and Debbie has passed a message from Rebecca that she can only see him in her lunch hour. Having not been in the office on Monday and Tuesday, Rebecca hasn't seen Brian since the weekend. Is he going to arrive with a bunch of flowers and apologise for events at the stock car racing? Some chance. Brian has been keeping a low profile since the Local Gold fiasco. Has he actually been doing any work in the intervening months? Retaining him as a member of staff continues to feel like a long-running act of charity and Rebecca wonders why she bothers.

A few minutes later, Brian enters her office without knocking. He's carrying bottles and is followed by his assistant brewer, William Clayton, and Dave Townley, their engineer. William is in his late twenties, a quiet family man who'd also previously worked for Ingrow Ales. Rebecca has the impression that he'd been personally recruited by Brian, and to his credit William works with his boss without ever showing signs of resentment. Rebecca is also pretty sure that he does the hard graft in that team. They sit down at the small round table and Brian plonks two bottles in front of him, William adding a third.

"All looking very serious, chaps," Rebecca says.

"How's Wilberforce?" Brian asks.

The men scrutinise her closely.

"The campaign's gone remarkably well, Brian. Partly because of your brilliant suggestion to use Saatchi's."

"It wasn't my suggestion, as you know – I was being sarcastic."

"The point is, the advert they produced has hugely impacted sales. We're thirty-five per cent up in the off-trade. And a stunning fifty-two per cent in the on-trade!"

Brian nods as if this is no big deal and Rebecca wonders where the conversation is heading.

"I take it you have seen the advert?" she asks.

"Oh, I've seen it. I thought it was pretty good, actually. We all did, didn't we, boys?"

"It was great," William says. "I loved it."

"Me too," Dave adds. "That stuff in the stadium when he runs off with the ball – genius."

"That was funny," Brian agrees. "And clever too."

This sudden outbreak of enthusiasm momentarily floors Rebecca. She can't recall Brian talking so positively about anything.

"And from what you say, it's been successful?" Brian continues.

"I've never seen anything like it," Rebecca says.

"So, you might want to try doing the same again. With something else?" Brian says.

Finally, Rebecca sees what lies behind this. She remembers offering up the vague possibility of a launch of Local Gold sometime in the future during the difficult meeting in April.

"If I think it's the right product, certainly," Rebecca says.

"We're sure it's the right product. I thought I'd asked you guys to bring glasses?"

"I'll go." William heads towards the corridor.

"This isn't about Local Gold, is it?" Rebecca asks.

"The fizzy marmalade?" Brian laughs. "No, we've got something much better."

"So, this is an ale, is it?"

"Yes, an ale."

"Would you excuse me a second?" Rebecca rises and leaves the room. She finds Sally having a cigarette in the box room containing the photocopier. "I don't know what he's up to, but I want your support," Rebecca says.

"Maybe we should get Roland in as well? The voice of a sensible male."

"Yes, check his room. And we'll need more glasses. Ask Debbie to come too."

Minutes later, they're assembled in Rebecca's office and Debbie brings in a second extra chair.

"Have we squeezed in enough people, or should we invite the royal family?" Brian asks.

"That's a good idea," Sally says, laughing.

"All right, Brian, perhaps you can tell us a little more about this product," Rebecca suggests.

"It's an ale. And it's new," Brian says. "Go on, William."

William opens the first bottle and fills all seven glasses halfway.

"Cheers, everybody," Rebecca says.

Somehow everyone manages to take a sip from their glass at the same time, except Brian who drains his with one glug before wiping his mouth on his shirtsleeve. Roland narrows his eyes, looks at Rebecca, and takes a more thoughtful mouthful. Rebecca stares at the murky liquid in her glass, drinks more.

"Could I have a top-up?" Roland asks.

The second bottle is opened and also the third, William pouring. Everyone is now sitting with a full glass.

"Is anyone going to say anything, or do you all have to consult a bloody lawyer first?" Brian asks.

"I would say," Roland begins, "and this is subject to a number of legal caveats! – that it's actually a pretty good ale."

"It's delicious," Sally says. "Very refreshing. It reminds me of the ales my dad used to drink, I'd take a sneaky sip sometimes."

"It's bloody good, Brian," Dave says.

"I like it," Debbie says. "It tastes oaty. And I don't even like ale as a rule."

"All right," Brian says. "So, we've got an 'actually a pretty good ale', we've got a 'delicious', we've got a 'bloody good' – wasn't it Dave?" – Dave nods – "And we've got a 'like it because it's oaty', or was that oaky, Debbie?"

"I don't know – either," Debbie says, embarrassed, and heads to the toilet.

"What about you, Rebecca? Cos you like to think that yours is the opinion which counts round here."

Rebecca drains her glass. "I do like to think that, Brian – thanks for reminding me. And I'd say we're going to need more of this stuff. Because I bloody love it!"

Dave and William are sent to fetch more bottles.

CHAPTER NINETEEN

19 SEPTEMBER 1979

"Y ou're a sly devil, Mr Sheridan," Rebecca says with a chuckle. "I had no idea you were even working on this. Talk about a closely guarded secret. I don't know whether to be delighted you've produced such a belter or mortified that I didn't know what was going on in my own brewery."

"You see," Brian says, "I'd describe this as a heavily roasted malt. It's got fewer hops so it's less bitter to the taste."

"And it's slightly nutty," Rebecca says. "This could be your finest moment, Brian."

Debbie returns to say that Rebecca's afternoon appointment with Morrisons has just been cancelled. The man has gone home sick. It's agreed this is perfect timing as more bottles are opened.

"Has it got a name?" Roland asks. "Names are all-important when it comes to marketing."

"Not yet," Brian says.

"How about Ingrown Ale?" Sally asks.

"Hmm..." Rebecca says.

"It's too much like ingrowing toenail," Roland says.

"You're right," Sally says. "The jokes would be unbearable."

"How about Yorkshire Terrier?" Rebecca suggests.

"Or Yorkshire Terror," Roland says.

"Spooky," Sally says. "Maybe My Ghostly Ale?"

"Do you have any ideas, Brian?" Rebecca asks, noticing his silence.

"Yes, Sheridan's," Brian says.

"Sheridan's, as in Brian Sheridan?" Rebecca asks.

"Well, it's my creation," Brian says.

"Sheridan's," Roland says. "That's pretty good."

"I like it too," Rebecca says. "Let's go with that."

William Clayton looks like he has something to add, and Rebecca briefly wonders whether she's just facilitated another moment of injustice in the workplace.

"Top the glasses up, William," Brian says.

They are still going at five thirty; at some point whisky and gin were added to the drinks available, and the conversation bears all the hallmarks of those conducted through the distorting prism of alcohol.

It isn't that Rebecca has forgotten that she's meeting Larry so much as she suddenly realises she's in no fit state to do so. And her announcement that she's meant to be going out with someone for a drink causes a ripple of laughter that gathers momentum and quickly turns hysterical. "I can't even drive myself to the pub," Rebecca moans.

"Is this your American friend?" Brian asks. "Rebecca's found herself a swanky boyfriend, I met him on Sunday."

"I didn't think you'd want to talk about that considering your own condition," Rebecca says. "I was worried you'd throw up in my car."

"Well, you'd know all about being 'with drink', wouldn't you?" Brian points out, not unreasonably.

Rebecca laughs, realising she's feeling more relaxed in his

company. Maybe the problem had been hers all along. Perhaps it was her being too uptight and judgemental.

"I certainly wouldn't recommend you having more drink, sis," Roland says. "He might try and take advantage of you."

"Don't worry, he's already done that!" Rebecca screeches, and the room erupts in a brouhaha of catcalls, cheers, laughter and lewd jokes. At this moment of mayhem, Nigel Liddelow, the bookkeeper, leads Mervyn Harris into Rebecca's office. Nigel looks around with evident disbelief, as if he's walked in on his grandmother in bed with the postman. The room goes quiet. Nigel explains that he was on the point of leaving for the evening when he heard "an uninterrupted buzzing from reception".

"That will have been the buzzer then," Dave says.

"Yes, I realised," Nigel shouts over the raucous laughter. "This gentleman has come here to see Rebecca."

Nigel and the uninvited guest are given a drink, the table and chairs are moved to one side to maximise space, and the party continues.

Mervyn approaches Rebecca, saying he was hoping to have a private word.

"Whatever you've got to say you can say it in front of my colleagues because they're all bloody marvellous," Rebecca announces. She insists on introducing Mervyn to everybody, explaining that they're celebrating the development of a new product, Sheridan's. He's fortunate enough to have been given a sneak preview. She hopes he'll attend the official launch and write a positive article or two.

They move over to the window and Mervyn admits to feeling confused as to whether they're ever going out together to have a drink.

"I'll answer that question in a minute. First, you can tell me what you were doing sitting in your car in my road with the engine turned off. It was a few weeks ago and don't shake your head like that."

Mervyn continues to deny it so Rebecca opens the window and peers out into the car park, seeing if she can spot a red Hillman Imp.

"I need my glasses, but I can pop down now and see if it's there if you prefer."

"I just wanted to speak to you," Mervyn says. "You were ignoring me."

"So, we've finally got the truth," Rebecca cries out. "And I don't ever want to see you loitering there again. Now I'll answer your question. We won't be going out for a drink as I've met somebody else. I'm seeing him tonight, in fact."

If anything, the news that Rebecca is unavailable relaxes Mervyn. He helps himself to more drink and gets into a conversation with Sally, although Rebecca could tell him that he's wasting his time with her too.

In the end, Debbie, who's spent most of the afternoon catching up on admin, offers to give Rebecca a lift to the pub. The celebration is still going as they leave.

"Give my regards to lover boy," Brian calls after her.

Rebecca is only five minutes late arriving at the Brownlee Arms. Larry is standing by the bar, and without her even saying a word, he laughs uproariously.

"Jeepers, what happened to you?"

"I'm a little the worse for wear," Rebecca says slowly.

They agree it would be crazy for her to drink anything else and Larry offers her a lift home. I'm so sorry, Rebecca keeps saying. He tells her not to worry. If he had been mixing drinks non-stop for six hours, he'd be in a similar condition. "Even the boss is allowed to get drunk once in a while."

When they get to Lidgett Park Road, she makes a run for the downstairs toilet and vomits copiously. I'm so ashamed, she says as Larry takes her upstairs, helping her off with her dress. Rebecca slides into her bed but has to get up a few minutes later to throw up again, this time in her en suite. Larry is there to escort her there and back. "Things are not good in the state of Denmark," he says with a chuckle, sitting on the edge of the bed.

Later, he goes to fetch a large glass of water and Rebecca sits up in bed to sip it. "I promise this won't happen again," she says.

He assures her that it's fine, and as she's starting to look a bit better, perhaps he should take himself off home. Rebecca becomes tearful, begging him to stay and look after her, and Larry spends the night beside her in her bed, a model of decorum and respectability.

Rebecca wanted Larry to have spent a second night before calling Simon, which she does the next day. It makes it more solid and official to have woken up together and shared breakfast twice, even if the second time was with a hangover. She waits until lunchtime before telephoning him at work from her office, straight away telling him that she's finishing their relationship. He calls her back a few minutes later when he's able to talk privately.

"I'm still taking it in, to be honest," Simon tells her.

"That's fine, but if you don't mind I've got a meeting in Pudsey to prepare for."

"I can't believe you've met someone you like more than me."

"It was bound to happen at some point, Simon."

He is sounding desolate, but she can't bring herself to evince any sympathy and tells him why. "I thought it was a bit ironic that you asked what I was doing on my birthday, and that evening I saw you drinking with another woman in the Cobourg."

"That woman happens to be my wife, and I was acting on your suggestion to take her out."

"No, Simon – I know what your wife looks like because I've met her."

He tries to protest, he tells her he doesn't know what he'll do without her, but Rebecca is in no mood to hear it. Maybe they'll bump into each other another time, she says, and finishes the conversation. She surprises herself sometimes just how brutal she can be.

CHAPTER TWENTY

13 OCTOBER 1979

Larry is generous. He'd pay for everything if she allowed him, which she doesn't, as she's determined that things should proceed on an equal basis. He's modest too about his achievements as a financial consultant. Their meeting has come at the right time for both, though Rebecca has many anxieties, the relationship feeling as fragile as a newly laid robin's egg. She's impatient to move beyond this stage to the comfortable familiarity of being a couple, even if this means sacrificing some of that early feathery excitement. The process of becoming an established item, while nerve-racking, is also oddly bureaucratic: specific boxes must be ticked; certain conversations must happen; experiences must be shared.

Buoyed by the returns from the afternoon's stock car racing, they invest a day in an outing to the coast, as Larry would "like to do the British seaside thing". They debated the relative merits of Whitby versus Scarborough, Blackpool versus Morecambe, Rebecca warning that while the view across the bay in Morecambe is glorious, everything in the town is closed down, falling apart or broken. "I'm guessing I'll feel right at home there," Larry said with a wry laugh.

They leave first thing Saturday, catching the train from Bingley, the journey scheduled to last two hours. Larry is straight away asking questions, wanting to know the ins and outs of her childhood, the dynamics of her family life. Was the boss always a high achiever? And how has financial success affected her relationship with her siblings? Rebecca explains that, if anything, she is treated with less respect by Roland and Eileen than at any time in her life, even though she is, quite literally, Roland's boss.

"He doesn't kowtow to me and is very tough on bad ideas, especially mine. I can talk to him about anything."

"Have you told him about me?" Larry asks.

"I may have mentioned my silver saviour."

"Silver saviour. Isn't that the guy who waits tables in a fancy restaurant?"

"Only if you're looking for a career change, Larry," Rebecca says.

They follow a lugubrious trail of passengers out of Morecambe station. Larry wants to visit the Midland Hotel nearby.

"It has art deco seahorses, apparently."

"That's right, above the entrance." He's clearly done his research.

"I've never seen art deco seahorses. I assume I'll be missing out unless I do."

They head there first, sinking into deep red chairs, drinking tea and chatting about twenties' architecture in a dining room that's seen better days. Afterwards, walking along Marine Road Central towards the seafront, they go past the Winter Gardens which Rebecca announces closed in 1977 following decades of decline. "I'll be combining the duties of tour guide and grim reaper today," she says.

It is a clear day, the blue-grey shadows of the Lake District visible beyond the bay on the left. Eventually they reach another landmark, the clock tower, standing alone and conspicuously red, as if embarrassed to be spotted in Morecambe in such straitened times. They buy ice-cream cornets and before Rebecca has even tasted hers, a seagull swoops from above with a force that makes her scream, batters it from her hand before savaging the cone and vanilla splodged on the paving. Rebecca cries out again, this time in frustration, raising her boot above the offending bird, but it performs a skilful take-off manoeuvre, carrying a sizeable portion of the booty away in its beak.

Larry places his hand on Rebecca's shoulder.

"Are you all right, love?" a woman in a headscarf and National Health glasses asks, before Larry can. "They're such pests, aren't they?"

Rebecca laughs. "I'm fine. It's just one of those things."

"Same thing happened to us," her husband in a tweed cap says. "Remember, June?"

"When we were engaged, yes. Before the war," she adds for Rebecca's benefit. "Though you saw the little beggar off."

"Well, I saw him coming."

"Colin batted it away, didn't you?"

"I stuck my arm out." Colin demonstrates. "And I bashed him."

"He did too."

Colin turns his square face and looks Rebecca in the eye.

"You can prevent these things, if you look out properly, you know."

Rebecca stares at him, amazed that her moment of misfortune has become a topic for public reprimand.

"I'll bet you fought in the war too," Larry says to Colin.

"Of course, he was a pilot," June says.

"Flew twenty-three missions."

"You'd have been proud to have carried out an air raid like that seagull just did," Larry says. Colin laughs uproariously while his wife rubs his arm affectionately.

Rebecca can't help noticing Larry's ability to put people at their ease.

CHAPTER TWENTY-ONE

13 OCTOBER 1979

They sit on the seafront, just the two of them. "In all seriousness, isn't it symbolic being attacked by a seagull?" Rebecca asks. "It doesn't feel like a good omen."

For him, Larry says, seagulls are the ultimate scavenger; they remind him of the need to make the most of what he has, which feels a lot right now. That skill at making use of older things means you can resist buying anything new. It becomes all about thrift stores and giving items a new lease of life. In his mind, this is what seagulls symbolise. Perhaps Morecambe is an example of that ethos in action?

"Do you even have seagulls in America?" Rebecca asks.

"Of course. It's the state bird of Utah." She's no longer surprised by the breadth of his knowledge but smiles in appreciation anyway.

They settle down to read their books. She is struggling with *The Dead Sea Scrolls and the Christian Myth*, a birthday present from her first cousin. Larry is apologetic for his choice, Stephen King's *The Shining*. "It's not highbrow, I know, but boy can that man tell a story."

They eat a fish and chip lunch, buy one or two trinkets and

spend more time on the beach. Larry produces a Frisbee from his bag and Rebecca is delighted that this time she tosses and catches with increasing swagger and panache.

On their way back to the station, they stop off at Brucciani's ice-cream parlour, admiring the porthole lamps and classic deco handles. Sitting at a livid orange Formica table, they order two Knickerbocker Glories from a girl who's not much more than sixteen. She commends their choice.

Larry wonders if they have time to pop into the waxworks museum nearby. They find it on Marine Road and pay the meagre entrance fee to a young man absorbed in reading *For Whom the Bell Tolls*. There are only two or three others inside and the place is in an advanced state of decay, a smell of chemicals and shoe polish permeating the building. They begin with the tawdry collection of historic figures and celebrities: Abraham Lincoln, William Shakespeare, Florence Nightingale and Benjamin Disraeli. Princess Margaret's wig is matted and clearly way too big.

"Remind me again why you wanted to come here?" Rebecca raises her eyebrows quizzically.

Larry chuckles as he stands next to the most recent addition, Terry Wogan.

"Hey! This guy's head has actually been stuck on someone else's body. You can see the join marks."

"It's that Morecambe thrift again," Rebecca says. "One minute reusing an ice cream, the next someone's head – or should that be their body?"

Larry links his arm through hers. "I've got a smart cookie here. I'll need all my resources to deal with you."

Upstairs, they enter the chamber of horrors, featuring Hawley Crippen, John Christie and Ruth Ellis, incarcerated in chicken-wire cages. "What an inhuman way to treat Britain's finest murderers!" Larry says.

"I think you'll find Crippen was one of yours," Rebecca points out.

Things take a further turn for the worse with the museum of anatomy, which a local pressure group actually campaigned to have closed down. They now appear to be the only people in the museum. The first room features torsos of life-size women, headless and legless, nine in total, presented as cross sections that claim to depict "the nine stages of pregnancy". Wander past them, however, and it feels more like an exercise in the macabre than the scientific; a celebration of sliced up naked women, gaping wounds and gleaming internal organs.

"I wouldn't bother even going into this one," Larry calls from the next room.

"What's in there?"

He reads from a sign. "'In these models you see the awful results of men leading immoral lives before marriage'."

There are a few seconds' silence, then she hears cackling.

"It's basically body parts, ravaged by venereal disease. Yuk!"

"I'll leave that one to you," she shouts back.

"Good call," Larry says.

She waits, looking at one of the pregnancy models, trying to work out which bit is the foetus.

"What are you actually doing in there?" she calls.

There's no answer. A couple of minutes later, he returns shaking his head.

"That was rancid," he says, laughing. "Let's go before I barf."

The train is barely out of the station when Larry lays his cards on the table.

"Next weekend you get to choose. Anything. Neither of us

was taken with that museum, I feel bad for suggesting it. In fact, you've had a lousy day all round. And it was all my idea."

"Don't be mad. I've had a great time."

"You've been savaged by a seagull. You've experienced the most sordid place on earth. I'm begging you, choose what we do next weekend."

"The thing is, I'm off to Grantham next weekend," she replies. "I'm staying with my cousin. There's something urgent that needs discussing."

"Are you going Saturday?"

"Friday after work. I'll get back Sunday evening."

"I see." He sounds genuinely disappointed.

"But–" Rebecca is thinking on her feet, "they don't have such a big place, but maybe you can come too? If you can stand a weekend with my first cousin and her baby? And her husband, of course. I'll check it will be all right."

"I'd love that. The more of your relatives I meet the better, seriously. As long as I'm not in the way."

CHAPTER TWENTY-TWO

14-19 OCTOBER 1979

Rebecca calls Alison the next day. It's no problem, Alison says. They'd love to meet Larry, although at some point over the weekend, she'd still like that private chat.

Rebecca doesn't see Larry in the week and time passes slowly. She also starts to feel anxious. What if Alison doesn't like Larry? What if her husband doesn't like him either? Years ago, she wasn't bothered by what people made of her partners but this time it feels different.

Alison and Ahmet live in a two-bedroom maisonette close to the centre of Grantham. When Larry and Rebecca arrive hungry around eight pm after sitting in heavy traffic, Ahmet immediately tells them all about their property. It's set over two floors and the bedrooms are both doubles. They'll find it surprisingly spacious and it's very handy for shopping. Rebecca will later joke to Larry that they might have been prospective buyers, being given the lowdown by an over-enthusiastic estate agent.

Supper is macaroni cheese with broccoli and cauliflower, cooked very much with Dana in mind.

"She clearly loves it," Rebecca says, beaming at the baby.

"We think it's important that she eats what we eat," Alison says.

"It's delicious," Larry says.

"How are you getting on with the book about the Dead Sea Scrolls? Or maybe you've been too busy?" Alison asks.

"I wouldn't describe it as a page turner," Rebecca says.

"I thought you'd enjoy the historical controversy." Alison sounds slightly annoyed. "When I read the review, I thought of you."

Afterwards, Alison settles the baby in her cot and she and Rebecca take a walk to the local church. Larry accepts Ahmet's offer of a whisky.

"It's because he's Asian," Alison tells Rebecca. "The bank manager said they might have agreed had it been for an Indian restaurant, but this was too risky a proposition. They hoped we'd understand."

"How irritating."

"And we're an intelligent family, trying to do the right thing. New enterprise and all that."

"What's the loan for exactly?" Rebecca asks.

"So, it's a healthy drinks and snacks outlet, on the high street. Things that aren't jam-packed with sugar. Things you'd be happy to give a young child."

"It sounds interesting," Rebecca says non-committally. "Are you sure Grantham's the right area for it?"

"Of course, you'd be surprised! By the way, Ahmet doesn't want to make a big fuss about this. He'd be really embarrassed if he knew I'd even mentioned it. He's a very proud man."

As both bedrooms were described as doubles, Rebecca had assumed that this would translate to a double bed, so is disappointed to find a single next to a zed bed with mattress. Larry improvises by joining them, somewhat clumsily, stretching a sheet across then tucking it in. Lying next to him, Rebecca tells him about her conversation with Alison.

"I've never asked for your advice before. But you are a financial consultant."

"How much is she thinking of?" He tucks a stray thread of her hair behind her ear.

"Well, it's strictly a loan. And she did say when it becomes profitable, I'll see my share and more..."

"Yes...? And...?"

"Twenty-five thousand pounds. Which I thought was rather a lot."

Larry breathes deeply several times. "It is a lot. I'm almost annoyed – on your behalf, of course – that she's had the temerity to ask."

"I'm not annoyed. She's my first cousin and we were close growing up. I always got on better with her than Eileen, much better, in fact."

"I understand. But even so."

"So, let's look at this as an investment opportunity." For some reason, she can't resist reaching out and stroking his beard.

"As opposed to helping out a family member?"

"For the moment, yes. Would it be a good investment?"

"We haven't seen the business case, so how can we tell? Presumably the bank's had more of the detail. And they didn't want to touch it."

"I see where this is heading. You financial consultants are a cautious breed."

They kiss on the lips. She slowly slips her tongue into his mouth.

"Not in everything."

"Okay," Rebecca continues, "so it's not a good business proposition. Based on what we know anyway. I could ask for more information. Or I could as you say treat this purely as a favour to my first cousin."

"In which case, would you be happy to drop twenty-five thousand pounds?"

"Hmmm..."

"Of your hard-earned money!"

"Not exactly."

"Me neither."

"I feel like I'm being pulled in different directions."

Larry kisses her on the forehead. "Sorry, I didn't mean to be overdramatic. I'm just thinking she has a nerve."

"Me too. But I don't make decisions last thing at night."

"Always a bad idea."

"Particularly if the thought of hanky-panky might make me rush the decision."

"I like that thought," Larry says, sliding towards her before slipping down the gap between the two beds. There's a thud and Rebecca laughs so loudly she wakes the baby in the next room.

CHAPTER TWENTY-THREE

21 OCTOBER 1979

On the Sunday, Alison recommends they go to St Wulfram's Church, with its celebrated spire and stunning vaulted ceiling. Larry is fascinated by the chained library, a concept he's never come across before. "It shows how much you Brits value reading," he says. "In the States, no one would ever think of stealing a book, let alone chaining it to the bookcase." He remains there long after the others have lost interest.

Rebecca, Ahmet and Alison are having a conversation about Margaret Thatcher. Rebecca is curious how the town has reacted to her triumph at the polls. Alison sends Ahmet off to buy bread and cheese for their lunch and asks Rebecca if she's thought any more about their earlier conversation on Friday night.

"Okay," Rebecca says. "So, I'm not going to lend you the whole amount. But I'd be interested in trialling some products locally."

"Right," Alison says, sounding both doubtful and disappointed.

"I'd be willing to put some money into that, and into a local advertising campaign."

"Thank you."

"And then we can evaluate the results and take it from there. Let's talk about the specifics on the phone."

She describes the conversation to Larry on the way home, how Alison was clearly not happy but equally did not want to spurn the offer. Oddly, Larry seems unhappy too, particularly when she mentions the figure she's decided on for the trial and advertisements. He does not stay for tea or coffee when they reach her house, making the excuse of an early morning meeting with a client.

She comes through her front door at nine forty-five. Her answerphone is blinking, showing one message.

The voice is male. Clearly drunk. For a moment she thinks of Brian but it's not him. The caller rambles for a few seconds about how he'd rather speak to her in person if it didn't seem so difficult. She suddenly realises it is Mervyn.

"You might be wondering why I care. Perhaps I can explain.

On 18th April I interviewed you and suggested William for your advert. We agreed to have a pint after you'd read my articles.

On 19th June we met at the Bluebell. You hadn't read the articles, but we made an arrangement to meet at the same pub on Saturday 30th.

On 24th and 25th June I left messages, confirming Saturday. You didn't call back.

On the 30th June I left another message. At six o'clock you rang me back and said you had toothache. Toothache!

On 31st July you had your party for Wilberforce Ale. You didn't invite me, even though I found the star for the advert. However, he was good enough to invite me.

On 19th September I visited you at work and you told me

*you'd met someone. The implication was that I should leave you
alone.*

*Today, the 21st October, I'm telling you I'm not leaving you
alone, because you're making a big mistake. I'll be in touch."*

There is the click of the call ending before the machine
beeps three times. Rebecca stands in the hallway, trying to
regulate her breathing. She picks up the phone and dials Larry's
number. Then she remembers that he won't even be home yet.

CHAPTER TWENTY-FOUR

5 NOVEMBER 1979

Bonfire night falls on a Monday and Roland asks Rebecca if she'd be up for an early drink in Whitelock's.

"So what do you think of the 'Flush out the Ripper' campaign?" Rebecca asks, after they've sat down at a tiny table near the stained-glass door.

"Those adverts?"

"Yes – 'The Ripper would like you to ignore this'. I heard on the radio that it's a really bad time to do this as the investigation's already behind on following up leads."

"It probably won't make any difference either way."

"I'm glad you're so calm about it. Most women I know are petrified of stepping out of their front door at night."

"I'm sorry, sis, I'm probably not the best company tonight."

"So what's wrong?"

"On Saturday I received a Dear John letter from a woman I only just met. I was due to see her that evening – she couldn't bear to even phone me. Am I that unattractive?"

"Of course not."

"You can be honest. You couldn't make me feel any worse about myself right now."

"Oh dear, Ro." Rebecca pushes her bottom lip out. "I haven't heard about this one! Are you very upset about her?"

"I don't suppose you'd be over the moon either."

"All right, fair point. What's her name and how did you meet?"

"Nicola. She's the friend of a friend of a friend."

"Maybe she's got something else going on right now. These things aren't always personal."

Roland finishes his beer in one gulp and checks how Rebecca's doing with hers. She holds up her hand. "I'm not getting shit-faced tonight. And I thought we might see some fireworks. East End Park would be closest, but Middleton and Roundhay would also be possible."

"I don't think I'm in the mood tonight."

He buys himself a pint and returns to the table. "This thing with Nicola came at a bad time. I spent the last couple of years lusting after Sally. I felt a right Charlie when I discovered she doesn't like men."

Rebecca is finding it difficult to hear him above the surrounding hum of conversation.

"If it helps, I had no idea either." She looks up towards the bar. Something is happening.

"How's Larry?" Roland asks.

Rebecca can't help smiling. "Larry is good, thanks. He told me last weekend our relationship feels very solid. And that he's already head over heels in love."

Roland nods sadly – as if the vet has just confirmed that his dog needs to be put down. "How long's it been now?"

"A couple of months. But it feels longer."

"Yeah, it seems like you guys have been going out forever. And you haven't even introduced him to me yet."

A policeman standing behind the bar calls for quiet. The barman bangs a glass on the wooden surface and calls, "Could we have a bit of hush please? There's a copper here and he'd like to make an announcement."

CHAPTER TWENTY-FIVE

5 NOVEMBER 1979

"Sorry to interrupt your evening, ladies and gentlemen," the policeman says. "There's a killer on the loose in Yorkshire and he's also making a habit of interrupting people's evenings."

This line works a treat and there is silence.

"I'm going to play you a tape of his voice, that's right, the voice of the Yorkshire Ripper. I'll let you hear it a couple of times, so please listen carefully. And while I'm doing that, my fellow officer will walk around with samples of his handwriting."

A board with scratchy slanting writing samples is being held up by a second policeman. Rebecca notices that it's Simon.

"And can I just emphasise this?" the first policeman continues. "One of you may know this sadistic murderer. He's somebody's husband, or neighbour. Maybe he's that strange chap working in the local corner shop. He could be a family man, a work colleague – he might be extremely good at his job! Perhaps he's living in your house."

Simon smiles at Rebecca and Roland as he continues raising the boards with handwriting samples above his head. He mouths, "See you later". Rebecca recalls having been particularly unpleasant to him in their last conversation, so is pleased to have an opportunity to smooth things over.

When the first policeman has finished playing the tape, Simon comes over and smiles broadly. "They've got a few of us back in uniform for this," he explains.

"How many pubs will you do tonight?" Roland asks.

"Probably a dozen. Maybe more."

A chair has become available next to Rebecca. Simon sits there and takes a sip from her beer.

"Oi!" Rebecca says. Roland gets up to buy more drinks.

"Just a half for me," Rebecca says.

"Unfortunately, not for me. On duty," Simon says, finishing Rebecca's pint.

While Roland is at the bar, Simon says he has a question, something he's been thinking about for a couple of months. Go on, she tells him, she's all ears.

"Why did you think I was with someone else, not my wife, at the Cobourg? On your birthday?"

"I told you. I know what your wife looks like. I had a long conversation with her. The woman you were with wasn't her."

Simon smiles in that patronising way he has. "And when exactly did you have this conversation with my wife?"

"At a Reclaim the Night march. Around April maybe."

"Yes, I drove past it."

"Your wife was there," Rebecca says. "She was wearing a straw hat and she told me all about studying art. At Jacob Kramer College."

"Right..." Simon is still smiling. "And what made you decide that was my wife?"

"Maybe it was something to do with her saying that her husband was a police officer working full time on the Ripper case, and that he kept disappearing from the house. Or even that his name was Simon."

"Okay, a few things. Number one. There are hundreds of us working full time on the Ripper case. I'd be amazed if there isn't another Simon, though I can't honestly say I've met one. Two. My wife doesn't own a straw hat, or any hat for that matter. She tells me she 'hasn't got a hat face'. Three. Molly didn't study art. When she draws a cat it looks like two overlapping circles in a maths exam question. She's an estate agent by the way. Four. She wouldn't go on a Reclaim the Night march. We've never really talked about her, have we? She's not political. Five. Molly wouldn't go on any march as she can't walk without a stick."

"What?"

"Not since her car crash, which I believe was 1974. She's very self-conscious about her walking."

Simon takes out his wallet and produces a photo of the woman Rebecca saw in the Cobourg. She is leaning on a gate.

"This is Molly. If you ever want to stop by my house, I'll show you our wedding photos."

"It's all right, I believe you," Rebecca says.

Rebecca is aware that she looks embarrassed. She is slightly annoyed at him for deliberately causing this, although she recognises it was important for him to put her straight. She licks her lips and turns towards the bar as if searching for her brother.

"I'm not ready to accept that we'll never be together again," Simon says.

Roland returns with the drinks. Simon immediately seems more cheerful and takes a sip from Rebecca's pint. "I could really do with one of these. Shame we have to earn a living."

"Is this new media campaign helping at all?" Roland asks.

"Is it helping? Okay, how can I explain this? Imagine a baker, in her kitchen, with thousands of orders to make. She doesn't have a list. Instead, the orders are all over the kitchen, scribbled on scraps of paper and her boss is passing her new ones all the time. She's got to make chocolate éclairs, quiches, wedding cakes, Cornish pasties, macaroons, doughnuts, jam tarts and Eccles cakes, and others too. And every order is overdue. There's a table in front of her, laden with complicated recipes in various stages of production. So, that was the state of the investigation before the 'Flush out the Ripper' campaign. And the adverts have produced a deluge of information, the equivalent of a lorry load of flour being tipped over the baker's head, and over the table with the complicated recipes, and over all the rest of her kitchen. But actually, none of this new information is helpful. The flour being tipped over the baker is five years past its sell-by date. And our baker had plenty of good flour before, which she now can't find, of course. Does that tell you if the campaign's helping?"

"I think it does," Roland says.

Later the same evening, Rebecca calls Pamela.

"Guess who's made a prime idiot of herself yet again."

"What have you done now?" Pamela asks wearily.

Rebecca tells her how she got completely the wrong end of the stick regarding Simon's wife. "I feel terrible."

"He'll get over it, he's a big boy. Or so I've heard!"

"I'm not in the mood for your humour, Pam."

"You sound stressed. Maybe you need a holiday?"

"I haven't been stuck in Leeds, you know. Last month I went to Morecambe and Grantham."

"Very exotic. I was thinking more about catching some winter sun. I'd be up for it if you would."

"It's a nice idea but I don't have time. We'll definitely do it next year."

"I was thinking. Talk about two lives changing beyond recognition. Look at us two since our little break in Harrogate."

"I wouldn't say beyond recognition exactly. We both have new relationships."

"Significant relationships."

"I suppose."

"Well, aren't they significant?" Pamela asks. "Seriously though, we talked about what could possibly be better for you. Well, now you've met Mr Right, you surely do have the perfect life."

"Except I've got this weird journalist on my tail. He refuses to accept that I won't go out with him."

"I'm sure you'll think of something. Sally says you're extremely clever."

"I might be clever. But that doesn't mean I know how to handle some weirdo who waits on my street and leaves threatening messages on my answerphone."

"Well, anyway, Sally thinks you're the cat's whiskers."

"How's your work?" Rebecca says, changing the subject, sensing that Pamela has a mental block engaging with this one.

"Slightly mad. They're thinking of copying the karate and judo thing the high school in Leeds are doing."

"I don't know about that."

"I'm surprised, it's been in all the local papers. Basically, they're teaching their pupils martial arts, because of the Ripper. Do you think that's sensible?"

"I've no idea," Rebecca says, irritated by the local papers comment.

"I'm just trying to make conversation."

"I know. It's just every conversation seems to go back to the bloody Ripper these days."

"That's true."

"I can't wait for that not to be the case," Rebecca says.

"Yes, I know exactly what you mean."

CHAPTER TWENTY-SIX

"How's work?" Ken Tobias squeezes his cloth then slowly runs it over his bonnet as if finely sanding his latest sculpture. The blue Pontiac Firebird is shining like the police box in *Doctor Who*.

"Work is good, thanks. We're thinking about an advertising campaign for a new product."

Ken smiles and stretches over his car to clean the middle of the roof. Doesn't he always do this when she tells him about her job?

"It's an ale called Sheridan's." Rebecca retrieves her sponge from the murky bucket; she can't be bothered to change the water now. "Look out for it in the supermarket."

"Don't suppose you have free samples?" Ken says.

"Afraid not."

"Need an actor for the ad?"

Rebecca laughs. "Sorry. We've already got someone in mind."

"You're no fun," Ken says. "Seriously though, when you bring out a new ale, what messages are you looking to get across?"

"We're just discussing this with our agency. Definitely to reassure people they're in safe hands. After all, we brought you Sailor's Watch and Wilberforce."

"Don't delay, it's a Wilberforce day," Ken says with perfect Yorkshire inflection.

Rebecca is always happy when people repeat her strap-line back to her. She resists the temptation to tell him that she wrote it.

"Which agency do you use?" Ken asks.

"Saatchi & Saatchi."

"No wonder. They did a great job on that advert."

"I thought so too, although to be honest they really just adapted our idea."

"How did you get the footballer?"

"William? He came through a journalist I know." She hasn't heard from Mervyn since the message on her answerphone in October. She'd considered giving him a call to pour oil on troubled waters, but didn't get round to it and was soon caught up in the rush leading to Christmas celebrations, some of which she half expected to see him at.

"So, what's your poison of choice?" Rebecca asks.

"We're working our way through a healthy stash of French reds we bought on a tour. It was just before Jill got pregnant."

"My boyfriend Larry always buys Californian wine. He must be more patriotic than I think."

"I've seen him around. Kind of sophisticated-looking, with a beard?"

"That's him."

"I really hope he doesn't like that Paul Masson crap."

Rebecca has finished her car. Ken is still working on his, although it looks immaculate.

"Have a great weekend," Rebecca says.

"Will do. What are you up to, by the way?"

Rebecca says Larry is coming over for lunch. They have no particular plans. Ken suggests they stop by for a drink later, if they're not busy. They settle on nine o'clock, unless Ken hears otherwise.

CHAPTER TWENTY-SEVEN

9 FEBRUARY 1980

L arry arrives at Rebecca's with flowers, something he's done only once before. Twelve dark roses and a second bunch mixing chrysanthemums, tulips and geraniums.

"They're beautiful!" Rebecca puts them on the telephone table and kisses him on the lips.

Larry tells her he's been to Otley that morning, on a recommendation from a client. He walked along the river and later came across this cute florist. How could he not buy her flowers on such a significant Saturday?

The explanation for this comes soon afterwards when Rebecca is clearing away the first course.

Larry says, "I was thinking we should live together. But not just that. We should get married. That's what I was thinking."

"I believe it's more traditional to go down on one knee," Rebecca says and carries the soup bowls through to the kitchen.

"I'm so embarrassed," Larry says when she returns. "I made such a hash of that!"

"You did rather."

"All right, take two." And now, holding a silver serviette holder he just found in the sideboard, he kneels in front of her.

"One knee," she says.

Larry adjusts his position. "Will you marry me, Rebecca – my dear, sweet, beautiful Rebecca?"

"You're overdoing it now." Rebecca hopes she isn't blushing noticeably.

"Not at all. Well, what do you say?" He stands up again.

"Is that my engagement ring?" She takes the serviette holder off him and scrutinises it.

"We can buy your ring this afternoon. Aren't you going to respond?"

"I'm thinking about it. It's a very kind offer."

Back in the kitchen, Rebecca is suddenly close to tears. In four months, she will turn thirty-five; this is the first proposal of marriage she's ever received. She's often thought the day would never come, believing instead that she'd be a single career lady, her life's work summarised in a moderately enthusiastic obituary in the local paper. Now, standing in her oven gloves, a very different life is opening before her.

Larry carves the chicken expertly, and as they eat it with roast potatoes, carrots and green beans, they talk, as normally as possible, about things other than his marriage proposal.

"I've told you about my neighbour, Ken," Rebecca says.

"The actor?"

"He's invited us over for drinks. He lives with this woman called Jill. And a baby."

"Sounds good. Are they nice?"

"I don't know him terribly well. We chat when we're washing our cars. And I've never said more than hello to her."

"Tonight's your chance to put that straight."

Rebecca has made raspberry and apple crumble which they barely touch. Not to worry, she says, they can save it – maybe they'll tune into *Grandstand* and eat it in front of that. Maybe, Larry says with a perceptible lack of enthusiasm.

Rebecca tells him to wait at the table. They need one more thing. She returns with a bottle of Bollinger.

"It isn't cold," she says. "But it's a good one. I won this industry award and never found the right occasion to drink it."

"And just so I'm clear," Larry says, "what is the occasion?"

"Please keep up, Larry. We've just got engaged."

Larry whoops and pops the cork, and they take it through to the living room, quickly consuming the whole bottle on the sofa with the zigzag pattern. They become increasingly giggly, then Rebecca leads him by the hand to the bedroom. Perhaps because of the drink, Larry finds it difficult to perform.

"Your little man isn't working," Rebecca says, disappointed, trying to nudge it into life.

"I feel bad to have let you down. But don't worry. I'll make up for it later."

They end up falling asleep in each other's arms, not waking until four in the afternoon.

"Come on, let's buy you a ring," Larry says.

They drive to a new jeweller in Lands Lane that Rebecca's heard good things about. She insists that a diamond is unnecessary, choosing an oblong sapphire elegantly set on silver instead.

"We're engaged," Rebecca says on the journey home. "This all happened so fast."

"I couldn't hang about. I seem to have several rivals."

"Rivals? What on earth are you talking about?" Rebecca laughs.

"There's Mervyn. And Simon. And this actor next door."

"Mervyn isn't a rival, he's a peculiar journalist. And I finished things with Simon months ago. And as for Ken."

"Ken wants to be more friendly."

"Oh, come on."

"Just kidding. Still, I realised I ought to stake my claim

sooner rather than later. Drive my flagpole into the earth and all that."

"It's not the Oklahoma Land Rush."

"It's similar." Larry chuckles.

Rebecca parks her car and stretches her fingers out in front of her. "I love it. Thank you so much. And you're sure it's okay? Pricewise?"

"It's fine. Why?"

They get out of the car. "It's just your work never seems that... busy. You're always at home when I ring."

"I work from home. It's where I see my clients."

"That must be it then."

He follows her into the house. "Hey, how about I play chef tonight?"

"That would be great. But I don't have much in the fridge."

"I'll work with what you have. It'll be rough and ready."

Like most things Larry turns his hand to, he's an excellent cook. The risotto is soft, creamy and infused with the salty flavours of mushroom and mature cheese.

"You've clearly learned the way to a woman's heart is through her stomach. This risotto is to die for."

Larry performs a little bow at the table. "What time are we due next door?"

"We've got ages yet."

"Just time for the snooker highlights?"

"I was thinking more along the lines of a more horizontal activity."

Later, Rebecca experiences an out of body moment, looking down at his head clamped between her thighs, his jaws wide open. After a quarter of an hour of frenzied fucking, this feels like an unnecessary indulgence – complimentary Turkish delights after a heavy meal.

"You can join me up here now," Rebecca says.

He pulls his head away but remains at the foot of the bed.

"Are you about to start a course in anatomy?" she asks.

"It's just the most amazingly beautiful thing–"

"Well, now you've seen it, let's have a shower."

They can both just about fit in the shower stall in her en-suite bathroom. Larry cups her buttocks, pulling her towards him, and they're doing it once again. Afterwards, they take it in turns to soap each other all over before showering off the suds. They sit on her bed with fluffy lilac towels.

"I'm completely sated," Rebecca says. "Don't even think about trying anything on later!"

"Me too," Larry says, picking up a hand-painted lamp that sits on her bedside table. "Does this thing work by the way?"

"No, it's Victorian. I bought it in an auction."

"It's quite beautiful – like you."

"Oh please, Larry. We'd better get moving."

By the time they're dressed, they're almost half an hour late.

CHAPTER TWENTY-EIGHT

9 FEBRUARY 1980

"Hi, lovebirds," Ken says, opening the door. He has a strange smile and Rebecca wonders whether he heard them making love in their bedroom. But she's not living in a terraced house in Armley. He surely couldn't hear anything with the distance between their properties.

Jill comes up behind Ken. "Aren't you going to invite our guests inside? Apologies for my oaf of a boyfriend." She pinches Ken affectionately on the back of the neck and they go through to the living room where there are bowls with peanuts and Chipsticks, and glass dishes with silverskin onions.

"Make yourself at home, guys," Ken says. "What can I get you to drink?"

Larry asks what he recommends, and Ken produces a wine from the Roussillon region.

"Careful, these Mourvèdres can be high in alcohol," Ken says. He passes Rebecca and Larry their drinks.

"I haven't had these in ages," Rebecca says, taking a handful of the tiny potato matchsticks and sitting down. "I remember tower-building competitions with my younger brother."

"The competitive spirit has never left her," Larry jokes.

"I've noticed when we clean our cars," Ken says.

"Oh, come on," Rebecca protests. "Yours is always much shinier."

"Yes, but you always finish first."

"That's because I'm lazy."

"Don't believe that," Larry says.

They're just raising their glasses to make a toast when Rebecca yells in pain.

"What is it?" Larry asks, concerned.

"I think I cut my mouth."

"I'm always doing that," Jill says. "Those Chipsticks are really sharp and they tend to overcook them."

"I'd forgotten how lethal they are," Rebecca says.

"I wouldn't buy them, but Ken thinks they're the best thing ever."

"You're in safe hands, Jill's a doctor," Ken says.

"You're not!" Larry is impressed.

"Yes, I'm a general practitioner for my sins."

"That's how we met," Ken says. "I injured my back filming and had to go for a referral."

"I soon had to pass him to one of my colleagues. Serious conflict of interest."

"Wow," Larry says. "We probably have in this room tonight, two of the most high-powered women in Yorkshire."

Now onto their third glass of Mourvèdre wine, the news of Larry and Rebecca's engagement has been shared, toasted, and her new ring duly admired.

"You've made a wise choice," Jill says. "It'll be so much easier living with a financial consultant than an actor."

"What!" Ken looks devastated. The others laugh as large tears well in his eyes.

"You see," Jill says. "Totally fake emotions."

Rebecca says, "It must be difficult to ever know what he's thinking."

"And actors are probably brilliant at having affairs," Larry says. "Cos they're so good at pretending everything is normal."

"As if either of us has the energy for affairs," Jill says.

"We're both getting woken six times a night by our demented baby," Ken adds.

"Having affairs is what actors do, isn't it?" Larry says. "I'm going to be keeping a very close eye on Rebecca."

Later, Ken turns the heat towards Rebecca for tempting so many vulnerable people, including actors, of course, into developing a drink problem. "If the devil were looking for a job, he'd certainly be interested in the alcohol industry," Ken says. Rebecca then cleverly switches the discussion onto how most doctors are ill-equipped to treat the large number of alcoholic actors created by the drinks industry, as they're all narcotics themselves. Jill is then forced to vigorously defend herself and her fellow physicians. She eventually passes the buck across to Larry, explaining that the doctors trying to treat the alcoholic actors are only driven to narcotics because of the stress of dealing with their financial advisers. And so the conversation goes on until Rebecca and Larry, weak with laughter, finally make tracks at two in the morning.

CHAPTER TWENTY-NINE

10 FEBRUARY 1980

The twins are excited about the trip to Bramley Baths, even though they regularly go there with their school. Rebecca had offered for her and Larry to take them swimming, but Eileen insisted that she wanted to go too. They are her children and, curious as it may seem, she also likes spending time with them.

"We're doing the race, yeah?" Archie says, as soon as he touches down on the back seat of Rebecca's car.

"Yes, we're doing the race!" Lindsay says.

"I hope it's not Mr King today – I can't stand him!"

"What's wrong with Mr King?" Rebecca asks, making eye contact with Archie via her rear-view mirror.

"He's just really bossy," Lindsay says. "In a really moany kind of way."

"'Geron wi' yer armstroke!'." Archie laughs.

"Yeah, 'Geron wi' it – tha's no speed!'."

"That's it!" Archie explodes with laughter. "'Tha's no speed'."

"Will you sit back, Archie? Your head's practically between your aunt and Larry," Eileen says.

Rebecca parks opposite to the pool and they cross the road.

As soon as they're through the turnstile, Lindsay and Archie make a bolt for the cubicles.

"No running!" Rebecca calls after them.

"They're all right," Eileen says. "They always do 'first in the pool'."

And indeed, by the time the adults reach the cubicles, the twins are announcing their progress.

"Jumper off," Archie calls out.

"Cardigan off," Lindsay calls back.

"Shirt off."

"Don't jump in the pool with your socks on this time."

"I won't. Pants off, trunks almost on!"

"Don't believe you," Lindsay says.

They emerge together, Archie leaping into the pool fractionally ahead of his sister, cheering with delight as he hits the water.

Rebecca and Larry use different cubicles for appearances' sake. By the time she emerges, Larry is swimming lengths, breaststroke one way and crawl for the return legs. She watches him, totally occupied by the task – neat, methodical, oblivious to the twins' pranks at the shallow end. Even when they're standing on their heads, walking on their hands along the bottom, he doesn't notice.

"This is the man I'm going to marry," she murmurs to herself as he exits the pool using the metal stairs, the grey hairs on his chest glistening, his body pale and compact.

"Doesn't Eileen like swimming?" He glances up at the gallery where she's now sitting.

Rebecca shrugs. Then lowering her voice, "She just likes to be different. Or you could say, bloody awkward!"

"Have you written any poems lately?" Rebecca asks Lindsay in the car.

It takes a while for Lindsay to answer, her mouth being full of crisps, Jammy Dodgers or Wagon Wheels. Rebecca sometimes wonders whether Eileen primes the twins to ask for as many snacks as they can eat whenever they're out with Aunty Becky. She couldn't help noticing the brief look of distaste that registered on Larry's face when Archie chose a Bovril and a 7Up to go with his chocolates and crisps as he was "that thirsty". She's sure no one else saw the same thing and is happy that Larry's retaining his status as special new member of the family. After he'd swum his lengths, he and Rebecca played raucous games with the children, then Larry taught them to swim underwater.

"I don't think I've written any more poems," Lindsay says hesitantly. "Have I, Mum?"

"No, but you've got the main role in your school play."

"Not quite the main role," Lindsay says.

"That sounds great," Rebecca says. "What play is it?"

Lindsay says, "It's called *The Thwarting of Baron Bolligrew*. But Archie has a different name for it!"

"Which Archie is not going to say," Eileen adds.

"It's quite funny," Archie says.

"It's rude, and you're not saying it!"

"I wouldn't mind hearing it," Larry says.

"I'll whisper it." Archie leans forward between Rebecca and Larry, then hisses loud enough for the whole car to hear, "The Thwarting of Baron Bollockscrew!"

There is uproarious laughter, none louder than Eileen's.

"Brilliant!" Larry says. "Did you think of that?"

"No," Archie admits.

They discuss the dates that it will be on, and Larry and Rebecca promise to put it in their diary.

Rebecca and Larry agreed in advance that they'd wait until tea to tell Eileen and the twins their news. While they're eating Rebecca's egg and cress sandwiches and chocolate layer cake, Larry bangs his fist on the table.

"Okay, your Aunty Becky has an announcement."

"After that, this is bound to be an anticlimax," Rebecca says to the three expectant faces. "It's just that Larry and I have become engaged."

"That was quick," Eileen says.

"I knew it," Lindsay says.

"Hold on," Archie says. "Not only did you promise me you wouldn't marry him–"

"Hardly," Rebecca interrupts.

"You definitely did, I remember it distinctly."

"I think we should at least congratulate Aunty Becky and Larry," Eileen says.

"It's not that I don't like him," Archie says. "I'd just rather they didn't get married."

"What's the second thing?" Lindsay asks Archie.

"What second thing?"

"You said, 'Not only did you promise me you wouldn't marry him', which means there's a second thing."

"Well, there isn't a second thing. Oh, yes there is!" This causes some laughter. "All right," Archie says, "I just forgot. The second thing is that you're not going to have children, are you?"

"That's a question, not a thing," Lindsay says.

"Anyway, what's the answer?" Archie asks.

Rebecca takes a large bite from her sandwich to allow time to consider her response. She and Larry have never had this conversation. He's looking at her, smiling, permitting her to answer on their behalf. How does Archie always manage to put her on the spot with these questions about her personal life?

Larry's clearly good with children but that doesn't mean he wants his own.

"Would you like us to have children?" Rebecca asks Archie.

"Of course I wouldn't. Because you'd just be looking after them and changing their nappies and all those other disgusting things, and we'd probably never see you for five years."

"I think you're being selfish, Archie," Lindsay says. "You need to look at it from Aunty Becky's perspective. She's never had children and she might want some."

"Well, to be honest, Larry and I haven't even discussed this yet, so it's too early to say."

CHAPTER THIRTY

5-28 FEBRUARY 1980

Rebecca's in her kitchen, having brought her radio downstairs for *Just a Minute* while she's cooking. The episode features Kenny Everett, who was the reason Rebecca left work earlier than usual, making sure she was at home in time to catch the show. He'd been mentioned by Andrew Storey, their new account executive at Saatchi & Saatchi, as being a possible star for the Sheridan's campaign. Storey explained that he went to the same school as Everett and that, without doubt, he could persuade him to appear for, say, a year's supply of free beer. "In any case," he added, as an aside to Roland, "it would be peanuts, or crisps, depending on your preference."

Roland thought the comedian was a great idea. Rebecca was less keen. Not that she admitted it, she couldn't remember who Everett was. She agreed, however, that Storey could check out his availability. That weekend, when she noticed the line-up for *Just a Minute*, she decided to tune in. As she listens, she recalls watching *The Kenny Everett Video Show* and finding it funny. She's suddenly excited by the possibility of him appearing in her advert and telephones Andrew Storey to ask if Everett is available. Everything goes silent for ten days, then Storey calls Roland to say that Kenny's definitely on board and that they'll discuss the details at their next meeting.

That same day, Roland mentions to Sally in the kitchen at Keighley Beers who they might be using for the Sheridan's ad. Sally tells Debbie and the news rapidly circulates around the office. Later, there's a triple rap on Rebecca's door. Brian, clearly seething, enters, followed by William Clayton.

Rebecca gets up from her seat. "To what do I owe this unexpected pleasure?"

"Don't try and be clever, you know what this is about," Brian says. "That mincing idiot. Are you seriously suggesting using him to sell my beer?"

"If you mean Kenny Everett – we are considering him, yes."

"I've heard it's more definite than that. What on earth are you thinking of?"

"Brian, Kenny Everett is a household name. He's been in adverts for Woolworths, Yellow Pages–"

"I don't care!" Brian is almost shouting. "Why wasn't I consulted? This is my baby."

"Because you're our head brewer. You're not in charge of sales and marketing."

"We're advertising beer here. To blokes from Yorkshire! He might be good at what he does, but he's as camp as a row of tents."

Things develop further when Roland and Rebecca attend a meeting in London to agree the concept and shooting schedule. Andrew Storey collects them from Saatchi's grand reception and leads them to a poky meeting room.

"If you think this is bad, you should see the rooms we actually work in," he says.

He serves them cups of tea in odd mugs that aren't clean,

then produces the artist's illustrations, laying them out in front of Roland.

Rebecca and Roland are intrigued by the concept of a man in a pub in conversation with a tiny Kenny Everett, sitting on the edge of the man's pint of Sheridan's. Kenny then starts to show off, balancing on the rim of the glass and calling out, "Look at me!" before falling into the murky liquid. As he swims around, he swallows rather a lot of Sheridan's. "This is completely delicious!" little Everett will shout as the man attempts to fish him out with a teaspoon. The strap-line – "Sheridan's, so good you could swim in it", is still under discussion, Storey says.

"I can just imagine him, hanging on to the edge of the glass like a trapeze artist whenever the man takes a sip," Roland adds.

"It's going to be brilliant," Rebecca says. "Are you sure it's not been done before?"

"Only by Lewis Carroll, and that wasn't to sell beer," Andrew says.

"I love it!" Roland says.

"That's what I like to hear." Andrew removes a sheaf of papers from a briefcase. He passes them to Roland. "This is the shooting schedule we're proposing."

"Looks good," Roland says, barely glancing at the papers.

"I'll have a look at that," Rebecca says. She studies the dates set aside over the first ten days of April. "They're rather spaced apart."

"Kenny's a busy boy. We have to fit in around his availability."

"And what about the costs?" Rebecca asks. "I haven't seen those yet."

"Okay, we'll put them in the post. Don't worry, there won't be any nasty surprises."

"Actually, they're at the back," Rebecca says. "It's coming in at a quarter of a million!"

"Really?" Andrew is adjusting his shirt collar.

Roland looks over Rebecca's shoulder.

"Everett's fee is two hundred thousand pounds," Rebecca says.

"It says that?" Andrew is looking sheepish.

"He must drink a fuck of a lot of beer," Roland says.

The meeting finishes soon afterwards, Rebecca saying they'll think it over. On the way home, she is furious.

"Did he think he'd get away with that? That we wouldn't remember what he promised?"

"Maybe Andrew will negotiate him down a bit."

"I don't expect Kenny Everett even remembers him from school. Anyway, they can forget it. Saatchi's just lost our business."

CHAPTER THIRTY-ONE

15 APRIL 1980

R ebecca has been focused on foreign sales and Roland has been distracted by a leak in the basement of his property. They only realise as the Sheridan's launch approaches, that they've completely taken their eyes off the ball with finding a new advertising agency.

Rebecca spends the first twenty minutes of the launch talking to Larry, Roland and Sally about the last celebration, her engagement party.

"It was quite a week," Rebecca says, "as Larry had moved into my place the day before."

"I remember," Sally says. "I had to find a cheap removals company."

"There didn't seem much point continuing to rent mine," Larry adds.

"The biggest problem was finding space for his belongings," Rebecca says with a laugh. "If that wasn't a test of our love, I don't know what would be."

"Going back to the party," Larry says, "I thought it was fitting that Roland arrived with a new partner at an occasion celebrating love."

"Nicola isn't technically new," Roland says. "I was seeing her last year. I told you about her, didn't I, Becky?"

Rebecca nods.

"It would have been nice to see Simon," Roland continues, then goes pale.

"It's okay," Rebecca says. "Larry knows exactly who Simon is."

"Yeah, I met him once. Hell of a nice guy."

"You did?" Rebecca says. "When was that?"

"A while ago. He was doing some house-to-house enquiries. Luckily for me, he decided I wasn't a mass murderer."

"But how d'you know that was him?" Rebecca sounds slightly put out.

"You showed me that photo – remember? To reassure me he isn't good-looking. Although I beg to disagree on that."

"So Simon won't be coming today?" Roland asks, deliberately changing the subject.

"Not invited," Rebecca says.

Roland had received a phone call from Simon a few weeks earlier, in which he'd told him about his depression since Rebecca broke things off. He couldn't believe it was all over, adding that he sometimes thought about doing something really stupid. When Roland asked what he meant by that, Simon had not responded.

The large function hall is filling up. Rebecca says they ought to mingle with the guests. Roland has been tasked with chatting to the pub landlords and anyone important from Morrisons. Sally and Rebecca are to make sure suppliers are looked after. Rebecca and Roland are to butter up the journalists and keep them apart from Brian Sheridan. Rebecca will handle Mervyn Harris who was invited as a goodwill gesture.

Brian must have spent the afternoon in the pub as he's past the point of no return when she bumps into him at nine o'clock.

"Brian, I wasn't sure if you were coming," Rebecca says. "You remember Larry?"

Brian nods and Larry briefly puts an arm around his shoulder.

"We're getting good feedback tonight on your ale – no one's got a bad word to say," Rebecca tells him.

"Where's Kenny Everett?" Brian asks. "I was expecting to see him, or at least one of those lovely cardboard cut-outs you people are so fond of."

"You're being rather loud," Rebecca says, smiling broadly. "How much have you had to drink?"

"Not as much as when you last introduced me to your boyfriend."

"Maybe not, but I'm going to call you a minicab."

"I thought we were discussing the launch," Brian says. "You were telling me how well it's going."

"I think it is, yes."

"So where are the VIPs?" Brian asks, peering across the room. "Where are the cast of *Emmerdale* or Jimmy bloody Savile? Haven't you got anyone important coming to this sodding thing?"

"Brian, do you have a coat in the cloakroom or are you going as you are?"

"What about Jimmy Adamson or the Chairman of Tetley's? No one here looks important to me."

"There are plenty of important people–"

"What's happening with the advertising campaign anyway?"

Roland comes over. "Is everything all right?"

"I think Brian should probably–"

"I'll go when I'm bloody ready!"

"I can give you a ride home, Brian," Larry says.

"Can someone tell me what happened to the advert? A few weeks ago, it was Kenny this, Kenny that."

"Shall we talk about this in another room?" Rebecca suggests.

"What's happening with Kenny fucking Everett?" Brian shouts. Larry puts a conciliatory hand on his shoulder. "Get off me, will you!" Brian growls.

"We're not using Kenny Everett – which I thought you'd be happy about. And we're not using Saatchi's."

"So, who are we using?"

Roland and Rebecca look at each other.

"Could someone explain what's going on here? You seem to be sabotaging the launch of my beer!"

"Listen, Brian," Larry says. "No one's sabotaging anything."

"So, where's the advertising? Or d'you want me to go round the streets with one of them cardboard signs, shouting, 'Hey, folks, wanna try some Sheridan's?' They'll know sod all about it otherwise."

This is the kind of thing Rebecca has nightmares about. The whole room seems to have turned in their direction, like film extras gawping or making embarrassed small talk. Brian is allowing Roland and Larry to lead him from the room, but not before freeing himself and leaping onto the stage. "Don't tell anyone about Sheridan's," he rasps. "It's all very hush-hush. It's the best kept secret in Leeds."

Later, after Larry has dropped Brian home and returned to the party, Rebecca sees Mervyn Harris's wiry frame gliding in front of pints of Sheridan's lined up by staff, like a vine creeping along a trellis. She watches him in profile draining a glass before coming over to where she and Larry are standing.

"Are you really naming your new beer after that old soak?" Mervyn asks.

"Hi, Mervyn!" Rebecca says with unprecedented

enthusiasm. "This is Mervyn, Larry – our friendly journalist. And Larry is my fiancé."

"I wouldn't trust a word she utters," Mervyn says.

"A little harsh, perhaps," Larry responds.

"My experience with Rebecca is she'll say, 'Let's do this', and 'Let's do that'. But none of it happens. You really believe she's going to marry you?"

"I do actually," Larry says, happy to meet him on his own terms.

"Just because you're engaged? I wouldn't count on anything with Rebecca!"

"Wow," Larry says when he and Rebecca get home. "Keighley Beers sure knows how to throw a party. Do you think Steven Spielberg would be interested in turning it into a disaster movie?"

"You can joke about it," Rebecca says, switching on the kettle. "But I'm feeling quite sick about Mervyn Harris. I mean, nothing ever happened between us for Christ's sake."

Larry says, "Give me his number and I'll call him. I'll take him for a drink and check him out a bit."

"Would you really?" Rebecca is genuinely grateful, immediately feeling supported.

"It's all part of the service. We'll have a man-to-man chat and I'll gently steer him away."

True to his word, Larry makes contact with Mervyn the next day and sets up a drink in a pub. Rebecca wonders why Mervyn agreed so readily. What has he got to gain from meeting Larry? In the run-up to the arrangement, Rebecca's relief at having Larry's support is replaced by a sickening dread that something awful will happen. She tells Larry that she's had a premonition. One sleepless night, at three fifteen, she begs him not to go. Larry holds her and gently laughs it off. It will be fine, he says. He's dealt with much worse than Mervyn Harris.

CHAPTER THIRTY-TWO

19-20 APRIL 1980

That Saturday evening, Rebecca had met up with Alison for a conversation that she didn't want to have on the telephone. They'd gone for an Italian meal near Grantham. Rebecca had driven over there as Dana's age made going further afield difficult for Alison. The trialling of six products, supported by advertising in the Grantham and Lincoln local papers, had produced an indifferent response from the public. Rebecca had also paid for an expensive programme of market research, something Alison had not considered: the evaluations from this were equally disappointing. Rebecca had been sceptical from the outset and had said something to this effect to Alison before. Now the various promotional and research activities had set her back a little over ten thousand pounds. She was not keen to invest more and arranged to meet Alison to draw a clear line under the project. Alison had remained reasonable, although the conversation became thorny when she suggested that Rebecca, despite all her business successes, had lost touch with ordinary people. Rebecca responded that she'd just spent a small fortune trying to understand the ordinary people of Grantham and Lincoln and it was abundantly clear they were not ready for healthy drinks and snacks.

Having passed the evening's challenging topic, Rebecca and Alison managed to reconnect as cousins who were once extremely close. They reminisced about the summer of 1963, when Rebecca, Roland and Eileen moved in with Alison's family in Armley after Mrs Ferguson died. Despite Rebecca having lost both parents in quick succession, Alison remembered this period as being fun and containing a huge number of laughs. One evening, they'd all got hold of a few bottles of Cherry B and drank them in Armley Park. They almost cried with laughter as they recalled the telling off they got from Alison's father after they'd crept home in the early hours.

However, the difficult parts of the evening start replaying in Rebecca's mind as she drives home. Perhaps this is what causes her to lose track of where she is going. She'd come off the A1 to buy petrol in Newark and it's after midnight when she pays. She realises immediately that she hasn't picked up the right road from the roundabout by the garage, finding herself on a dark country road, too narrow to make performing a U-turn anything other than a dangerous manoeuvre. Recalling the fateful roundabout as best she can, she thinks there was a sign for a place beginning with the letter L. It can't be too long before she ends up there, or some other town. Either way, she'll then take out her map and assess the situation properly. The country road is going on forever. She's driving slowly, her beam switched on so she can see a bit further ahead, when she feels the car sputtering. She continues for a minute then an eerie silence descends as the engine cuts out – her immediate efforts are concentrated on bringing the car to a safe halt at the roadside.

Rebecca turns the ignition to restart the car. The engine is completely dead. She waits, then tries again. Nothing. Of course, she's using precious battery power to keep the headlights on, which will make starting the car even more difficult. She switches them off. Now in total darkness, Rebecca locks her door, leans across and locks the passenger side too. What on earth is wrong? The Opel Kadett is less than four years old. There have been no recent problems, although the other day, on her way to work, the car juddered for a mile or two. She'd put the aberration down to a bad batch of fuel. Perhaps she has a flat battery and waiting a few minutes will be all that's needed for it to fire back up into life. But didn't her mechanic replace her battery in the MOT in November?

Rebecca feels panic rising from the pit of her stomach, constricting her chest. She is lost on a country road in a broken-down car. She doesn't know where the nearest town or village is, or even the nearest farmhouse. What's more, the road is narrow and she's worried that a car travelling swiftly might go into the back of her. Things can't get much worse than this.

The road is lit up for a few moments as a car drives past. Then darkness again and Rebecca tries to think what best to do. She turns the key in the ignition and there is no glimmer of life. The problem is serious. She won't be able to start it again. She will need to summon help or else spend the entire night sitting alone on a remote road in total darkness.

Another car approaches slowly from behind and Rebecca decides against putting her arm out and waving it to a stop. As the car passes it goes slower still, inching stealthily forward like a grass snake. The driver is male, in his thirties perhaps. He's actually stopped in the middle of the road next to her and is peering into her car. He winds down the window on the passenger side. She winds hers down. Maybe he will offer help, but instead he holds up something in his left hand and smiles inanely.

"Would you like a..." – he chuckles mid-sentence – "would you like a pork pie, love?"

He is not offering to help, he is offering a pork pie, or very likely something else. She shakes her head. Slowly, the car reverses, it is behind her now, the lights getting smaller as its distance increases. Maybe he's taken a wrong turning too. The car has stopped again, and it juts inwards. He is parking it just a few yards behind her. Surely he will get out and ask whether she has a problem, but nothing happens. The man remains seated in his car. The headlights flash several times, as if he's trying to draw her attention to something. Does he seriously expect her to get out and ask him what he wants? She waits in the car, her heart knocking inside her chest. He must have switched on his beam as her whole car is now lit up by his headlights. She turns around and gives him her most ferocious stare. He is now holding up a pie in each hand, beckoning her with his head to come over. He wants to share an impromptu meal in his car. She faces forwards again, sending a clear message that this won't happen. She takes surreptitious peeks in her rear-view mirror, checking whether he's still sitting there.

He will get bored eventually. But what if he tries to break into her car? She has no idea who this man is or what he's capable of. She tries summoning photofits of the Ripper to mind. She's sure that in most he has a beard whereas this man is clean-shaven. He's flashing his headlights on and off, deliberately intimidating her, and she's finding it difficult to breathe. She reaches to the back seat and grabs her crook lock. It is metal and could be used for self-defence. Should she hold it up for him to see, or would this provoke him further? She sits, absolutely still, waiting, clutching the crook lock.

The man's pulling out from behind her again now. Inching towards her Opel Kadett, he once again stops in the road next to her. She won't give him the satisfaction of turning, but she hears laughing. She involuntarily turns. The man is holding up what looks like a cricket bat, pushing it forwards as if playing a defensive shot, then hooking an imaginary ball to the boundary. He's clearly crazy, hitting fantasy balls all around him from his seat. Is this how it will end, clubbed to death in her car by a madman with a cricket bat? She is strangely calm now, facing forwards, waiting, but nothing happens. She wills him to get it over with or go. Again, he drives his car forwards. And again he stops, this time pulling it directly in front of hers. A full minute goes by. His lights go off and there is darkness once again. And then she's jolted sharply in her seat, her chest impacting uncomfortably against her steering wheel; he's deliberately backed his car into hers, she's not injured, she may be bruised but what on earth will he do next? His lights go back on and he inches forward, then raising his cricket bat in a mock salute, he tears off up the road. She thinks he was driving a Granada although has no idea of the colour or number plate. But he's gone. For the time being anyway.

She feels shredded inside.

It is one thirty and the temperature is dropping. In an effort to appear businesslike and stylish for her conversation with Alison, she'd chosen her Joan Walters summer jacket, a flowery blue number she's owned for two years. She curses her choice as it provides little in the way of insulation. She did not bring a coat. She does not carry a blanket in the car; there is nothing to wrap around herself. She will have to leave the car at some point, but not for a good while in case that lunatic has parked further up and is waiting for her. She could walk the other way but she drove at least a few miles after Newark. She will wait an hour or so. Surely, he'll be gone by then.

CHAPTER THIRTY-THREE

20 APRIL 1980

Attempting to keep warm, Rebecca rubs her legs vigorously and then her arms. This helps but it becomes tiring. She needs a distraction. If only she could read a book or listen to the radio. There is nothing to do other than sit there and try not to let her temperature drop too much. Without even thinking about it, she begins singing "Ding Dong Merrily on High", her favourite Christmas carol. Crazy as this is, she belts it out at the top of her voice and finds some comfort in doing so. She's fairly sure she knows all the words but loses her place once or twice. After singing it three times, she moves on to other favourites, "Go Tell It on the Mountain", "God Rest Ye Merry Gentlemen" and "The First Noel".

As suddenly as she began, Rebecca tires of the activity. How ridiculous to be singing Christmas carols in April. If she could find a telephone box, she could call Larry. Between them they might work out where she is, and he could collect her. She takes her purse from her handbag and is relieved to find plenty of coins. It is past two o'clock. She is so cold that she must leave the car.

Her jaw tensing, she unlocks the door on the driver side and gets out. She is carrying her handbag and carefully places her car key in a zip compartment. The last thing she needs is to lose this. Then, thinking better of it, she withdraws the key and sets off slowly, holding the point facing outwards, keeping to the side of the road. The stars provide only the faintest illumination although her eyes have adjusted sufficiently to make out the rough course of the road ahead. Progress is slow. She will not come off this road. If it leads to nothing, then so be it – she cannot risk getting lost. She must be able to return to the car, if only to sit out the rest of the night.

At any given moment she expects someone to leap out from the darkness, as silent and deadly as a vampire. It is now two-twenty. She feels light-headed and realises she has been holding her breath. She's been walking just over fifteen minutes. There is a buzzing sound directly in front of her. She stops immediately, ice running down her back. The noise is repeated, as if someone is winding up an old clock. It must be a bird rather than a person making this sound. There are birds other than owls that have nocturnal song. She once did an ornithology project at school; corncrakes and nightjars habitually sing at night. The buzzing sounds again, and this time, certain that it is a bird, she resumes walking.

The road banks and curves to her left. She tries not to think about the Ripper creeping up behind her. What were the thoughts of his victims in the moments before he struck them on the head? Were they even aware that anything was amiss, that their lives were about to be cut prematurely and tragically short? She must think about something else. Work. What is to become of Sheridan's after the unfortunate launch? Should she still be formulating a plan for advertising or should they just cut their losses?

She can make out the line of a fence, which could mean fields belonging to a farmer. What would she give for a cup of tea provided by the friendly wife of a farmer? A rudimentary bed in a spare room? She'd pay thousands, more than she just spent on Alison's health products. She continues slowly, bending to her left. A red telephone box. Finally! It might have just been placed there by God Himself. She doesn't know where she is, but she hopes they'll be able to trace the call. She's sure she read that they can do this, in a *Reader's Digest* at the dentist perhaps?

She takes a handful of change from her purse and lifts the receiver. Instead of the purr of the dialling tone, there is an awful high-pitched drone. She rattles the hook several times but still no dialling tone.

"Fuck it!" Rebecca screams. "Fuck it! Fuck it! Fuck it!"

She tries dialling 999, in case this number itself is a call to action overriding any technical malfunction. Nothing. She smashes the handset repeatedly into the cradle, screaming as she does so. Tears fill her eyes.

"Okay," she says to herself and steps out of the telephone box.

"I couldn't get that thing to work either," a male voice says.

Without even looking to see who is there, she sets off running in the direction of her car. The voice was young, almost chatty, maybe it was the lunatic from earlier, maybe not, but either way, anybody prowling at this time is most surely disturbed and dangerous. She sneaks a glance behind her, she cannot see him, but still she keeps on running.

Large raindrops have begun falling. She misses her footing and her ankle buckles outwards; she manages to straighten it and keep going, but each step painfully impacts on her. She has to stop running but continues moving at a brisk pace. She looks around and this time there is a shape navigating the curve some twenty yards behind her. Is that the man following? Her heels are sensible rather than high, but she whisks them off and continues in her tights. She lands on something, a sharp stone, or worse, a piece of glass. She doesn't pause... Surely the car isn't too far now. She looks behind again and cannot see anything. Perhaps she was mistaken before – perhaps it was a trick of the darkness. The rain is heavy and every part of her clothing is sodden. The glass, if that is what it is, is more painful than her ankle. She'll face all these discomforts as she sits out the rest of the night in the car. And she needs to pee, but she isn't going to stop in case he's following her. At last, she sees her car and picks up the pace. Looking around, she impulsively squats by the passenger door, a small stream of liquid running between her feet. She has finally been reduced to animal status. Rebecca Ferguson, millionaire businesswoman, unceremoniously pissing at the side of a country road at three in the morning, terrified that she will be attacked by a crazed predator: what an ending that would be. She finishes and, without caring, uses her sleeved arm to quickly wipe herself.

Back in the locked car, she wonders how long before it becomes light. Maybe three hours. She pulls her tights off and extracts the small piece of glass from the heel of her right foot. There is some blood. She is so wet and cold it will be impossible to sleep. But when she shuts her eyes, she does start drifting. She is startled by a sharp tapping on her window.

CHAPTER THIRTY-FOUR

20 APRIL 1980

Rebecca jolts to her right and looks directly into the pale eyes of a man.

"You didn't have to run away. I'm not dangerous."

"Go away," Rebecca says. It's been a long and difficult night, and this is the best she can do.

"I'm getting absolutely soaked out here. Can't we just talk?"

She winds her window open less than half an inch. "I'm not in the mood for conversation."

He pokes a little finger through the window, flexing it at its tip above her head.

"I am human, you know."

"So is the Yorkshire Ripper."

"I'm not him, I'm Duncan Salisbury, and I'm drenched."

"Then go home."

"I had an argument with my family. I'm nineteen years old. I was kicked out. I've been sleeping in the woods since Wednesday."

"I can't help you."

"I'm so cold. And hungry too."

"I can't help you."

"When you read about me in the newspapers, Duncan Salisbury, found dead with exposure, then it will be on your conscience."

"I'll live with it."

"You'll regret it for the rest of your life."

"I don't know what you think I can do for you."

"You wouldn't have a sandwich? You could pass it through the gap in the window."

She cannot help laughing at the ridiculous nature of the question.

"If I had a sandwich, I would have eaten it. I have nothing. I don't even have a sodding blanket to wrap around me. Now leave me in peace. Go back to wherever you were before. Forget I exist."

"Can I come in, keep you company? It's a horrible night."

"I'm not keen."

"I'll just sit next to you; I won't be any trouble."

"If you were me, would you let a strange man into your car?"

"Ask me anything about myself. I've got three A levels and I'm having a year out before university."

"What are you going to study?"

"Maths and philosophy."

"Where?"

"Nottingham."

"What were your A level results?"

"What grades do I need to get into your car?"

"That isn't funny. What did you get?"

"A, B, E. E in history. I'm not great at essays. I miss the cornerstone arguments. Can I come in now?"

He is well-spoken enough and clearly intelligent. She leans across, about to unlock the passenger door.

"What period in history did you cover?"

"Disraeli, Gladstone – the Eastern question. And we did the National Socialists as a special subject."

"Who was in charge of propaganda?"

"Goebbels."

He's just a teenager with family problems. Educated. What's the worst he can do? She unlocks the door, and he walks around the front and gets in.

"Thanks. I owe you one."

"You can sit here until it's light. Then you can walk me to the nearest town."

"Maybe we can get your car going."

"This car isn't going anywhere." To prove her point she turns the key in the ignition. It doesn't make a sound. "Where is the nearest town?"

"Laxton," he says. "It's a village but it's not too far. A few miles."

She turns on the overhead light. Why didn't she do this earlier? He has pale, deeply puckered skin, long hair soaked through, an oily line running down the side of his denim jacket.

"Sit there and be quiet," she tells him. "I'm too tired to talk."

"I understand. What's your name by the way?"

"Why do you need to know? Oh, what's it matter. Rebecca."

"Thanks, Rebecca. I'm really grateful. Do you want me to fix your car?"

"How will you do that?"

"I don't know," he says vaguely. "I could look under the bonnet."

"Do you know about cars?"

"Not really."

"It's dark out there. And pouring with rain. How are you going to see anything? Let alone fix the problem?"

"You're right. It's impossible."

"It wasn't an incredibly helpful offer."

"Sorry."

There is silence. She can feel her teeth chattering. Jesus Christ, what a night. Strangely, she feels safer with the young man in her car. She turns to look at him. He is rubbing the growth of hairs on his chin.

"I need to shave."

"How old did you say you are?"

"Nineteen."

"I'll be thirty-five in two months' time."

"You're ten years younger than my mum."

"So, what was the argument about?"

"You don't need to know."

"We could sit here in silence if you prefer."

"I thought that's what you wanted to do."

She can see how this young man would quickly test the patience of any family. He speaks without thinking, makes offers he has no right to make. And then has the nerve to challenge, as if she's the one lacking reason and consistency. But aren't all teenagers like that? Perhaps she was too.

"All right," he says. "I found my dad's collection of dirty magazines. He caught me looking at them."

"Where did he hide them?"

"It was such a cliché. Under the mattress, his side of the bed. It was practically the first place I looked."

"Not exactly original, I grant you. So, you were looking for them?"

"Of course."

"And what did you think?"

"They were amazing. I'd never seen things like that before. *Fiesta, Men Only, Knave, Club International*. He's got loads."

"It's not how real women are, you know."

"Yeah, but some have got Readers' Wives! They're more normal-looking."

"It's not how real women are," she repeats.

"Maybe. Do you mind talking about this stuff? There's no one else I can talk to about it."

"As long as you don't expect anything to happen."

"Of course not. You're old enough to be my mother."

"I take it you've never had a girlfriend."

"Not a proper one. I've kissed girls at parties and stuff. Copped the odd feel. But that's about it. How about you?"

"I'm engaged. To an American. He's called Larry."

"We could do it in the back seat," he says. "It might keep us warm."

"What did you just say?"

"It wouldn't mean anything. I won't tell Larry, if that's what you're worried about."

"All right, you can get out now," she says. "I mean it, now!"

"Oh, come on, I was only joking."

"No, you weren't." She looks at him directly – he is red-faced, biting his lip.

"All right, I wasn't. But even so, it's fine. We'll just sit here."

"I said nothing's going to happen. And I meant it."

"I've heard when women talk about sex, they want it really."

"It isn't true. A lot of things you hear about women aren't true."

"All right, I'm sorry."

"You're just a little boy. What makes you think I'd be interested in you? You're pathetic."

"Okay, Rebecca, I get it. You don't have to humiliate me."

"We can talk, and that's it."

"I get it!"

There is a long pause.

"By the way, I saw you weeing. By the side of the road."

She huffs loudly, choosing not to respond.

"You were, weren't you? I saw you."

"Yes, so what?"

"Nothing. I saw you, that's all."

"Well, if that's what turns you on, I feel sorry for you."

"It's not. I'm not into that kind of stuff. Disgusting."

She is more amused by him than anything. And she wouldn't have been able to talk so frankly about sex at his age.

He sniffs a few times and there is silence. She can feel her eyes becoming heavy. It's after half past three and she has had no sleep.

"Duncan – it is Duncan, isn't it?"

"It is Duncan," he says.

"If I close my eyes, can I rely on you to be good?"

"Of course." He sounds mildly offended.

"And by good, I mean not trying anything on."

"No problem."

"I don't want to have to defend myself, but I will if needs be."

"I get it. I'm shutting my eyes too if it makes you feel any better."

She turns off the light, closes her eyes and within minutes falls into a fitful sleep. She is woken by the rising sun burning through her eyelids. The passenger seat is empty. Duncan has gone. And so, she soon discovers, has the purse from her handbag.

CHAPTER THIRTY-FIVE

20-26 APRIL 1980

When Rebecca arrives home in the early hours on Sunday, courtesy of a mini-cab driver, she is gratified that Larry is up and about and extremely concerned for her welfare. He's spent the entire night awake and when she walks in he pulls her to his chest, holding her a full minute before finding his money and scurrying out to pay the driver. He listens to her tale of woe while he makes breakfast, and explains the steps he'd taken, including calling the police as well as Roland, Alison and Eileen. He found the last three numbers in her address book.

"The police said they were onto it, but I was desperate. I'm not sure Eileen appreciated the three am call! It was Archie who answered which probably made it worse, but I thought you'd gone round there for some reason. Blood's thicker than water and all that."

"What on earth did Archie say?" Rebecca laughs.

"He was pretty bemused. 'Let me know if you find Aunty Becky', I think."

"Oh dear."

"Then I spoke to Roland. And we talked about driving to

Grantham to see if we could find you or work out what had happened. But we figured it would be better to stay home by our telephones."

"Makes sense."

"I'm sure he thinks I'm nuts," Larry says. "I told him Alison probably talked you into leaving me and you'd driven to a hotel while you considered your next move."

"Very dramatic. But not really me, Larry. I wouldn't ever pay for a hotel if I could avoid it."

He laughs. "Don't forget, I'm still getting to know you."

"I'm still getting to know myself. I started singing Christmas carols at the top of my voice, just to keep cheerful."

"That's hilarious."

"You find out all sorts when you're facing a life and death situation."

"Anyway, I should call everyone I spoke to, tell them you're back, including the police."

He does so while Rebecca continues eating toast and jam and drinking the remainder of the pot of tea. She also scours the latest *Yorkshire Evening Post*, looking for car dealership adverts having vowed never to drive the Opel Kadett again. After that they both go to bed and sleep until mid-afternoon.

That evening, over dinner, Larry questions her about her fear of being attacked by the Ripper. Hadn't she broken down in Nottinghamshire, not Yorkshire?

"And what about the man waving his cricket bat around from his seat? I suppose because it was outside Leeds, it was silly of me to be concerned – a hysterical overreaction no doubt!"

"All right, all right," Larry says. He apologises for his thoughtlessness and they are quickly friends again.

The following Saturday, Rebecca part-exchanges her car for a fudge-brown Datsun 280C. She tells the salesman how the advert had leapt from the page as it emphasised the reliability of all cars made by the company.

Her intention had been to buy the Datsun Laurel. However, the salesman is good, and she is persuaded of the benefits of electric windows and radio aerial and an autochange stereo cassette player – the Japanese are brilliant at all that stuff, he tells her.

"What's an autochange cassette player?" Larry asks Rebecca later.

"I've no idea," she replies.

CHAPTER THIRTY-SIX

28 APRIL 1980

Two days later, Rebecca wakes in a panic, a line of piranhas is swimming inside her, darting between her ribs and nibbling at the shipwreck of her emotions. It's Monday and they are due to go to Ingram Road Primary School that evening to see Lindsay in her school play. Next week, Larry will be meeting with Mervyn Harris. This weekend they have an appointment with a hotel in Harrogate – a possible wedding venue. Arrangement is following arrangement – arrangements piling up and into each other, a steady stream leading inexorably to the most significant arrangement of all, her wedding to Larry. And yet she hasn't asked the fundamental question, the one question which no woman in her right mind would marry Larry without first having asked. It's obvious to her now as she lies next to his bulky sleeping form. It will be the start of an important conversation, one that needs to take place. She's tempted to wake him to begin it, but surely she would appear insensitive, or worse than that, needy. He's making rasping noises in his sleep as if struggling to draw sufficient oxygen into his lungs. A battlefield of emotions plays out on his face, his lips twitching, forming silent words – there is movement behind his stretched eyelids. He is dreaming, but what about? Perhaps he's in the grip of a nightmare. As she watches, fascinated, Larry wakes with a start and straight away it's clear that all is not right.

He has the most terrible headache, he tells her. She rises half naked from the bed and runs around her house in a flurry of activity, making tea – he always needs tea first thing – fetching her most powerful painkillers, and then bringing him brown toast with butter which he eats sitting up in bed, barely able to speak. The conversation that seemed so important minutes ago must wait; his needs have outweighed hers. After eating half of the toast, he puts the plate to one side. His head is still pounding, and she fetches a flannel drenched in water, first placing a towel underneath his head. His feverish forehead keeps heating the flannel up, she finds herself continuously dipping it in and out of the bowl she's brought to the bedroom, cooling it then replacing it on him.

"I didn't know you get migraines," Rebecca says.

"It's not a migraine," he groans. "There's no nausea or flashing lights."

She smiles to herself, comforted somewhat that even in his dire condition, his pedantry has not deserted him. As the flannel is proving ineffective, she soaks a large towel in the bathroom sink then wraps it around his head. This is great, he tells her. But would she mind resting the tips of her finger and thumb over his closed eyes? – not too much pressure please, yes, there, that's just right. It's clear this service has been performed before, perhaps by a worried mother, or more likely, by Sarah, his wife. How is it that she knows so little about Sarah? She was a schoolteacher, a few years younger than Larry, and they were married eighteen months before her untimely death. She collected *Life* magazine, having been given many of the earliest issues by her father. And that's the sum total of her knowledge. Rebecca understands why this is a sore subject, but surely her instincts are right. She must ask Larry why Sarah took her own life.

He eventually falls back to sleep. She is still gently pressing his eyes through the wet towel and her left arm is tired. Perhaps she can withdraw now? She pulls her hand away, but he stirs, so she has to replace it. Another twenty minutes goes by, the aching in her arm is almost unbearable. Again, she slowly pulls it away, willing him not to wake, and manages to safely leave the room.

She telephones Roland and explains the situation. She's going to be late coming into work. But not just that, would he and Nicola mind taking their tickets for the performance tonight?

"Are you going to be nursing him all day?" he asks, slightly incredulous.

"He has the most terrible headache, Roland. I don't know – I just don't know..."

"It's a headache, Becky. We all get them. And if he's asleep, just come into work. He'll be fine."

She hums and haws, then takes his advice and sets off in the courtesy car provided by the garage, but the word *aneurysm* keeps popping into her head. She's uncertain what the symptoms would be, but a blinding headache is at least a strong possibility. Even though she has left Larry a note, she considers ringing him as soon as she arrives, assuming he's not already dead. It's not normal for her to see possible catastrophes in all that surrounds her. She wonders what lies behind it.

She manages to wait two hours before she calls him at home. He is up and about, feeling much recovered and is "looking forward to Baron Bollockscrew". Roland is interested in going too with Nicola, so Rebecca calls the school. At first they say the performance is sold out, but when they realise that it's local entrepreneur Rebecca Ferguson calling, they're sure they'll be able to find extra seats for her brother and friend. She will meet Larry at the school. The important conversation will have to wait until they get home.

Rebecca is slightly embarrassed by the reception she receives upon arrival that evening. She really just wants to know whether Larry has made it to the school and how he's feeling, but she is dragged to the side of the entranceway and detained by what practically amounts to a welcoming committee, leading to a ten-minute conversation with the very intense headmaster, Mr Colverton. He is keen to expound on his own views on the advancement of ladies in modern-day society, citing Margaret Thatcher's and Rebecca's achievements as testimony to what is possible. He asks whether Rebecca might be interested in giving an inspirational talk to their older girls, at a date and time convenient to her, of course. Rebecca says she would be, although, for her, it's not about being a man or a woman, it's about being the best person for the job. That's the criteria she uses.

"Indeed," Mr Colverton says, standing so close to Rebecca she smells garlic on his breath. He insists on taking her home address to contact her about the matter.

Rebecca also cannot help thinking, as she chats about the growing opportunities for women in society, that no Yorkshire woman can step out at night without the fear of being brutally done to death by a lunatic armed with a hammer. There's an irony which does not escape her, and she considers telling Mr Colverton about her night in the Opel Kadett. Instead, she signals to Larry, who is amongst the latest wave of parents coming through the door, and makes her excuses. Soon afterwards, they are joined by Eileen and Archie, and by Roland and Nicola who tells them she's been offered the position of history lecturer at Leeds University. Rebecca says she was just talking about women getting fabulous jobs, and Roland says how proud he is. It will be so much more interesting than what he does, he says, smiling at Rebecca.

CHAPTER THIRTY-SEVEN

28 APRIL 1980

The English department has done well in coaxing lively performances from the young cast. Rebecca has doubts about her ability to appreciate or judge theatre. She is aware of the audience's rapt enjoyment, and the joke about Lindsay's character, the thieving magpie, being "a bird of loose morals", provokes so much laughter that the next few lines are drowned out.

In the interval they drink weak tea served with Nice biscuits. Eileen holds forth about the play being half fairy tale, half satire, very much in the tradition of radical working-class theatre. And the magpie stealing the baron's things is, apparently, not theft but a class action in the vein of Robin Hood. Rebecca wonders how her sister learned to analyse the arts. She's hoping that Larry will step up to the plate and match Eileen's flamboyant discourse, but, despite saying he has recovered from his headache, he's subdued and irritable. Thinking about it, Larry has not been at his best lately. The previous week she'd caught him scowling as he read an official-looking letter. When she asked about it, he looked distracted and said it wasn't important.

The conversation is now all about Lindsay's performance; her shuffling movements and squawking voice, her subtlety and proficiency. She is a cut above the other actors.

"No wonder she didn't want me to test her on her lines. She's hardly got any," Archie says.

In the second half, Rebecca does her best to engage more critically with the drama so she can join in the discussion afterwards. Is Baron Bolligrew's rapid conversion from despot to respectable citizen realistic? Perhaps she could make a comparison between the duke's efforts to rid the tyrant Bolligrew of his last remaining dragon, and the Yorkshire police's apparent inability to snare a modern-day dragon, or would that be too contrived?

In the event, Eileen and the twins leave quickly after the play ends, and Rebecca and Larry drive home separately. Rebecca parks in her driveway, leaving space for him to pull in behind. She waits in her car, the memory of the night spent sitting in the Opel Kadett returning to her. And the young man she allowed inside. Why did she even do that? Does she have a death wish? She was too ashamed to tell Larry that part of the story, let alone report the theft of her purse to the police. Larry's orange Vauxhall Viva pulls into the driveway behind her. They climb out of their respective cars.

"What did you think of the play?" he asks.

"I wasn't convinced by the baron's character transformation. I don't think that happens in real life."

"Boy, you were taking it seriously." They go inside. Rebecca starts making Horlicks, their new nightly ritual.

"You weren't yourself tonight," she says, facing him and putting her right arm on his shoulder.

He nods in agreement.

"Are you worried about something? Meeting Mervyn perhaps?"

"No, *you're* worried about me meeting Mervyn. Remember?"

She smiles. "You definitely haven't been yourself."

"I'm sorry. Even Larrys have their off days, you know."

"Of course. And it didn't exactly get off to the best start for you."

"Yeah, I'm just about ready for bed."

He's standing with his drink, his eyes asking whether she's coming up too.

"Before you go, Larry–"

"Yes?"

"There's something I've been meaning to ask."

"Oh. Should I sit down?"

"Yes, why not."

They get out the foldaway chairs and sit on opposite sides of the square table, their mugs of Horlicks in front of them.

"I feel like you're about to issue the police caution – the one they use on your detective programmes," he jokes.

"No, nothing like that."

"So, what does the boss want to discuss?"

"It's just you never really talk about your wife. I hardly know anything about her."

"I suppose I don't."

There is a pause, each waiting for the other to speak, the clicking of the red wall clock gently orchestrating their discomfort.

"So, what d'you want to know? It's not the easiest thing for me to talk about."

"I understand. But you weren't married long. It seems that it all went wrong rather quickly."

His grey eyes narrow as he considers this. "Let me put it this way. Sarah was a complicated person. There was a lot I didn't know when we got married."

She's not going to let him off the hook that easily. "That must be the case for most couples."

"Of course. But Sarah – in fact, her whole family – did a pretty good job persuading me she was quite different from the person she actually was."

A look of petulance has taken up temporary residence on his face.

"Different in what way?" Rebecca asks as gently as possible, sensing that she needs to coax the information from him.

"Well, I had no idea about the anorexia nervosa when she was a teenager for a start. I don't blame anyone for this, but those images didn't make it into the family album."

"I suppose we all try to present the best parts of ourselves. It's like advertising, isn't it?"

"I totally get that. But I'm talking about a complicated history here – she was mentally ill, Rebecca. She had powerful feelings of helplessness that started in her teenage years which became unmanageable. I had to find all that out for myself after we married. And it didn't take long, believe me."

She wants to say that he could have found those things out before they married, by talking in the way they're doing now, but doesn't want to stall the conversation.

"So, when did you find out?"

"Driving down through California on our honeymoon, beginning with an unstoppable outburst of tears on 17-Mile Drive. An hour-long conversation about suicide as we walked across the Golden Gate Bridge. Her refusal to go into Mexico as she was convinced we'd be knifed to death by the locals."

She nods. A picture is indeed beginning to build.

"Can we take these upstairs?" he asks. "We'll be more comfortable."

"So, you both talked about her depression?" Rebecca is

leaning against the wooden headboard, enjoying that feeling of hardness on her back.

"Sure, we talked about it. And it wasn't the first time she tried to kill herself either. I'm not saying she didn't intend to do it. I'm damn sure she did. You don't jump off a balcony onto your backyard patio unless you mean business."

Rebecca takes a sharp intake of breath. These details are new and shocking.

"They told me at the funeral they pulled her out the family car in the garage on her seventeenth birthday, just as it was filling with fumes. That was something I didn't know either."

"And she talked about suicide as something she might attempt in the future."

He nods. "Sure."

"My father never talked about it," Rebecca says. "That made the whole thing harder to deal with."

"Harder than finding your wife's dead body on the patio with her skull smashed open?"

"I didn't mean it to sound like that. I wasn't trying to trivialise... I'm sorry."

He finishes his drink. "I'm sorry too. I overreacted. I understand. His death must have seemed like it came from nowhere."

She nods.

"So, does that answer your questions? I'm kind of keen to get some shut-eye."

She smiles. "I just wanted to know whether it was because of problems in your marriage."

"I really don't think so."

"You've reassured me. Thank you."

"We loved each other very much. I'm trying to be as honest as I can here."

"I know you are, Larry."

She switches off the bedside light, turns on her side to face him and puts her hand over his chest, entangling her fingers in his hairs. The regular inflating and deflating slow as he drifts into sleep.

CHAPTER THIRTY-EIGHT

30 APRIL 1980

The fateful Wednesday evening has come around and Larry is in a pub in the centre of Leeds with Mervyn. Anyone observing Larry's relaxed demeanour could not possibly imagine Rebecca's fears for his safety which led up to the meeting. He'd half expected a phone call from her work, or a last-ditch attempt to persuade him to cancel but she seemed reconciled when saying goodbye.

"I know exactly what you mean about pressure from family. When you're growing up. I know all about that," Larry says.

"I don't want to burden you with my problems," Mervyn says.

"You're not. At all." Larry gives him a reassuring wink across the table. Mervyn sips his Tetley's.

"I was always brought up not to do that," Mervyn says.

"Winking?"

"No – burdening other people."

"Oh. Me too, funnily enough. In my family it was my grandfather," Larry continues. "He lived with us throughout my childhood, in fact he didn't die until I was – what? – twenty-eight maybe, thirty even. He called the shots in our household."

"My mother did. My father was always working."

"Of course she did. Because you're Jewish, right?"

Mervyn looks like a store detective just slapped a hand on his shoulder. "How did you guess?"

"My boy, I knew so many Jews in the States, I'm practically an honorary member of the tribe myself. How shall I put this? I'm one bar-mitzvah away from being your next rabbi."

Mervyn chuckles, visibly relaxing.

"So, what was your dad's work?" Larry asks. "Don't tell me, a family business."

"He was in sales. Left the house early, often away overnight–"

"Like Willy Loman?"

"Perhaps."

"And your mother wanted you to do something more respectable – 'You don't want to end up like your father! Why not be an accountant? Or a lawyer! God forbid that one of my sons should actually become a lawyer!'."

Mervyn laughs. "She wasn't that much of a stereotype."

"Allow me some artistic licence here. I suppose what I'm saying is that we're men of a certain age, we've been around the block a few times, yeah? I'm turning forty this year. Share the same birthday as John Lennon as it happens – exact same day."

Mervyn nods. "I'm a few years younger."

"You're probably Rebecca's age. We should talk about her by the way. But no rush."

Mervyn pats the top of his head nervously, his curls flexing like spring coils.

"How did you end up in journalism, Mervyn? You don't get too many Jewish journalists."

"What about Bernard Levin?"

"Well, obviously Bernard Levin."

"My parents were *Daily Mail* readers. It seemed he had a column every day."

"Okay, so I'm getting a picture, nice Jewish family growing up in...?"

"Manchester..."

"Growing up in the suburbs of Manchester – and you're the youngest of three brothers, yeah?"

"I have two older sisters actually – but close."

"Close enough. And young Mervyn is the quiet one. Always reading, and not just the *Daily Mail* delivered by the paperboy. 'What is it with you and books?' your mother no doubt said. 'What's to learn from books?'."

"I'll tell you what it was," Mervyn says, becoming almost loquacious. "My family loved to talk about the news. Local news, national news. And politics! They were the things we were passionate about. But you're right, I was also the dreamer in the family."

"There you go!"

"I'm the reporter here, Larry. You're very good at information gathering, perhaps you're in the wrong career?"

"Ha-ha. And I agree we're not actually so different. I grew up in Seattle. And the constant thing my teachers told my parents was that I was lazy. Clever. But lazy. Would never achieve my potential unless I knuckled down."

"And now you're engaged to Rebecca." Mervyn's change of subject is as sudden as flicking a light switch in a cellar.

"I am. And I believe you said she'd never marry me."

Mervyn stares at him, his eyes too close together, like a bush-baby, Larry thinks. "Is that what I said?"

"You don't remember?"

"I was acting strangely that evening."

"It's fine," Larry says. "Everything's cool. From tonight, I'm thinking of you as a good friend."

Mervyn smiles and Larry tries not to look too obviously at his teeth, which he's sure Mervyn is sensitive about.

A little later, after Larry has bought two more pints of Tetley's, they return to the subject of Rebecca.

"I'll be honest," Larry says, "she's not been having a great time recently. Her car broke down on a country lane at the weekend and she was worried about being murdered by the Ripper!"

"Was it at night?"

"The middle of the night, yes."

"Any woman would be terrified in that situation," Mervyn says.

"Sure, but in Nottinghamshire?"

Mervyn's eyes narrow as he drains half of his pint.

"Kind of crazy they haven't caught him yet, eh?" Larry continues. Mervyn nods. "I mean, we've had ten or eleven deaths, and they're just the ones we know about."

"You think there are others?"

"I'm damn sure about it. This guy's intent on killing women – he could be doing it anywhere. What happens when he goes on holiday?"

"But we'd know about it, surely," Mervyn says. "The police would say, wouldn't they?"

"Depends how much faith you have in the police. You're a journalist. You know about cock-ups and conspiracies."

"Yes, but they can tell who his victims are."

"Like I say, I don't have that much faith," Larry says. "They suck at catching him so why would they be any better deciding who he killed and who someone else killed? It's one big mess if you ask me."

"It's pretty depressing if you put it like that," Mervyn says.

"I'd never heard of him until I moved here. And then

discovered my whole street was obsessed. Two victims lived there, yards apart."

"Awful."

"Sure is," Larry says. "I used to sit in the playground where they found Jayne MacDonald. Surprisingly peaceful. Nice spot to read a book."

"Really?" Mervyn raises his eyebrows.

"Yeah, till I found out what happened there. But then I thought, what the hell? – it's a playground! A suntrap. And I carried on reading there. But the point I'm making – and maybe not very well – is with all this in the background, Rebecca doesn't need some guy parked in her street, leaving weird messages, and generally scaring the bejesus out of her. I know you two were meant to go out one time and it didn't happen, but hey, buddy – isn't it time you moved on?"

Mervyn nods. "It won't happen again," he says.

"Don't worry about it," Larry tells him. "It's forgotten already."

"You probably don't know what it's like going a very long time without a girlfriend," Mervyn says. "When the chance came along, I got a little over-excited."

"I know all about that. I was alone for years after my wife died."

"You were married?"

"Yeah, crazy woman – really, a headcase. She did me a big favour and topped herself."

Mervyn's face freezes.

"Mervyn, I'm joking!"

"She didn't kill herself?"

"Yeah, she did, but it wasn't..." Larry stops and looks at the table. Mervyn is scrutinising him, his pint of beer halfway to his mouth. "Oh, never mind," Larry says. "Maybe we should change the subject. What do you English like talking about? Oh, yeah, soccer, isn't it?"

———

At ten thirty-five that evening, Rebecca hears Larry pulling into the drive. She sneaks a glance through the living-room window as he gets out and he looks fine, if not a little serious.

Once inside, Larry reports back that he's now slightly worried about Mervyn himself. There is something not quite right there and they'll need to keep a close eye on him.

"You didn't manage to warn him off?" Rebecca asks, wondering what Larry achieved.

"Yeah, I did that. But then, apart from his encyclopaedic knowledge of Leeds United, he became overly interested in my late wife, which I thought was slightly odd."

"Sorry about that."

"Not your fault! But he's a strange guy, you were right on that point. I left feeling uneasy, that's all I can say."

They don't talk about Mervyn for another month or two and Rebecca doesn't see him until August. But in May he drops her a line to say he's started doing some research which will be of interest. Remembering he was writing a book on Tetley's, she assumes it's to do with this, some records relating to her father's employment perhaps.

CHAPTER THIRTY-NINE

20 AUGUST 1980

The nature of Mervyn Harris's research becomes clear on the third Wednesday in August. Rebecca meets him at nine thirty in the evening, in the Great Northern Hotel bar on Richardshaw Lane. They'd originally agreed on eight thirty, but she called him to put it back, having decided to go out first for a meal with Roland and a Nottingham businessman offering to co-sponsor an event.

Mervyn has been trying to arrange this for over a month, his phone calls increasing in frequency and urgency, Debbie's neatly handwritten messages piling up on one corner of her desk. Rebecca has been preoccupied with her wedding since they set a date. It will be in the winter on Saturday 17 January, although Larry would rather they'd made it earlier. Rebecca was determined, however, that 1981 would start with a celebration. She had finally called Mervyn back the previous week from work. He said he needed to make her aware of some things he'd discovered. About her father? she asked. He'd tell her when he saw her. He wouldn't talk about it on the phone. There was no time to lose. She told him she couldn't see how it could be that urgent. Her father had been dead for years, after all. There was a pause before his monotone reply. "This isn't about your father."

Having had the meeting with Roland and the businessman, Rebecca had said goodbye to them at the restaurant, driven to Pudsey, parking just off the main road. She's been waiting in the bar for less than a minute when Mervyn arrives.

"Does Larry know where you are tonight?" Mervyn sounds flustered.

"It's none of your business." She hasn't told Larry but there is no way she's about to reveal this to Mervyn. Not when she still finds him so creepy.

"I'm sorry, but we need more privacy than this. I know a quieter place."

He moves towards the door, turning to check she's following. Once outside, a lamp-post casts an ominous shadow across his face.

"Where are we going then?" Rebecca asks.

"It's a quieter pub, just a few minutes away." He has a navy-blue BOAC bag slung over his shoulder.

They continue without speaking. Why hadn't she told Larry who she was meeting? She'd thought about it even though Mervyn had insisted she keep it a secret. It was mainly because Larry would have been unhappy after his warnings to her the night he met Mervyn himself. Rebecca had considered various options, in the end leaving a note saying she'd be back late due to an evening meeting. That way she didn't have to talk to him about it.

On the other side of the road is the Oddfellows Hall.

"Shall we go in there?" she asks.

"If it's okay with you, the place I'm thinking of will be better," Mervyn says. He tries to smile reassuringly, but his face is fairly locked with tension.

"Well, I'm really hoping it's nearby. I've had a long day and I don't want a late night."

"It's just a few minutes," he says.

At this time, the neighbourhood is neither quiet nor humming with activity and Rebecca is glad for the few passers-by. A middle-aged woman heads towards them, her eyes quickly scanning both Rebecca and Mervyn as she passes. Rebecca isn't too anxious to notice her black gabardine overcoat; something smart like that could go over almost anything.

"How's the book going?" Rebecca asks Mervyn as they walk.

"What book?"

"The book on Tetley's. You told me you were writing one."

"I abandoned that months ago," he says, as if she really ought to have known.

"Are you working on anything else?"

"We'll talk in a minute. I'm trying to remember where this place is."

"Do you even know what it's called?"

"The World's End."

They've now been walking for almost ten minutes, and she can't understand what was wrong with the other pub they passed. There is a scream and a revving of engines as several teenagers bomb past them on mopeds, then disappear into the night.

Mervyn turns left into an altogether quieter street.

"Where are we heading, Mervyn?" Rebecca repeats.

"I'm pretty sure it's round here."

"Unless you find this place within the next two minutes, I'm going home."

"You need to hear what I've got to say. You really do."

"Yes, but..." She sees a pub on the other side of the road.

"This is the one," he says.

Rebecca follows Mervyn inside, and he puts his bag on the table in front of him. "You're going to need a stiff drink," he says. "How about whisky?"

"Whisky is fine." Rebecca masks her nervousness as best she can.

CHAPTER FORTY

20 AUGUST 1980

The pub is almost empty, save for a handful of men in their seventies sitting silently in one corner, staring gloomily into their pints. If the World's End landlord ever wanted an image in keeping with the name of his pub, he need look no further than these morose gentlemen.

Mervyn returns with two large whiskies and unzips his bag, withdrawing a tape recorder.

"If you're thinking of recording this, don't even bother to ask," Rebecca says.

"I'm not," Mervyn says. "How much do you know about Sarah Hudson, née Postlethwaite?"

"I can't say I've heard of her," Rebecca says dismissively.

"Well, you ought to have done. She was married to Larry."

"Larry *was* married to a Sarah, that's true. His surname is Appleby by the way. Presumably it became hers too."

"Is that what he told you?"

"Mervyn, where are you heading with this one?"

"I've done my research, I can assure you. Larry let slip his date of birth when I met him, and I started from there. I've spent a small fortune on transatlantic phone calls and postal charges."

He reaches into his bag, fumbling ineffectually. Rebecca can't help but think this is an elaborate exercise in time-wasting. What's he going to produce next from his box of tricks?

He passes her a photocopied sheet. A State of Washington licence, "To solemnize the rites of matrimony", dated 20 April 1974. The names on the certificate are Laurence Hudson and Sarah Postlethwaite, although the man has written Larry Hudson when signing. His date of birth looks correct.

"It looks like his handwriting," Rebecca says. "I'm slightly confused, I must admit."

"How much do you know about the death of his wife?" Mervyn asks.

"I know she killed herself. In a rather horrible way."

"Well, I suppose that's what the coroner thought too."

"Yes, exactly," Rebecca says.

"But her relatives mounted a campaign to have that verdict overturned."

Rebecca's ribcage feels like a wall that's shrinking and compressing everything inside. "I expect it was hard for them to accept she killed herself."

"They're convinced Larry murdered her and pushed her dead body off the balcony to make it look like suicide. And they've assembled a lot of evidence. He inherited plenty of money by the way. That's why he doesn't need to work."

"He does work. He's a financial consultant."

"I looked into that too. Me and some friends took turns to monitor your house for a week. We didn't see a single client arriving. And apart from a couple of trips to the shops, Larry hardly went out."

"I'm pretty sure he speaks to clients on the phone."

"He certainly spends a lot of time in front of the television.

You can see into your living room from a certain angle. Some days he did nothing else."

Rebecca gulps from her whisky and attempts to make sense of the thoughts overcrowding her brain.

"But the relatives' campaign hasn't been successful, has it?" She cannot prevent the tremor in her voice.

"No. The coroner is adamant that he will not review the decision."

"Well, there you are then!"

"This story was local news. Your fiancé had his photo in the paper, although I've not received a copy of that article. And then he suddenly left Seattle. No one there has seen him since."

"Look, Mervyn, this is all very interesting and thanks for your close attention to this matter—"

"We're here, Rebecca. You might as well listen to what I've got to say. And to the conversation with Sarah's mother."

"But the coroner wasn't interested. That's good enough for me."

"Another court is looking at Sarah's will, which her relatives have also challenged. Anyway, I'll find the relevant part."

He presses play on the tape recorder, intermittently winding it forwards. Sarah's mother is setting out her side of the story in a telephone call with Mervyn. From the fragments Rebecca hears, she is doing so in detail. Rebecca is angling forwards to hear better, and the tight curls of Mervyn's hair brush her forehead as he leans suddenly over the tape player.

"All right, this bit," he says.

In the recording, the mother is talking about how her daughter persuaded them to transfer a large sum of money into her bank account two months before she died. She and her husband also agreed to register Sarah as official owner of their holiday property in San Diego. Sarah argued at the time it would avoid her paying inheritance tax in years to come, but her parents now believe Larry was behind these out of character demands. Mervyn in the recording is helpful and solicitous, respectful of the mother's grief, gently prompting when needed. It was the unusual financial transactions shortly before her death which formed the basis of arguments to contest Sarah's will. The mother says she is pleased to have had some success earlier that year when a judge ruled certain financial assets Larry inherited should be frozen. Rebecca immediately thinks back to his recent concerns around money: the peculiarity of his reaction when she was considering helping Alison with her business venture; his reluctance to talk about booking a holiday.

"So, what are you saying, Mervyn? That he's planning the same fate for me too?"

"I'll leave you to judge that. But somebody looking at this objectively might think you're the type of person he would have in his sights."

They are done soon afterwards, and Mervyn walks her back to a bridge close to where they met. She thanks him for his time.

"It doesn't sound like you're particularly grateful," he says.

"Would you be?" she asks.

"It doesn't matter anyway. You can contact me whenever you like. I'll provide any information you need."

She waits for him to go before heading off in the other direction towards her car.

CHAPTER FORTY-ONE

20 AUGUST 1980

Larry is watching a late film on television when she returns, so she soaks in the bath and reflects on how preposterous it all is. There will be a good explanation for all of Mervyn's silly points, if she just gives Larry a chance. Larry can explain anything. But isn't that the problem perhaps? He's too bloody clever. To make the death of your first wife look like suicide to the extent the local coroner believes you is more than just clever, it's verging on genius. And that is probably what Larry is. She can't simply dismiss the evidence produced by Mervyn as fantasy and fabrication. Deeply uncomfortable as it is, she must accept the possibility that she's engaged to a wife killer.

It's nearly midnight when she comes down to the kitchen. Larry is making hot drinks.

"How was it? Your meeting?"

For a second she thinks he's found out about Mervyn but then remembers the business discussion over a meal before.

"It was good, thanks. An interesting project. I'll tell you about it when I've got the energy."

"Sure. And the car was okay? I assume so as you're not sleeping in a country lane tonight."

"Very funny. The car is perfect. Reliable, trustworthy, what more could I ask for?"

"Listen," Larry says, suddenly serious. "I don't want to spoil your evening, as you're obviously feeling relaxed after your bath. But I took a couple of weird phone calls tonight."

"Who from?"

"Okay, so let me get this right. It was a solicitor, no, a duty solicitor, calling from a police station. First time he was asking for you, second time he'd gotten permission to speak with me."

"What was it about?"

"I was wondering that when he first introduced himself. Then he mentioned Brian Sheridan, who is in a police cell right now. This guy's representing him. Brian apparently attacked his wife this evening, the neighbours heard screaming and called the police."

All around her there is violence to women. "Is she okay?"

"She will be, although she may have a broken rib. Terrible business, eh?"

She feels her eyes filling with tears and fights it. He puts his beefy arms around her, pulling her towards him, bear-hugging her. A part of her wants to hug him back, another part wants to head upstairs, pack an overnight bag and go and stay with Pam, Roland, Sally, anyone.

She pulls away from him.

"Do you know Brian's wife?" Larry asks. "You seem upset."

She shakes her head. "And what the hell was the solicitor doing calling me?"

"That creep wants you to put up bail."

"Brian? He can shove it."

"That's what I thought. I'm not sure how he even got your number."

"All the managers have that. In case of emergencies."

They go up to the bedroom and it's just her luck Larry is

feeling randy. To refuse him might arouse suspicion. She doesn't feel like kissing him so instead pulls the covers away and stares at it, the head purple. Is this the penis of a murderer?

"Hey, it's not so warm in here," Larry complains. "And I'm feeling kind of vulnerable in this position right now."

She takes him in her mouth. It would be so easy to bite right through his flesh.

CHAPTER FORTY-TWO

21 AUGUST 1980

The afternoon after they met, Rebecca takes a telephone call at work from Mervyn Harris.

"If this is more of what we were talking about, I'm not interested," she says when she recognises his voice.

"Have you heard what happened? Last night?" Mervyn asks.

"If you mean my colleague being arrested, I have no comment."

"I don't know anything about that. What I'm talking about happened in the area we met, the exact same area."

"Well, I haven't heard anything – because I'm trying to run a business here."

"She was a civil servant working in education in Pudsey. Within five minutes of her home apparently."

"You're talking in riddles, Mervyn. Can you please just tell me what happened?"

"She was called Marguerite Walls, and they're saying she probably died defending herself against an indecent assault. She'd been battered on the head, and quite possibly strangled too. They found her in a garden in New Street which is a short walk from where we were drinking."

"You seem to know a lot about it."

"I'm a journalist, Rebecca."

"Was it the Ripper?"

"He hasn't been mentioned. But from the timings, I reckon she was murdered just while we were in that pub. Her body was found this morning by the police. The owners discovered some things in the garden, shoes and a skirt, a cheque book, that sort of thing."

"That's terrible," Rebecca says. She suddenly remembers the woman they passed. "Was she wearing a black gaberdine coat?"

"I've no idea what coat she was wearing."

"And they're sure it's not the Ripper."

"They say not. But I have my doubts about that. They said she'd been working late in her office. In an effort to clear things before going on holiday. She won't be going on any more holidays, that's for sure."

Rebecca is distracted by a terrible thought. Larry had said there was something not quite right about Mervyn. "How do you know it happened while we were in the pub?"

"I'm going by the timings."

"Am I your alibi, Mervyn? Maybe she died *after* we left the pub."

"You're being ridiculous now, Rebecca, and you know that."

"Well, you certainly seemed in a strange mood when we parted."

"I was attempting to help you last night. You're in a dangerous situation and I'm trying to keep you safe. You don't seem to understand the scale of the problem."

After this conversation she considers phoning the police and telling them about her meeting with Mervyn, just around the

THE COMPANY SHE KEEPS

time the woman died. But then she realises she'd have to explain what she was doing in a pub with him in Pudsey in the first place and thinks better of it. She has quite enough on her plate right now without complicating things further.

In the days that follow, she notices people aren't talking much about this latest killing. Police confirmation that it's not the work of the Ripper relegates it to an item of less interest, as if the only murders that really matter are those committed by him. All other local murders are, of course, unfortunate, but not a reason to lose sleep, even if they're every bit as brutal as those perpetrated by the man dominating the headlines.

CHAPTER FORTY-THREE

22 AUGUST 1980

After a second sleepless night in a row, Rebecca tells Larry over breakfast that she's going on a business trip to capitalise on Wilberforce's recent success. The Byron Stevenson advert achieved such sensational results they've been re-running it nationally throughout the summer. A follow-up ad is under consideration with their new agency. Now is the right time to push forward into northern Europe, she says.

"Are you changing your name to Napoleon too?"

"Very funny."

Larry breaks his eggshell with a teaspoon. "Which countries are you visiting?"

"France, obviously! And Belgium and West Germany."

"Northern Europe beware!" He sounds jokey enough, but Rebecca wonders whether there isn't also an edge to his comment. "And how do you do that? How do you start selling your product in other countries? I honestly wouldn't know where to start."

"You sign a distribution deal, preferably with a local company with a gap in their portfolio."

"Sounds sensible. And they market your beer for you?"

"Hopefully, along with their own. Essentially, you need them to get it into the big supermarkets – your Carrefours and your Edekas. So I'll be meeting potential distribution partners. Typically, they're chief executives of breweries the same size as mine, sometimes bigger."

"Do you speak French and German? You've probably told me, but I forget."

"Conversational French," Rebecca says. "But I have an interpreter I use in Germany. I'm flying out on Thursday and start by meeting Jean-Marc, possibly the smoothest Parisian you're ever likely to set eyes on."

Larry chews his toast and raises his eyebrows. "Is that a fact?"

"He's also sixty-eight years old and happily married," Rebecca says.

"And you're going next week? That's fast."

"I know. Sally's been juggling dates and hotels, not really keeping me up to speed. I only got the itinerary yesterday."

"And what are the dates again?"

"So I leave on the twenty-eighth and come back the following Thursday. It'll be busy."

"If I'd have known earlier, I might have joined you. Taken in the sights, a few art galleries..." His sentence tails off. He looks disappointed, slightly hurt even.

"I did think about that. But when I got the details, I assumed you couldn't take time out at such short notice."

"You're right, I can't."

"I literally got the dates yesterday, Larry."

"I understand."

"Frankly, it'll be back-to-back meetings, so no fun at all. And I use evenings to prep for the next day, unless I'm being frog-marched to some god-awful tour of a brewery. Or worse still, a drinks party."

Larry smiles. "Are you going alone?"

She nods. "Roland was coming but he had to pull out at the last minute."

"I thought it had only just been arranged."

"I meant it doesn't fit with his schedule."

"Shame."

"I may fly Sally out if I really need her, but I'll probably be fine."

He pauses. "I'll miss you."

"You will?" She tries to sound light-hearted.

"My heart is shattered, but for the sake of appearances..." He flips his broken and empty eggshell in its cup, leaving the pristine end facing upwards.

Rebecca laughs. "And I'll miss you too. How's your work by the way? I haven't asked for ages. Do people want financial advice in a recession? You'd think it would be more important than ever."

"They do. And they don't. But it's fine. Ticking over."

"That's a relief." Rebecca smiles. She gets up, carrying their soiled crockery to the sink. "I don't really know how you conduct your business." She's peering through the window into the back garden, as if the answer might lie somewhere out there. "Are people coming here the whole day? Or do you go to their work?"

"Mostly, it's done on the phone."

"Oh, right." She rubs at a smudge on the window with a tea towel. "I pictured you poring over columns of numbers with stressed heads of departments."

"Really? I much prefer fax. Quite a few of my customers have invested in one. I tell them it's the future. Sure, we might meet once in a while. But generally, they don't want to see me. Why would they?" He laughs.

She turns to face him once again.

THE COMPANY SHE KEEPS

"And I make sure my American clients phone here, if you're worried about that," Larry says, meeting her eye.

"I'm not. You can use the phone as much as you like, as you know. The bills are not an issue."

"The boss is way too generous with her resources. I've always said that."

"I wasn't quite so generous yesterday."

The day before, Rebecca had received an early morning phone call from Brian Sheridan's solicitor. Brian had been released by the police, so finding bail money was no longer necessary. Rebecca was surprised the solicitor had had the decency to ring until she realised he was touting for extra business. He'd done his homework and was well versed in her career history.

Instead of heading straight to work she had stopped by Brian's house. He'd answered the door in his pyjamas. Over coffee he'd told her how it was just a silly row but for some reason he'd seen red and clobbered Vera with his plaster-cast arm. He'd broken it a few weeks ago. "I might as well have hit her with a piece of lead piping – this thing is like a rock," he said with a chuckle. "Now it's a waiting game to see if the buggers charge me."

"There was something about the whole conversation," she tells Larry. "The way he talked about it so calmly, while poor Vera was still lying in hospital. Short of having a screaming fit, I lost it. I know it's unprofessional, but I did."

"What did you say?" Larry asks.

"I said how disgustingly proud he seemed about putting her in hospital. That she'd presumably married him because she loved him and thought he'd protect her. I asked if it's acceptable for a husband to attack his wife with his plaster-cast arm?"

Larry nods as if to confirm that her reaction was more than reasonable. "How did he take it?"

"I might as well have been Germaine Greer standing on a soapbox in his kitchen. I should hear the way she goes on at him, he said. Then I'd understand. I very nearly fired him on the spot. I still might, to be honest."

"I don't think you can do that legally," Larry says. "It's not a work issue, it's a criminal matter."

"It's my company–"

"People have rights," he interrupts. "Employment law and criminal law are two separate things."

She waits until she's sure he's finished. "It's my company and I'll do what I bloody well like!" And with that Rebecca goes upstairs to get ready.

CHAPTER FORTY-FOUR

22-28 AUGUST 1980

Rebecca spends the days that follow going over her plans for her forthcoming trip. Has she forgotten anything? Are all bases covered? Larry has said he will drive her to the airport early in the morning, and this is fine. He can see her onto the actual plane as far as she is concerned.

In the event, Larry does not do this, preferring to stop directly outside the main airport building, not even turning into the car park. This hasty drop-off may be a result of her raising the subject of Sarah's relatives on the way there. She asked whether he was in touch with any of them. His response was restrained enough. Things hadn't been easy in the aftermath of her death, he told her. But a muscle in his forearm twitched as he tightened his grip on the steering wheel. Before she gets out of the car, she leans across and presses her lips firmly into his. He allows this to happen without really responding.

"I'll see you in a week," she says.

"Have a good one," Larry says.

Now out of the car, Rebecca stoops back in before closing the door. "I love you, Larry," she says.

He nods and smiles. "I love you too and don't forget it."

She walks away, carrying her bag towards the terminal building, her back drenched with sweat.

"You don't seem your normal ebullient self," Jean-Marc says, over lunch in a Parisian brasserie. They are speaking in French and Rebecca has been struggling to keep up with the conversation as well as she usually does.

"Shall we try in English?" he says, in English.

"If you don't mind. I'm just really tired."

"And you do not like your pot-au-feu?"

"It's fine. It's just me – I'm not on top form today."

"And everything is all right at home?"

She has known him since she took over the failing Ingrow Ales three and a half years ago. He was already distributing Sailor's Watch in France, and she flew out to meet him in her first month. Since then, he has become more like a friend than a business contact, and she'd dropped him a line when she became engaged to Larry, adding that he wouldn't be surprised to hear that Larry is from the state of Washington. It has been Jean-Marc's long-standing joke how stupid English men must be, if not one of them has yet had the sense to marry Rebecca.

She assures him everything's fine at home, and they resume their discussions of Wilberforce beer. Jean-Marc tells her he saw the advert while he was on a recent business trip to London.

"It's not so easy to sell your English beer here. But that doesn't mean I'm not keen to try with this one. I am sure I was offered it years ago, but now it's doing very well, yes?"

"It's been incredible," Rebecca says.

"In time we would remake the advert. Of course, yes. It is very good but it is very English." He almost spits out the last word and she smiles. "And I didn't recognise your footballer. You need Michel Platini, somebody French anyway."

"Yes, but then I'd need a famous Belgian footballer, and a famous German footballer."

"A famous Belgian footballer? You really must be unwell!"

"You know what I mean. I'd have to remake the advert for the Belgian and German markets too."

"Maybe, yes. If these countries are important to you. My view is that if you break into these, then you have Austria, Spain and Italy queuing for a slice of the cake also. Luxembourg too, but who cares about Luxembourg? I have friends in these countries. I can introduce you."

He smiles, confident in his abilities, his judgement and his connections. Even now, with his unruly grey hair almost touching his tailor-made jacket, he is an attractive figure. They agree he'll send her a contract, not dissimilar to Sailor's Watch, and they'll speak on the telephone next week.

He sees her to Gare du Nord station. "You must take care, Rebecca. I have been worried about you today." He kisses her on both cheeks and affectionately pats the back of her head before walking away.

There is a small kiosk on the pavement where Rebecca picks up an Eiffel Tower postcard. She attaches a stamp she bought earlier, writes a short greeting, posts it and takes the train to Charles de Gaulle. She is in good time for her flight to Frankfurt. This time she stops only to buy a scale model of an Opel Rekord Caravan which she sees in a shop window, and a postcard of The Römer, on which she writes a pre-prepared message. She puts the card in an envelope and sends it to Sally's home address. She returns to the airport where she has two hours to kill before her direct flight to Seattle.

CHAPTER FORTY-FIVE

29 AUGUST 1980

The flight time is eleven hours, so she will land at seven pm local time. Everything so far has gone to plan. Larry will receive the postcard from Paris in around three days. On Wednesday, Sally will fly to Frankfurt with the second postcard. She will send it to Lidgett Park Road from there. It won't arrive until after Rebecca is back but this is part of the plan to reinforce the message that her trip proceeded as she'd described. Rebecca will also give Larry the toy Opel car from Frankfurt as a joke present when she returns. Meanwhile, she will have called him from her Seattle hotel, mentioning a meeting at a brewery in the abbey of Saint Benedict, Belgium, before saying she's late for another appointment. She's sure it's just the police who can trace calls, and only if they last more than three minutes. But Larry is clever enough to have found his own way of doing it, so she'll keep the conversation short regardless.

Rebecca doesn't think Larry was suspicious, although his speed of thought and analytical powers are daunting. She is proud of her thorough preparation and the manner in which she carried out the plan under pressure. She has surprised herself and almost wishes there was somebody she could tell about it. Honesty has always been second nature to her: it turns out she's also an accomplished liar. And the trick she's discovered, quite by chance, is to lace her servings of deceit with as much truth as possible. Perhaps that is how Larry operates too, a master alchemist mixing the volatile compounds of fact and fiction, in order to create his own personal gold – credibility. In Seattle, she must not be distracted whenever she finds the truth in what he has told her. She will need to recognise it to understand the lies.

As Rebecca watches the cabin-crew members' safety presentation, she reflects that she was given little option but to behave in the way she has. Whether she likes it or not, she is entering a different state of existence with its own regulations. Here, she will have to continue to play dirty, possibly in order to survive. As the aeroplane soars into the sky, the impact of that realisation is crushing. There is no turning back.

Half an hour later, the woman sitting next to her is also presented with a crushing revelation. The vegetarian meal she ordered has not been loaded onto the flight. She will most likely go hungry until they land in Seattle. The head of the cabin crew arrives to apologise for the oversight. He also makes clear there's little he can do personally and strides back down the aisle.

Rebecca turns to her neighbour. "This may not be the most tempting offer ever, but please have my roll and butter. And this pudding, whatever it is."

"You're too kind." The woman cocks her head to one side appreciatively. "I'm guessing custard sponge, although it's an odd colour. You really don't have to give up your dinner."

"I'm not particularly hungry," Rebecca says. "This is my third flight today and I've had a meal on each. As well as lunch in Paris."

The woman, who is about her age, smiles warmly. "Three flights in one day. You must be a sucker for punishment."

"It's a long story," Rebecca says.

An air hostess delivers a Coca-Cola and peanuts, "With the compliments of the crew." The woman folds out her table. "Look at me now," she says. "I'm awash with gourmet food and drink."

They laugh and Rebecca is relieved to have found a friend so quickly.

"I'm Cherry, by the way."

"Rebecca." She puts out her hand and Cherry shakes it. She has wavy brown hair, the darkest eyes and most pronounced eyebrows Rebecca has ever seen on a woman. The overall effect is captivating.

Cherry says she was visiting her father in Frankfurt. He is on marriage number four, and she doubts this latest union will be a success either.

"His wife's a native Frankfurter, if that's a word, and twenty-two years younger. Pop says he's too old to learn German."

"It sounds like a match made in heaven."

"And what are you doing heading for America's wettest city?"

"Is it really?" Rebecca asks.

"It rains every day, so you're gonna feel right at home! I'm betting you're on a business trip. You're certainly well-dressed."

Rebecca thanks her. She's unused to receiving compliments about her clothes. She's still wearing the dark-blue velvet skirt suit she'd put on for her lunch with Jean-Marc.

"It's more of a family odyssey. I'm meeting some relatives of my fiancé."

"Is he out there already?"

"No, he's in Leeds. His work's too busy for him to join me."

192

Cherry nods. "But you're checking out his family before taking the plunge. Very sensible."

Rebecca takes rather too big a swig from her Coke and it fizzes over her face and even up her nose. Cherry is quick to pass a napkin.

"Here, you still have a few droplets..." She dabs at Rebecca's chin. "There. Order has been restored."

Rebecca smiles, embarrassed.

"So, are you meeting his folks tomorrow?" Cherry asks.

"I haven't arranged it yet. It's complicated."

"Families, secrets, complications. I know the territory..." Cherry laughs.

Rebecca had called Mervyn and taken down the relevant addresses and telephone numbers. It would have been too risky to call anyone before she departed, so she hid the information in the lining of a suitcase she stores at the top of her wardrobe. It can only be reached by standing on a tall chair and the note appeared undisturbed when she packed for the trip.

"I'll sort it out when I arrive," Rebecca adds. From what she'd gathered from Mervyn, Sarah's mother has been simply going through the motions since her daughter's death. It's unlikely she will be anywhere other than home when Rebecca calls.

"How long are you visiting for?"

"Just a week."

"Well, listen," Cherry says. "I live close to the Space Needle, if you're at a loose end tomorrow evening?"

"I'm staying at the Fairmont Olympic?"

"That's ten minutes away. Drop by and I'll mix some cocktails."

"That sounds fabulous," Rebecca says. And she means it.

After the meal they both use their overhead lights to read. Rebecca is making good progress with Howard Zinn's *A*

193

People's History of the United States, which Larry purchased after reading a review in *The Guardian*. He finished it in a day or two and recommended it to her, and Rebecca took a subversive pleasure in packing it for this trip. After reading one and a half chapters, she begins to tire and turns her light off to sleep. She is woken by an announcement from the captain that the plane will be landing in thirty minutes. Before they disembark, Cherry hands Rebecca a piece of card on which she has neatly written her address and phone number. Don't forget to call, she tells her. Friendship as always surfaces in the most unexpected places. Perhaps this trip won't be without some pleasure after all.

CHAPTER FORTY-SIX

29 AUGUST 1980

There's plenty of traffic as Rebecca's taxi trundles due north into the city. It is fifteen miles from the Seattle-Tacoma airport to her hotel, and from time to time the Duwamish River is visible on the left-hand side. The driver, a self-confessed "history nut", explains that the first European-Americans arriving in the area found the Dkhw'Duw'Absh people strewn across many villages. They'd been living by the river for over a thousand years. "Of course, the white folk soon put a stop to that. There's good evidence we deliberately burned their longhouses."

"How awful. When would that have been?" Rebecca asks.

"Less than a hundred years ago."

"As recently as that?"

"Yep. The things folk do to other folk in the name of progress."

Rebecca mentions the book she's reading, and the author's theory that most histories of America have ignored the real story of the American Indians.

The conversation comes to an abrupt halt as they arrive at her hotel, glamorous and imposing, its dominant position on the street corner affirming its serious intent. Inside, the lady at the reception desk is both welcoming and efficient and Rebecca is soon in her airy third-floor room, her bag arriving seconds later. Despite sleeping for several hours on the flight, she now has another night ahead before she can begin her research.

It is too late to make phone calls and she doesn't fancy more American history right now. She does, however, have copies of both *The Los Angeles Times* and *The Seattle Times* which she picked up at the airport. She reads about a dynamite bomb in a hotel casino, which explosive experts were trying to make safe. She is struck by the behaviour of gamblers in nearby hotels who refused to leave, even though they knew a massive explosion may be imminent. Instead, they continued with their cards and even cheered when they heard the blast of the bomb, returning to their gambling immediately afterwards.

Rebecca watches television for an hour and then gets ready for bed. All things considered, she doesn't sleep too badly. First thing in the morning after breakfast, she walks the five minutes down 4th Avenue and arrives at the three-box structure that is Seattle Public Library.

The library has copies of *The Seattle Times*, transferred to microfiche and dating back to the mid-1890s. A man with a ponytail, who looks like a throwback to the sixties, demonstrates how to operate the reader. "It's a precious resource to the city," he says. "Please use it with care."

He leads Rebecca to the filing cabinets housing the microfiche. "Each roll contains a month of the newspaper. You'll just have to spool through until you reach the bits that interest you. Unless there are particular dates you've already identified," he adds doubtfully.

Rebecca feels a flush of pleasure that she has indeed brought a list of dates embedded in a fake itinerary for her trip and considers putting the man straight on her level of preparedness. Instead, she settles for a simple, "It's fine, thank you – I know the months I need."

Unfortunately, when it comes to the very first microfiche, she has problems feeding the acetate into the machine. Expecting the worst, she approaches the same librarian for assistance.

"The ends can become gnarled," the man concedes, snipping off the offending two inches with scissors. He feeds the microfiche into the reader and returns to his desk.

The month that Rebecca has selected is October 1975. She knows Sarah died on the 29th. Rebecca starts to spool through the month, only realising after ten minutes that the machine has different speed settings, and that the fastest reaches the end of the month in seconds. Having got to 30 October, it occurs to Rebecca that any reporting of the death will not have happened until November and, even then, is unlikely to be of interest. She needs to jump forward in time and discover whether Mervyn has presented an accurate picture of the challenge to the coroner's verdict.

She returns to the filing cabinet, this time selecting February 1977. Back at the microfilm reader, she once again has problems loading the acetate. The librarian is now leaning over a large ledger, assiduously making notes, his head angled – quite deliberately, Rebecca assumes – to avoid seeing anyone approaching his desk. Rebecca clears her throat and the man looks up with a pained expression. Rebecca decides not to apologise.

"I'm having trouble loading the microfiche."

"But we've only just loaded it." He manages to look both baffled and condescending.

"I now need a different month," Rebecca says.

"My apologies, I thought you knew which month you needed."

"I do. And I now need a different one." She is hoping the broken record technique will help.

The librarian again cuts off the creased end of the microfiche and Rebecca spools forward, stopping at an article reporting a local petition by relatives of the deceased Sarah Hudson, requesting that the coroner's verdict be looked at again. There is nothing else of relevance that month, so Rebecca successfully loads April 1977. This time she finds an article noting that the verdict of suicide recorded in the death of twenty-four-year-old Sarah Hudson has been upheld, but that relatives are vowing to continue their campaign to see that justice is done. There's also a photo of Larry, his beard bushier in those days, his hair longer. The caption reads *Larry Hudson: widower or murderer?*

Rebecca studies the article, reading it several times. She has been thinking recently about Mervyn telling Larry at the Sheridan's launch that he can't trust anything she has told him. This wildly inaccurate remark had in retrospect given Rebecca hope that the person who could not be trusted was Mervyn himself. The argument seemed more compelling when considered in the context of his peculiar behaviour, parking in her street and leaving bizarre messages on her answerphone. Rebecca had even built an alternative narrative in her mind in which the tape of the conversation with the mother was the work of an actress following a script, and the contact details provided by Mervyn all fabricated in the belief that Rebecca would never follow them up. The newspaper article in front of her, and the one from February, are a sharp rebuttal to this flight of fancy. Indeed, they confirm Mervyn's research was accurate. What she now needs to establish is whether the allegations against Larry have any substance. It's quite possible that Sarah's family are deluded.

CHAPTER FORTY-SEVEN

30 AUGUST 1980

She has arranged to go round to Cherry's after dinner, which she eats in the hotel. Rebecca feels distracted as she tries choosing an outfit from the limited selection at her disposal. She opts for her trouser suit, then recalling Pamela's criticism last year that trouser suits are all she wears, changes it for a pair of jeans and a blouse.

"How was your day?" Cherry asks when Rebecca is settled in an armchair with an Alabama slammer. "Did you manage to make contact with the relatives?"

"Yes, I'm going over there tomorrow evening." Sarah's mother had been surprised but perfectly amicable when Rebecca called. Rebecca had been completely open about who she was, the fact of her engagement to Larry and her recent discovery of his controversial past.

"Perfect – I hope they give you a good welcome."

"Thank you," Rebecca says. "And have you been working today? I didn't ask what you do for a living."

"I'm a copywriter."

Rebecca laughs. "In an agency?"

"I used to be. I worked on some of the Boeing ads in the

199

mid-seventies. But now I'm freelance, which I love. What's so funny by the way?" She's now smiling herself.

"I'm sorry. I've been doing nothing but working with advertising agencies for my own business. I've always loved that world. At school, I used to copy slogans off buses on my way home. I almost met a boyfriend that way, in fact I did meet a boyfriend, but that wasn't until years later. I'm rambling, I'm sorry."

"Don't worry. I could listen to your cute English accent all night."

Later, happily inebriated from the cocktails, they take a walk to the Space Needle where Rebecca buys two liqueurs in the lounge. As she takes her receipt and change, zipping the coins in her purse, she makes a mental note not to bring home any dollars or cents.

"You look worried," Cherry says.

Rebecca confides she has serious doubts about her relationship. "I think you even sensed that on the plane," she adds, without going into further detail.

"I guess marriage is always a massive commitment. To anyone other than my father, that is."

They take the elevator ride to the observation deck.

"I come up here to remind myself how insignificant we all are," Cherry says, the surrounding skyscrapers and office blocks diminishing to specks of fluorescent dust in the distance.

"We arrive on this planet alone and we leave alone," Rebecca says.

On the walk back, Rebecca feels a surge of joy to be away from Yorkshire, and away from Larry, and away from the troubles that have trailed her in recent months like an aggressive stray dog in the park. She is in fact feeling so relaxed and happy she barely notices that she and Cherry are linking arms. Is it friendship or something else? – she hardly cares, such is her feeling of giddiness and relief.

If she has the time on this trip, Cherry suggests, there's a fantastic national park nearby. "We can pack some food, a knapsack, take a tent, sleep under the stars and forget we're part of this crazy merry-go-round I call runaway capitalism. Have a look at your calendar, what do you say?"

Attracting the attention of two passing late-night women joggers, the closest of whom gives her a secret smile of sapphic understanding, Rebecca shouts, "I say, yes. Yes, yes, yes!"

CHAPTER FORTY-EIGHT

31 AUGUST 1980

Rebecca gets a cab from the Fairmont Olympic to 19th Avenue in the Capitol Hill neighbourhood. The driver sucks in his breath as he looks up at the impressive blue and white four-square house.

"That's a classic," he says, "a real classic."

Rebecca pays and heads up the wide path, towards the American flag outside the house. A lady is waiting in the shadows on the gable porch, half hidden by one of the massive square columns. She steps forward, tall, white hair almost down to her waist, her eyes anxiously appraising Rebecca. She's clearly been keeping an eye out for her arrival.

"Hello, I'm Rebecca."

The lady doesn't smile. "I'm Katherine. Come in and we'll talk about Sarah. I can make tea in the English style, if you prefer it that way?"

"That would be nice," Rebecca says.

The door must have been caught by the wind, opening slowly of its own accord as they approach it. Katherine goes inside and Rebecca follows.

"You're really engaged to Larry?" Katherine says. "Walter

and I couldn't believe that's happened so soon after he killed Sarah."

Rebecca feels hope. The fact Katherine talks to her immediately about Larry murdering Sarah – immediately, as if this is an established and undeniable fact – at the very least suggests she is not of completely sound mind.

"It's almost five years since Sarah died, isn't it?" Rebecca says, as neutrally as she can.

"Don't linger in the foyer. Come through, dear. Walter! The young lady is here."

They turn right into a huge room with hardwood flooring and animal-skin rugs, the space easily accommodating a long table that could seat sixteen, perhaps twenty, people. Walter joins them via another door; he's shorter than his wife with wispy hair and a bold sandy moustache.

"It's good to meet you," Walter says, as Katherine scuttles off to the kitchen. "It's nice to have a Brit in the house. My forefathers were from England, going way back."

Rebecca smiles, shakes his outstretched hand and tells him what a beautiful house they own.

"It was built in 1909," he says, and then, as if she'd asked about its heritage, "a reaction to mass production and the Victorian era, I guess. All about wooden craftsmanship, Prairie-style."

"It's so spacious," Rebecca says.

"We have twelve bedrooms, at least we did when I last counted. We have an extended family, so this table comes in handy at Thanksgiving."

"I bet."

"And the house being this large means I hardly ever need go into the office. I have a room for press conferences here and a decent workspace for my secretary."

"I see." Rebecca is wondering what on earth this man does for a living.

"Here, we'll perch round this corner." Rebecca sits down, Walter remains standing. "Katherine will be back in a minute."

As if she'd been waiting on this cue, Katherine sweeps in and places a tray with three anaemic teas in china cups in front of Rebecca. "Please help yourself," Katherine says. Rebecca takes one. She is representative of the Yorkshire school of thought on tea: "Strong, one sugar; leave the bag in if you don't mind."

Walter continues. "We've been in correspondence with a guy called Mervyn, a friend of yours presumably?"

"I know him, yes. He gave me your contact details – I hope that's okay."

"We assumed he had," Katherine says, "although you didn't say on the phone."

They're obsessed with the minutiae. This happens perhaps when a chasm opens in people's lives. They try to fill it with a welter of tiny details.

Walter and Katherine look at each other, and then, as if controlled by the same marionette operator, they sit simultaneously, either side of Rebecca. They each take a tea from the tray. The situation feels more under control now they're all seated together.

"I really just wanted to meet you and perhaps hear your side of the story," Rebecca says.

"You've obviously heard what Larry's got to say," Walter says.

"He hasn't told me much to be honest."

"So, we'll start at the beginning," Katherine says. "We were impressed when we first met Larry, weren't we, Walter? He was intelligent, sophisticated... cultured."

"A million miles away from the boys Sarah had been knocking around with."

"And, yes, he was older," Katherine says. "But we didn't see that as a bad thing."

"How did they meet?" Rebecca asks.

"He was her financial adviser," Walter says.

"That's right, dear."

"She'd come into some money, a trust we set up when she was born–"

"Yes, when she was born," Katherine overlaps.

"And she wanted to be independent – not follow what we said the whole time."

"She liked to do things her way."

A realisation strikes Rebecca with the force of a blow to the solar plexus. If you're looking for a suitable candidate to marry, kill and inherit from, what better way than selecting from the people you advise financially? It's the perfect career choice if those are your intentions.

"And he was good with our grandchildren," Katherine continues, "Sarah's nieces and nephews. They were younger then–"

"They called him Uncle Larry."

Rebecca is only half listening. Maybe it's too easy to rationalise after the event, to make the facts fit a version of history.

"Shouldn't you get the photos, Walter?"

"In a minute, honey."

Rebecca wills herself to focus back on the conversation. "And when did they meet?" she asks.

"Oh, that would have been in the fall."

"She means which year," Walter says.

"How silly of me. 1973."

"And they were married about six months later," Walter adds.

"So it all happened very quickly," Rebecca says.

"Super quick," he agrees.

She remembers her sister commenting on how quickly she became engaged to Larry too.

"She was in love," Katherine says. "We didn't like to stand in her way."

"We couldn't," Walter says. "She was as stubborn as hell."

Katherine smiles vaguely.

"Would you say Sarah was happy? Growing up, and as a teenager?"

Katherine and Walter glance at each other across the table. "You take this one," Katherine says, as if they're fielding questions in one of their press conferences.

"I'd say she was happy," Walter says.

There is silence.

"And her teenage years were healthy and normal, is that a fair description?"

Walter frowns, raises his shoulders slightly. "You show me a teenager, any teenager, and I'll show you a mass of contradictions."

"But on the whole?" Rebecca says. Extracting information feels like skewering a wriggling fish.

"She would never have taken her own life!" Katherine says.

Soon afterwards Walter disappears and returns with three or four photo albums. The first shows pictures of Sarah as a toddler. Here she is, red-haired, on a sofa, her hands stretching out towards her brothers on either side – Bill and Mark. Katherine is behind the sofa, smiling proudly, her hair jet black in those days.

"You see how happy she was." Katherine's voice trembles.

Here, Sarah is playing ball in the backyard with her eldest

sibling, Maud, and in this one, lying on her front, her chin resting on the patio.

"Looking for ants," Walter says.

"She loved ants," Katherine says.

"She was overjoyed when we got an infestation one summer."

"Until Walter poisoned them all."

"I had to, honey."

"I know," Katherine concedes and then sobs. "Excuse me a moment." She quickly leaves the room.

"It's been hard for her," Walter says.

"I know – I can't begin to imagine."

They continue looking at the albums. It takes a few minutes to reach the teenage years, Sarah now less happy-go-lucky, a crop of acne on her forehead in this one, a cross look, perhaps at her parents, in another.

"Larry told me she became anorexic." Rebecca is determined to at least confirm or explode one piece of information.

Walter nods. "Hell of a worrying time."

"It didn't last long." Katherine returns to the table wearing a woollen shawl and carrying a box of tissues.

"Long enough. The weight was melting off her like summer snow."

"And do you have any pictures of Sarah and Larry together?" Rebecca is immediately annoyed with herself for steering them away from this important subject.

"We have them all, don't we?" Katherine says. "We can't bear to discard them. Maybe we should burn the ones with him in."

Several pages of one album are devoted to Sarah and Larry's engagement party in this very house. There's an image of Larry at the same table in the seat where Walter is sitting, with Sarah to his right in Rebecca's chair. Walter explains that their wedding has its own dedicated book, but Katherine cannot bear to open that anymore.

It is strange to be looking at pictures of a younger Larry in the arms of another woman, though she feels no envy. Is this a sign of something? At one point Rebecca automatically says, "That's a lovely one," before realising it may not be appropriate. Katherine and Walter do not seem to notice.

Walter starts talking about the early morning in October when Larry phoned the house in tears. "There was this diabolical groaning noise over the phone, like a wild animal in pain. I barely made out what he was saying – there had been an accident, a terrible, terrible accident. We know it was anything but, now. He's one hell of an actor, I'll tell you."

"But what makes you so sure Larry deliberately killed her?" Rebecca asks.

They explain about the money they transferred to her account, the holiday home in San Diego. Rebecca, who's heard all this on the tape, asks them how they feel about those financial transactions now.

"We'll never forgive ourselves," Walter says. "Had we not agreed, it might have delayed him murdering her. Something could have happened to intervene." He turns to Katherine as if to seek her agreement, but she is rising from her chair again, her thin frame shaking silently as she leaves the room.

CHAPTER FORTY-NINE

1 SEPTEMBER 1980

Mount Rainier National Park is south-east of Seattle, encompassing nearly four hundred square miles of wilderness, lakes, rivers and glaciers. Bears, goats, deer, elk, eagles, beavers and mountain lions live in a wary alliance of nature within the park. But the centrepiece is undoubtedly Mount Rainier which local native Americans called "the mountain that was God".

Rebecca has made two decisions before setting off with Cherry. First, she is going to tell her the whole Larry saga. She feels the need to talk it through with someone she can trust, someone with a fresh perspective. So far, she's only told Sally, and that was in the context of passing on complicated instructions for when she was away – what Sally was to say, for example, if Larry called the office: everyone else at her work believes she is in Europe right now. The second decision is to ask Cherry to accompany her on Tuesday evening. The Postlethwaites have invited her back for dinner, and this time they've promised she will meet other family members, and again Rebecca needs an impartial view. Are Sarah and Walter's theories anywhere near the truth of what happened or has grief caused them to veer off reality's cliff edge? From what she has seen and heard so far, Rebecca is inclining towards the latter.

By the time Cherry has picked Rebecca up from her hotel and they've driven to the park, midday is approaching. As they begin hiking, the sun is pleasantly warm but not overbearing. Rebecca hasn't done anything like this since she was a teenager. Her father would sometimes take the family for walks in the moors, and a rare holiday in better times was spent in the Cairngorms in Scotland. Neither Rebecca nor Cherry are bothered about climbing to the top of Mount Rainier. They agree that scaling heights is a particularly male preoccupation. As long as the views are beautiful, the company good, and they can watch the sun rising and setting, they'll both be more than happy.

Cherry is keen, however, for there to be some challenge, so has selected her favourite hike, the Tatoosh Trail. She promises Rebecca extraordinary views of the lake, steep and dramatic rises, an abundance of wild flowers and the odd wild animal. There are hardly any other hikers, so Rebecca begins the story of how she met Larry while out with her sister and her twins in Roundhay Park. She checks that Cherry doesn't know Larry, and although it would have been coincidental if she had, it's a relief when Cherry confirms she's never been friendly with anyone of that name.

"I wasn't expecting to meet somebody significant that day," Rebecca says. "When I see Eileen, I'm usually in damage limitation mode."

Although Rebecca has only known Larry a year, there is much ground to cover. They've been walking an hour and are sharing salty snacks and water on the ridge of a hill by the time she reaches the meeting with Mervyn, the marriage licence, and the tape recording. Cherry sits staring at Rebecca, nonplussed. "Is this really true?"

Rebecca nods. "All of it." And then adds, "I only wish it weren't. I'm basically here to discover whether I'm engaged to a murderer."

"It's so incredibly scary," Cherry says. "How do you even begin to deal with that?"

"Some mornings I don't want to get up. But that in itself could look suspicious."

"So what do you do?"

"I climb out of bed and get through the day as best I can. And at night I crawl back under the sheets exhausted."

Later, Rebecca broaches the subject of her return visit to Walter and Katherine's house.

"I'm sure they wouldn't mind if you came along too. They live in a mansion and are ever so hospitable. I can't decide what to make of them. Of course, I feel desperately sorry they lost their daughter in dreadful circumstances. But I suspect the tragedy tipped them over the edge."

"It can happen," Cherry says.

"They were reluctant to admit that Sarah had any problems growing up. Katherine even tried to gloss over her anorexia."

"I can see why it might be helpful to have a second pair of eyes."

"Helpful is an understatement. I can't afford to get this wrong."

"As long as they're okay with me coming, I'd love to support you," Cherry says.

"If only dealing with everybody was as easy as this."

Later, at the perfectly positioned campsite, they assemble the tent in good time to watch the sun going down.

"I'm glad you know how to do this," Rebecca says. "I wouldn't have a clue."

"I've built this little beauty many times with many girlfriends." Rebecca realises her expression has changed as

Cherry adds, "Don't worry, I'm fully aware of your proclivities!" And then changing the subject rather too obviously, "By the way, if you haven't had a chance to see the old Rainier Brewery in the north of Seattle, it's a pretty neat building."

"I'll look out for it," Rebecca says.

Cherry has brought the cocktail ingredients to mix Sicilian Sunsets. "I'll try to make them look like the real thing," she says, gesturing towards the glowing orange palette daubed over the Mazama mountain ridge.

CHAPTER FIFTY

1 SEPTEMBER 1980

The sunset has finished and it's getting dark by the time they finish their cocktails. Cherry clears her throat as if she's about to make an announcement. "I should probably have explained this before," she says. "But if you see a bear, you should always back away slowly, preferably in the direction you came. Never run in front of a bear, just walk. And keep looking at them, so you can see how they're behaving."

"Is that likely?" Rebecca asks.

"Not really. Basically, don't turn your back on them."

"I won't," Rebecca says.

"And we're going to put all our food outside the tent in a barrel. So, if a bear stops by, he won't come into the tent."

They undress in near darkness in the narrow confines of the tent. Cherry keeps the fly sheet open so they can sit up in their sleeping bags and enjoy each star revealing itself in the sky, whilst sipping a second cocktail.

Rebecca is again immensely gratified that this trip, which portended only adrenaline-fuelled anxiety, is holding moments of beauty, companionship and peacefulness. "I'm so glad they forgot to pack your vegetarian meal," she tells Cherry.

JAMES WOOLF

"Me too!"

"And I think this is the best of both worlds. Remote and magical. With showers and toilets."

"They're always a bonus."

"It's completely dark," Rebecca says.

"Know any ghost stories?"

"Not really. Do you?"

"I have a true story. Something that happened locally and was in the papers this year. It's kind of spooky."

"That could fit the bill," Rebecca says.

"I don't have all the details, but I'll do my best."

"It sounds intriguing."

"So, one day," Cherry says, "a few years ago, a girl from Seattle, a teenager somewhere between the ages of thirteen and nineteen, almost certainly met a man. And I'm sure she was excited to meet this man."

"Is this girl you by any chance?" Rebecca asks.

"Let me continue," Cherry admonishes. "I can't say too much about this girl, except she's sporty and has well-developed neck muscles. And she's possibly of Asian or American Indian heritage. She probably left Seattle of her own accord, and may have travelled down south with this man, somewhere close to Clark County perhaps."

"And this is a true story, you say?"

"Yes, all true."

"It's just you don't seem to know much about her," Rebecca says. "Or even what actually happened."

"That's a fair point. You'll have to bear with me. I do know she came from a good home and regularly visited the dentist."

"I don't mind if you make up bits here and there," Rebecca says. "To plug the gaps."

"All right, I'll do that. So she's seventeen years old and her mother, Kim Lee, is Chinese, and her father, Arthur, is

214

American. And she meets this guy in a hotel bar in Seattle. In the Olympic Hotel."

"It's a nice bar, I peeked inside."

"She's there with a group of girls celebrating a friend's birthday and they think they're being awfully sophisticated."

"But they can't drink alcohol," Rebecca points out.

"They've brought fake IDs. There's always someone in high school with a sideline making them. And the girls are having a great time when Morgan comes into the bar."

"Now I'm interested," Rebecca says. "And who is this Morgan character?"

"Well, he's average-looking and over twice her age. But our girl's fascinated, because he's dirty and loud-mouthed and flirts with all her friends. He kisses three including her, but he tells her she's his favourite. And the girls find him sleazy and disgusting but at the same time primal and sexy."

"So what happens?" It's getting colder now and Rebecca pulls her sleeping bag up to her shoulders.

"At the end of the evening, to the girls' chagrin, Morgan disappears. He doesn't take any of their phone numbers. But unknown to the others, he's waiting for our girl a little way down the street, and he offers her a ride in his truck. And they drive a little, and perhaps there's even a little kissing and cuddling in the back – I'll leave that to your imagination. And when he drops her home, he suggests they take off together the very next day for a trip to Clark County. He has a delivery to make, and he'll pick her up bright and early. 'Be sure not to tell your mom and dad', he says, 'they'll never let you go otherwise'."

"I worry about the direction this is heading," Rebecca says.

"She's waiting for him as arranged," Cherry ignores the interruption, "and, closing the front door as silently as she can, she joins him in the truck. And they're heading south and she's trying to make conversation, about his job, and where he grew up, but today Morgan is testy and unforthcoming. And when she asks which hotel they'll be staying in, he laughs coarsely, and tells her he doesn't stay in hotels. He sleeps in the back of his truck and he's kind of expecting her to do the same, unless she has a problem with it. And the girl says of course she doesn't – that will be just fine. This world is new to her and for all she knows it's normal for young girls to be sleeping in the backs of trucks belonging to men they've only just met."

There is silence which is interrupted only by the faint chatter of other campers some distance from their tent.

"And what happens next?" Rebecca asks.

"So we jump forward to 24 February 1980, a father and son – let's call them Ned and Ivan – are panning for gold in Fly Creek. It's probably a hundred miles or so south of here."

"And they find something, don't they?" It's like the time she heard the radio report of the murder in Halifax. She wants to hear the inevitable, yet she's dreading it too.

"They found bits and pieces. A skull that was intact. A few bones scattered across a dumping area of about one hundred feet. There was no actual body. Or any of her clothes."

Somewhere far away there is the soft mewing of a mountain goat.

"Investigators believed at first that the remains belonged to Jamie Grissim," Cherry continues. "She was a sixteen-year-old who disappeared on her way to Fort Vancouver High School in 1971. But they checked the dental records and there was no match. Detectives scoured other missing persons reports, but they weren't able to identify the remains."

"Why not?" Rebecca is indignant. "Didn't Kim Lee and Arthur report their daughter missing?"

"Those names were invented, remember? We don't know who our girl is. We don't know anything about her, except she was a teenager with strong neck muscles, possibly Asian or Native American."

"So the hotel bar and Morgan–"

"All made up. These bits of a skeleton they found; they really have no idea who they belong to."

"But how could that happen?" Rebecca asks.

"It's a mystery," Cherry says.

Rebecca is feeling upset now and slightly confused. "I'm not sure why you told me this story," she says. "You know my situation. It doesn't seem like the most sensitive of choices."

"It's just a spooky story," Cherry says and lies down in her sleeping bag.

"No, not when you think about the position I'm in right now."

"Okay, so maybe I did tell it for a reason. Not all crimes are solved. Some never will be. It's not a game you're involved in, Rebecca. This is serious. Maybe Larry did kill his first wife and maybe he'll get away with it. You need to tread very, very carefully."

"I realise that," Rebecca says. "That's the whole point of my trip."

"Yes, but even if Sarah's relatives seem odd and don't always make perfect sense, isn't it still a hell of a risk to go back to him?"

"He's also the person I fell in love with. And I don't know what's going on. And that's why I asked you to come along with me to the Postlethwaites, to get your view. I didn't want to hear weird upsetting parables."

"I didn't mean to freak you out – I'm sorry. I care about you. That's all."

"And I'm sorry too. I'm just upset about that poor girl. They don't even know who on earth she was, or her name, nothing. I find that terribly sad."

The conversation threatens to bring the evening to

something of a chilling conclusion. Rebecca can't shift from her head the thoughts of the unidentified bones still lying in a police station or laboratory, as she lies next to Cherry in the tent. She rolls her sleeping bag towards Cherry and asks if she would mind hugging her. The two women hold each other tightly for some time and Rebecca apologises that her tears may be soaking Cherry's hair.

CHAPTER FIFTY-ONE

2 SEPTEMBER 1980

The next day, Rebecca calls Larry from the Olympic Hotel. He has been reading *The Guardian* and is fascinated by the unfolding story of Craig Crimmins, a stagehand at the Met, who has just been arrested in the Bronx and charged with the murder of violinist Helen Hagnes Mintiks. She had been taking part in a performance accompanying the Berlin Ballet at the Metropolitan Opera House. The orchestra had just played an extract from *Don Quixote* which finished at nine thirty pm with Mrs Mintiks holding a C note for several seconds. It would be the last note she ever played. Larry mentions that the violinist had been bound, gagged and naked, then hurled down a ventilation shaft. Her body was found eleven hours later, dangling from a steel ledge in the shaft. Rebecca tries not to focus on any similarities with Sarah's death, which are pure coincidence after all, or the pleasure Larry is taking regaling her with the details. Their conversation is brief as Rebecca had planned. She has no time to tell Larry about any fictitious meetings in Belgium and Germany before Cherry collects her; the call is almost wholly taken up with talk of the violinist's murder.

The Postlethwaites are also discussing news stories when Rebecca and Cherry arrive for dinner. There's quite a crowd as they are shown in by Katherine and seated at one end of the long table. Walter is holding court, amusing everyone with his reflections on the presidential campaign. He acknowledges the new arrivals with a gesture of his hand before continuing.

"You heard what Reagan said in New York? I watched it on the news. 'The lady standing there has never betrayed us'. I thought that's a strange way to talk about Nancy, and right in front of her too! But then the camera panned across the bay, and I realised dear old Ronnie was talking about Liberty!"

Laughter ricochets round the room, rising and falling in pockets, as if the joke is being circulated via a faulty system of telegraphic communications.

"You're a regular stand-up comedian, Pop!" Rebecca recognises Bill, the adult version of the elder of the two boys she saw in the photos.

Katherine now introduces Rebecca and Cherry to the assembled gathering. As well as Bill and Mark, Bill's wife Alexandra, and Maud, the eldest of the siblings, she points out two long-standing friends of the family, Joan and her husband Vaughan. Rebecca wonders how forthcoming Walter and Katherine will be about Sarah with ten around the table.

"But what Reagan said about Carter was absolutely true," Walter continues. "He's betrayed the working men and women of America. The humiliations ordinary folk have to endure these days earning any kind of living – it's unforgivable."

An elderly black woman in a traditional pinafore enters carrying a huge tray laden with ten bowls, each brimming with minestrone soup. Such is the tray's weight that she struggles to keep it level, and indeed as she approaches the table, it tilts forward slightly and some soup escapes from two of the bowls, the liquid trickling onto the table. Walter's voice is a model of restrained patience.

"Take your time, Nina, that's it... slowly does it."

The help continues unassisted and places the tray without further mishap onto the table, then wipes the spillage with a napkin. Rebecca notices Cherry's open mouth and they exchange a look of mutual disbelief.

Katherine may have picked up on this, as she says, "Nina is with us evenings only these days, and on special occasions."

While Nina serves the soup and then pours wine from a tall carafe, the conversation fragments into chit-chat between neighbours. Cherry and Rebecca make small talk with Alexandra, who tells them she has come straight from a life-drawing class. "How these models just sit there with no clothes on in a room full of men and the odd woman! But she said she was a dancer too, so it's in the blood."

Towards the end of the first course, Mark says, "I have some news." He's sitting closest to Walter and although he's intending to share his announcement, his voice remains low. At the opposite end, Rebecca finds it difficult to catch all that he goes on to say, something about him deciding to study in Los Angeles.

"So when you've done your degree, you'll be able to translate the gobbledegook lawyers talk," Katherine says.

"That's kind of why I'm studying law, Mom. We're looking for some justice here, aren't we?"

"So much of what they tell us about Sarah is incomprehensible," Katherine explains to Rebecca.

"Unless you speak Latin," Bill says.

"Aren't you going to explain why we have our two guests with us here tonight?" Walter says.

"Of course," Katherine says. "Rebecca here is engaged to marry Larry Hudson."

"We're aware, Mom, that's why we all came along," Bill says.

"And you're going ahead with that, knowing what he did to Sarah?" Maud says, looking askance at Rebecca across the table.

"I only found out that might have happened a couple of weeks ago."

"Might have!" Maud says. "You don't think I'd know what happened to my own sister?"

"I'm here to learn more – that's what I mean," Rebecca says.

"You should have invited Isaac Stillman!" Bill says to his mother, who holds up her hand as if pleading guilty to an oversight.

"What do you want to know anyway?" Maud says. "If you're already marrying him, it's too late, isn't it?"

"Give the girl a chance," Walter says.

"We'll answer any questions you have," Katherine says.

"And who's your friend?" Maud says.

"Exactly as you say. She's my friend," Rebecca replies. She hasn't warmed to this woman and is already struggling to remain civil in her responses.

"And you have Joan here too," Walter continues. "You know who Joan is?"

"I'm afraid I don't," Rebecca says.

"She's Larry's younger sister." Rebecca feels a lurch inside her stomach. "She hasn't spoken to him since she discovered what he'd done."

The woman sitting opposite smiles self-consciously and Rebecca tries to smile back. She has the same grey eyes as Larry.

"Thank you for coming too," Rebecca manages to say.

CHAPTER FIFTY-TWO

2 SEPTEMBER 1980

"Perhaps you'd like to hear about the coroner's verdict," Katherine says. "Because that's important."

"Yes, that would be useful," Rebecca says. "I don't really understand how your system works."

Bill whispers furiously to Katherine, "That's why we needed Isaac! He was critical of the way Paul Moorhead dealt with it!" Katherine nods meekly, again acknowledging her mistake.

"Paul Moorhead was the coroner who handled the case. And Isaac Stillman is another coroner we've got to know," Walter explains.

"Could I ask a question?" Cherry says. "Was there a jury in her case?"

"No, and that was one of the problems," Bill says. "That and the fact that, according to Isaac, Moorhead didn't properly allow for the possibility that Sarah was already dead when Larry pushed her off the balcony."

Rebecca becomes aware of Katherine passing quickly behind her and leaving the room.

"Not the possibility. She was dead," Mark says.

"Obviously," Bill says. "But Moorhead was fixated with her injuries, which were catastrophic, clearly."

"And he made adverse comments about Sarah without informing us first," Maud says. "And he wasn't meant to do that."

"You're missing the most important thing of all," Walter says. "Moorhead was conflicted. He shouldn't even have been on the case."

"Conflicted?" Rebecca says.

"He should have recused himself," Mark says.

"He was at James Garfield High School. Same as Larry," Walter says. "Okay, he was a few years ahead, but he denied knowing Larry and we know that was a lie. We challenged him, of course. We challenged the fact he sat on that case when we discovered they both went to James Garfield's."

"Larry said he never knew him either," Bill says.

Rebecca has a sensation of light-headedness. She has drunk her wine too quickly and the flow of information across the table feels overwhelming. She should probably engage Larry's sister in conversation. She is surely the person who knows him best, but all this about Paul Moorhead could be important too if only she could focus.

As if sensing the problem, Cherry picks up the slack. "I think you need to be very clear about this. Rebecca and I are outsiders, remember. We don't know the details. You say the coroner lied about whether he knew Larry. And that Larry also lied. What makes you so sure?"

Walter looks at Cherry and nods, as if her speech has won her a badge of respect. He turns to Larry's sister. "Go on, Joan. You're in the best position to explain."

"Larry used to do orienteering," Joan begins. "It was the only thing he really made an effort in, which annoyed the teachers because it was a very good school."

"Still is," Walter says. "It's the high school to go to if you're gifted and from Seattle."

"Jimi Hendrix went there," Bill says. "Though Larry said he didn't remember him either."

"Oh, please," Walter says. "He wasn't gifted."

"Yes, so Larry went on to represent the State of Washington in orienteering," Joan says. "And when Sarah died, I knew the name Paul Moorhead was familiar. But I also knew he wasn't a friend of Larry's. Larry could talk to anyone, but he had only one or two friends."

"And Moorhead was much older," Walter says.

"But I knew I knew that name," Joan says. "So I looked inside this drawer of Larry's high-school memorabilia, it was all still there, years later."

"All his orienteering records going right back to when he first started running for the school team," Walter says.

"Yes, from when he was eleven," Joan says. "And there it was in the school newsletters. Paul Moorhead. Paul Moorhead. Paul Moorhead. He was the team captain. That's how I knew his name."

"He used to select Larry," Walter says.

"Yes, week after week," Joan says. "How would he not remember that?"

"That was a great piece of detective work!" Walter says. Joan flushes with the praise. Rebecca looks for the first time at Joan's husband, Vaughan, diffident and removed. He has not said a word all evening.

Later, Rebecca has been to the toilet and on her way back passes Joan in the corridor. She delays returning to the dining room and when Joan comes back out, asks whether she could give her a minute of her time. They open another door and Joan finds the light switch. Rows of hardback novels on mahogany bookcases line three of the four walls. The other has a large street-facing window.

"How can I help?" Joan says, as if she's not at all sure she can.

"It's just you know Larry so much better than any of those people and I would have kicked myself if I hadn't taken the time to speak with you personally. All of this has come as such a shock. Larry has shown me nothing but kindness since I met him."

"The thing you have to remember is that Larry can make friends with anybody."

"I've noticed that too."

"There was this boy at his school, always in trouble with the teachers. And later with the police. Ryan Westlake, he was called. He used to make the other boys' lives a misery, Larry's too for a while – Ryan locked Larry in some freezing outhouse at school for a whole day. But Larry was crafty. He found a way of talking to Ryan. And he began to love Larry. He'd drop by our house to see him after school or weekends. And Larry always made time for him. Our parents were concerned, but Larry said it was okay. They were just having conversations. Or sometimes they might go out and Larry would watch him smoke. But he made one thing clear. He absolutely hated Ryan. He'd just decided it was better for Ryan to like him. And he never had any more bother from him."

"Could I ask about someone else? Larry tells me he has a brother in the UK, but I've never met him."

"Yes, he does," Joan confirms. "Kirk. He's the eldest. Larry doesn't like him, but to be honest, he's not alone in that. Kirk's strange. We're a strange family when you think about it."

"Does Larry ever speak to Kirk, do you know?"

"He probably would if it's useful for him," Joan says. "He's always been strategic with people."

"I can see that, but it doesn't make him a murderer."

"He doesn't have real feelings for anyone. We realised after a while he was the same with everyone, whether they were family or not. It was all about what he could get from us, how much money he could extract from Mom and Dad. But he's charming; he could talk us round to anything."

"There's just so much information," Rebecca says.

"I didn't want to believe he killed Sarah either. But the more I looked into it, the more sense it made."

Just around ten thirty, as Rebecca and Cherry are leaving, Katherine reappears with their coats which she'd hung up elsewhere. She's now wearing the same woollen shawl she put on during Rebecca's first visit.

"Ever since Sarah died, I've never been able to get the right temperature. I'm either too hot or too cold. I can't understand why that is."

From the dining room, talk of Walter's birthday drifts through to where they're standing.

"So I bought you this attaché case when I was in Los Angeles, Pop," Mark is saying. "It's from Renwick of Canada, but I got a good deal."

Walter's response cuts right through the approving murmurs. "Jesus Christ! – I can't understand you boys sometimes. Why on earth would you buy me that when I'm practically retired?"

Cherry screws up her face before recovering and thanks Katherine for the lovely meal. Katherine opens the door and, looking embarrassed, tells Rebecca and Cherry it's been a pleasure having them over.

CHAPTER FIFTY-THREE

3 SEPTEMBER 1980

Cherry rests her knife and fork while she considers. "If it's a question of picking somebody for a team, week after week. Then seeing that person at the matches. Coaching them maybe. You'd remember, wouldn't you? And Larry would have stood out. He later represented the State in orienteering. That's what she said."

Rebecca looks at Cherry's incredibly dark eyes. "I suppose so. But you must admit Walter's reaction to the birthday present was strange. He'd been on best behaviour all evening, then when we stepped out of the room, he became himself."

"I hadn't thought of it like that," Cherry admits.

It is Rebecca's last night in Seattle and Cherry has prepared a spicy pasta Napoletana for her at home.

"That's the thing though," Rebecca says. "The whole family is weird. And poor Katherine takes the blame for pretty much everything."

"I did feel sorry for her," Cherry says, wiping her chin with a napkin.

"This is absolutely delicious! Thanks so much for your hospitality. Again!"

Cherry laughs. "It's my go-to recipe when I don't have much in the cupboard. So... What will you do when you get home?"

"I first have to decide about Larry."

"You're still not sure?"

"Should I be?"

"From what I heard, the evidence is almost conclusive. I know the family are strange, and that's not surprising. And they had their problems before Sarah died, for sure. But Larry's sudden disappearance. The fact nobody, except his parents, have heard from him since. I mean, why didn't he even contact his sister Joan?"

"Well, she supports Sarah's family's side of the story."

"That's my point."

Rebecca nods. "He's meant to have a brother in the UK too, not so far from where we live. I've never been introduced and it's not for want of trying. But according to Joan, Larry never got on with him either."

"Is that a fact?" Cherry tops up their glasses with white wine. "I know it's not my decision, but there's a lot pointing towards his guilt. And they've kept everything, haven't they? The bank statements showing the money was transferred, that postcard from Mexico. When she mentions to her parents that Larry just jokingly asked how much they were worth–"

Rebecca stops eating. Raising a finger to her bottom lip, she stares at the table in silence.

"What is it?" Cherry asks. "You read that postcard too."

"It's something Larry said. I just remembered."

"What was it?"

"He told me that on their honeymoon, Sarah refused to go into Mexico because she was petrified of being stabbed by the locals. But they did go to Mexico."

"Unless he just forgot."

"Larry doesn't just forget. Anything."

"Listen. If it were me, I'd be satisfied he murdered Sarah. Not one hundred per cent. But enough for me to get right out of the relationship."

"I'm pretty convinced he's guilty too," Rebecca says.

Cherry exhales with relief. "Thank the Lord for that!"

"And that's what makes it more important than ever that I return to my house and make sure he doesn't suspect a thing. He's not going to get away with this."

CHAPTER FIFTY-FOUR

4–5 SEPTEMBER 1980

Rebecca flies to Frankfurt the following morning. During her two-hour turnaround, she chats with an English woman awaiting a flight to Heathrow. The woman tells her she's just become engaged and promises to send her at least three photographs of the happy bride and groom on their fantastic day. Rebecca does not mention her own engagement.

She is fully expecting to take a taxi home from Leeds airport upon her arrival on Thursday evening. Her heart quickens as Larry approaches her in the concourse. He got her landing details from Sally, he says. Knowing how exhausted she'd be, he thought he'd make her life a smidgen easier. Not for the first time, an image of him pushing a slender Sarah over a balcony railing plays in her imagination. This time, however, it's as if an old movie has been restored to full technicolour glory, the details so much more vivid now she's met Sarah's family. Larry is perkier than he has been in months, running round her like a badly trained sheepdog, almost falling over himself in his attempts to carry her bags, open doors and do whatever needs doing.

"I'm so glad to have the boss back," Larry says, closing the boot. "This week has dragged something rotten." His enthusiasm seems genuine enough. Then Rebecca remembers Walter's comment about him being one hell of an actor. "So what shall we do to celebrate your return?" he continues.

"I'm very tired," Rebecca says. "I'm going to have a shower and an early night, but let's catch up tomorrow night."

He tries to persuade her to slow down a little, to at least take tomorrow morning off work. Rebecca says that won't be possible. There's so much to do following her trip.

The reality at work the following day is somewhat different. There's a telephone call Rebecca is desperate to make, one Larry must know nothing about. Apart from that, she has no meetings, or anything much to accomplish before the weekend. Work is a distraction right now. As she cannot make the call until the afternoon, she first tries to get hold of Simon. A colleague says he's away on training, so she leaves a message. The rest of the morning is spent reading mail, reviewing sales figures, and waiting.

Rebecca has already arranged the call through the Postlethwaites and she makes it from the privacy of her office at nine am, Vancouver, Washington time. Sally and Debbie have been instructed she should not be disturbed. The phone barely rings before it is answered.

"Hello?"

"Mr Stillman?"

"Rebecca," he says. "Very pleased to make your acquaintance, I'm only sorry it's not in happier circumstances. Please call me Isaac by the way." His voice is smooth and authoritative. Straight away Rebecca feels she's in the hands of a professional.

Isaac tells Rebecca he was highly sceptical when the Postlethwaites first approached him about their daughter's death. As a coroner, he's encountered several relatives with wild and eccentric theories.

"When did they first contact you?"

"It was some months after a verdict of suicide had been recorded. The parents and eldest son arrived one morning at my office. I'd read about the case in *The Seattle Times* but I wouldn't have expected to find common ground with the bereaved family. But over time I became convinced that Larry is dangerous. That he literally got away with murder. In my view at least," he says.

Rebecca takes a moment to get her thoughts in order. "There's one thing that puzzles me though, Isaac. No one has said – at least not to me – how Larry might have killed his wife. If she was already dead when he pushed her off the balcony, wouldn't her real cause of death have been apparent in the autopsy? I can't help but think that's a gaping hole in the Postlethwaites' argument."

"It's a good point. And it would be a hole, as you say. But I have a theory," Isaac says.

There is crackling on the line, then it goes silent. High-pitched laughter outside her room distracts Rebecca further.

"Can you keep the noise down?" Rebecca shouts. "Are you still there, Isaac?"

"I am indeed. Can you hear me okay?"

"I can hear you. You were talking about your theory?"

"Yes. So it's my belief that Larry suffocated Sarah."

"What makes you say that?"

"For a start, homicidal smothering is difficult to detect. I expect Larry knew as much."

"Was there any evidence?"

"That's the thing, Rebecca. We just don't know. Because the coroner, Paul Moorhead, didn't look for it."

"I'm probably being slow, but can you explain that a little more?"

"I had a private conversation with Moorhead. I asked if he hadn't checked for the telltale signs: subconjunctival haemorrhage, or high levels of CO_2 in the blood, perhaps some subtle bruising to the face? Or was there any trace evidence, such as fibres around the nose and mouth of the deceased? He didn't want to get into the detail. Eventually he admitted he hadn't looked out particularly for those things. His words, 'hadn't looked out particularly'. Based on her brain injury, he said it was crystal clear she died from the injuries sustained landing on the patio."

"Does that mean he didn't do his job properly?"

"Again, this is one person's view. At the very least, it was insufficient. And quite possibly negligent."

"But it's not easy to just suffocate someone, is it?"

"Sarah Hudson was very slight. From what the family say, she always had been."

"Yes, I've seen photos."

"So it would have easily been possible for Larry, a bulky man, to have climbed onto her back while she slept, perhaps tying her hands behind her first, and then asphyxiated her by leaning hard onto her head, pushing her face into the pillow. We're told her suicide was first thing in the morning. Larry's story is that he woke alone and soon discovered her on the patio. My view is he deliberately woke early and killed her before she could even defend herself."

"But with all due respect, Mr Stillman – that's just a theory, isn't it? Because there's no evidence of suffocation."

"The evidence wasn't ever looked for. That doesn't mean it wasn't there."

"And the family told me that Mr Moorhead shouldn't have

been acting. That he had a personal connection with Larry from their school days. Do you have a view on that?"

"I do. Had it been me, I wouldn't have accepted the work."

"So presumably you supported the family in their challenge?"

"I added my weight to their campaign, yes. But Moorhead is a big cheese and others quickly closed rank around him. I was chastised by colleagues – criticised in an open letter. I distanced myself, decided not to push it further. It is my livelihood, after all."

"You distanced yourself," Rebecca says. "Does that mean when it became awkward for you, you decided to stay silent?"

There is a pause on the line. "That's exactly right," Isaac says. "And I'm sure you'd have done the same."

"No, I would have continued to speak up about it," Rebecca says. "But I guess not everybody is too worried about due process being done. Thank you so much for your time, Mr Stillman."

CHAPTER FIFTY-FIVE

5-7 SEPTEMBER 1980

"You have a letter," Larry says, almost as soon as she walks through the door. "It came this morning and I must admit I was curious."

Rebecca hangs her jacket in the hallway.

"Your name's typed on the envelope, so it could be important. But it's been sent here. So that means it's personal. Not a work thing."

"Larry – why don't you just give me the letter?" Rebecca doesn't like the sound of it. She's also feeling tired and would rather just go to bed.

He retrieves it from the kitchen, and she's relieved to see a Leeds postmark.

"Now, what I'd really like is a nice cup of tea," Rebecca says, moving into the living room and dropping onto the sofa. "Perhaps you could make it while I read the letter? All week I've been drinking the most terrible tea. The French in particular have no idea."

He smiles from the doorway and heads back to the kitchen.

"It's nothing very exciting," she tells him when he returns. "Just this headmaster from Ingram Road Primary School."

"Baron Bollockscrew."

"That's right," Rebecca says, noticing his instantaneous recall. "This tea tastes slightly odd."

"I made it the same as usual."

"Maybe the milk's on the turn."

"Could be," Larry admits. "It's been open a few days. And I don't always remember to refrigerate it."

"I'll make a black coffee later." She puts the tea to one side. "Yes, so Mr Colverton wants me to do a motivational talk for his older girls. To inspire them to aim high in their future careers."

"It's taken him long enough to write to you," Larry says.

"Exactly. His girls will need to be a lot more proactive if they're ever going to achieve anything."

That weekend Rebecca feels something of a prisoner in her own home, as Larry is adamant they spend time together. Saturday is anything but relaxing as he's decided he doesn't understand England's political system and insists she explain everything in detail. He's heard Jim Callaghan is likely to resign as Labour leader, so who'll be taking over? And who decides when a general election takes place? The day is a curious mixture of knowledge sharing, domesticity and tension.

Sunday is somewhat better. Larry goes out early to buy the quality papers and they spend the day in the living room, drinking vast quantities of tea which they have with toast and hot muffins, discussing articles or reading in silence. Rebecca is drawn to the story of Sandra Page who wants to marry a convicted murderer before he dies in prison. She decides not to say anything to Larry about that story.

"I think you should use this Geoff Capes guy in one of your macho beer adverts," Larry says, propped up on his elbows on the carpet reading *The Observer*. "Apparently he's the strongest guy in the world."

"It looks like he needs a bra," Rebecca says, peering over his shoulder from the sofa.

"Listen to what he has for breakfast! Three pints of milk, cereal, half a loaf of bread, six eggs, half a pound of bacon, mushrooms, tomatoes and a can of beans."

"What!"

"So we can eat our muffins with a clear conscience."

Later he's fascinated by a page telling them what television they can look forward to over the autumn. "I quite like the look of *Play Your Cards Right*. Is that any good?"

"It's okay," Rebecca says. Panel games are not her thing.

"I can tell you're not keen. Hold on, *Nobody's Perfect*. A new comedy series about the ups and downs of an Anglo-American marriage. We'll have to look out for that one!"

Rebecca is not sure whether she should be concerned that Larry barely touches her all weekend and doesn't initiate anything sexual. She is certainly not disappointed.

CHAPTER FIFTY-SIX

8 SEPTEMBER 1980

Simon calls Rebecca back after the weekend and she asks him to come to her office. But not in his police uniform. She also tells him she's booking his appointment under the name Crispin Garrod.

"That's fine," he says. "Shall I arrive with my monocle and magnifying glass?"

"Very funny. I'm also putting you down as working for Whitbread."

It feels strange seeing him the following afternoon. He is shown into her office by Sally, who gives Rebecca a knowing wink. His hair is shorter than she likes and noticeably thinner. She is sure he has more wrinkles on his forehead too.

"So how are you?" she asks, after she's recovered from him kissing her boldly on the lips as soon as Sally is out the door.

"Oh, not too bad, Becks. Been better to be honest. I haven't seen you for ages. And it's taken a while to get over the shock of you being promised to someone else."

"Well, bigamy isn't recommended for detectives."

"I didn't think you wanted to know me anymore. Until I got your call, of course."

"Shall we sit down?"

He looks at her intently and stoops to sit at the small table. Rebecca sits opposite.

"How's work?" she asks.

"The chaos continues. A lot of us think the Ripper killed Marguerite Walls, but the top brass are convinced it wasn't him."

"Yes, I heard something about that." Rebecca again thinks that if it wasn't the Ripper, it could have been Mervyn, unless they are one and the same person. Perhaps it wouldn't be too late to tell the police about her meeting with him that night after all.

"She was a civil servant," Simon tells her. "She was found in the garden of magistrate, Peter Hainsworth. Anyway, it's probably another cock-up in a long series of cock-ups. And as usual, the killer is left free to go about his business."

"The question, I suppose, is will there ever be justice?" she says. "Or will it be like Jack the Ripper, taunting the police with his letters, and then disappearing forever?"

"Oh, we'll catch him. Eventually. Give us a few months, or maybe years."

"Very comforting," Rebecca says. "Do you want tea?"

"Maybe later. I want to know what this is all about. Why I've been summoned to the Ferguson empire."

"I don't know where to start, to be honest."

"The beginning is traditional," he says.

"You're really going to have to take this seriously. I've just come back from Seattle, where I was trying to work out whether Larry killed his first wife. The coroner's verdict was suicide. But many people disagree. There. I said it. And I started at the end."

Simon looks genuinely shocked. He confesses he doesn't know what to say and again asks her to tell him the whole story.

It's three fifteen pm when she begins with the meeting with

Mervyn and the background to her trip to Seattle. It's four thirty pm by the time he's finished asking questions.

"I sensed things might not be perfect," Simon says. "But I had no bloody inkling of this. I'm dumbfounded to be honest."

"I was too. But then I realised I'd have to get past that. And quite quickly."

He wipes his palm down over his forehead, past his nose and over his chin. "Jesus Christ, Rebecca. What do you want me to do?"

"I just want your advice. I don't want you to do anything. Not yet anyway."

"My advice is to get the hell out of that relationship!"

"I thought you might say that. But you haven't met her mother in Seattle. You haven't seen what this has done to her."

"I've met the families of murder victims. I've seen the toll it takes."

"Yes, and I don't want him to get away with it."

"But from what you say, there's nothing more to be done. The family will keep trying, no doubt. That battle could grind on for years."

"Why has he picked me, Simon? Think about it."

"I could name one or two pretty good reasons." His eyes glint mischievously.

"Not those reasons! I'm a single millionaire businesswoman. It can't be a coincidence."

"Ah, the penny drops. No wonder people were surprised about my promotion. So, you're going to entrap him?"

"Yes! I'm pretty sure he's not going to do anything until we're married. He was very insistent about that happening as soon as possible."

"So you've got time to plan things. But I still don't understand what you're going to do."

"I'm thinking about confronting him. Telling him I know

what he's up to. In the hope he'll let his guard down. But there will be people around me, to protect me."

"And he won't know about them."

"Obviously."

"All right, go on."

"And I'll have tape recorders. Or cameras."

Simon remains seated, frowning. Weighing it up. "And you don't think he'll do anything before your wedding? Because that's the risk."

"I don't think so, no."

"When is that?"

"January the seventeenth."

"And if he makes it look like you've killed yourself, are you sure he wouldn't inherit before?"

"I don't think so because of what's in my will."

"Take legal advice," Simon says. "He's bound to have researched it."

"Good point."

"I really hate to see you putting yourself in danger. But if this is what you want to do, your plan could work. *Could* work."

"You think so?" Rebecca cannot help feeling a little proud.

"It could be the only way he's tried for Sarah's murder," Simon admits. "If he confesses to killing her, of course."

"And I thought you were going to tell me I was mad."

"You are mad. Completely. But this situation is fucking mad."

"I'll tell you what you can do, though. You can be there, ready to intervene, whenever I need you."

"Of course. That's a given."

Rebecca exhales a long wavery breath. She leans forward to cover her eyes with her hands. "Thank you."

"And I might be able to get hold of some decent recording

equipment. Set it up all over your house so you don't need to worry where the conversations happen."

"That would be amazing. We just need to make sure Larry's out the house for a few hours."

"Of course. But rest assured, by the time we've finished it will be like an episode of *Hawaii* bloody *Five-O*."

"I'm glad you're finding this so funny. I could be dead by the end of the year."

"Sorry. Defence mechanism."

Rebecca stands. She walks round the small table and leans to kiss him on the forehead. He raises his head upwards, pulls her towards him and they are kissing again, his tongue right inside her mouth. She pulls away and shakes her head, smiling. Simon is now unbuttoning her blouse and, cupping her in his hands, presses his face into her chest. She disentangles herself once again and does up her blouse. She strokes his thinning hair, kisses him on the lips and goes over to the telephone.

"Sally? Mr Garrod and I would like some tea and biscuits, please."

CHAPTER FIFTY-SEVEN

9-21 SEPTEMBER 1980

Over the next ten days, Rebecca confides in Pamela and Roland, and also Sally who was only told a few details before the trip to Seattle. They each agree to support her and be there for her when needed. Pamela thinks Rebecca is insane for carrying on living with Larry. She should surely put her personal safety before any quest for justice. Sally takes the opposite view, that doing whatever she can to bring Larry to trial must be Rebecca's priority. It's no surprise when she also mentions that she and Pamela have split up. Roland can see both perspectives and asks if it's okay to speak to Nicola about it.

"Under no circumstances!" Rebecca says. "This goes no further."

"Okay, Becky."

"And I'm not telling Eileen. I thought about telling Alison but she's been very distant recently."

Rebecca's brain is so overworked, it is unsurprising that sleep is the first casualty. Falling asleep is not a problem, but a cycle emerges of her waking at two each morning, her mind like a stoked fire, going over all that's happened and all that may yet happen, while she lies next to the man who has stirred up this anxiety and whose own sleep, judging by the rasping and snoring, is unaffected.

One night, two weeks after her return, she awakes with a feeling of dread. Something from a dream alarmed her, something she cannot bring to mind. It is connected to Cherry. Cherry was in her dream, but why this sudden feeling of panic? She lies silently, trying to relax sufficiently to enable the details to permeate her consciousness once again. The dream starts to return in fragments, snipped frames from the cutting-room floor. Two liqueurs Rebecca purchased. In a lounge. The Space Needle! She dreamed of her drink with Cherry there. Rebecca feels like she is approaching the summit of her anxiety. But why would this innocuous drink with a friend have caused her to wake with such powerful foreboding?

She goes over what happened there. Her talking about her problems in a general way, perhaps testing Cherry to see if more might be disclosed at a later time. Cherry mentioning commitment, making a joke at her father's expense. But still what Rebecca is searching for eludes her. She had bought the drinks, put the receipt and change in her purse. She had given her remaining dollars and cents to a hobo at the airport who looked like he could use a meal. She'd given away the dollars, but the receipt... The receipt for the liqueurs, which surely had the price in dollars and probably the words Space Needle, or at the very least a telltale logo. Could she really have brought that back to Leeds and left it lying in her purse? It was in the zipped compartment and presumably safe there from prying eyes. But even so, it must be destroyed. There is no chance of further sleep that night unless this happens immediately.

She rises from her bed and silently crosses the room. Larry makes a ratcheting sound; how does he even do that? She heads down the stairs and waits in darkness in the hall, checking there are no further noises from upstairs. After another minute, she makes her way to the kitchen where her handbag rests on a chair. She pulls out the purse and unzips the compartment. There is no receipt. The receipt is missing. She has no recollection of having taken it out.

CHAPTER FIFTY-EIGHT

6 OCTOBER 1980

"Miss Rebecca Ferguson was born on the twenty-sixth of June 1945 and grew up in a small two-up two-down near the Wellington Road in Armley. She attended Roundhay School for girls, where she took history, mathematics and chemistry A levels before studying for her degree in psychology at Sheffield University. From these modest beginnings, Miss Ferguson rose to become one of the leading businesswomen in the country, and almost certainly the most notable in Yorkshire. She remained loyal to Leeds and now lives in a lovely house, not too far from where she went to school. I think I'm right in saying that, Rebecca?"

"Yes, less than five minutes away." Rebecca feels herself blush as she looks out at the assembled faces. She has never enjoyed public speaking which is too closely associated in her mind with acting, something she avoided whenever possible at school.

"What a lovely life Miss Ferguson must live, girls! Able to shape the direction of Keighley Beers, whilst retaining an active interest in her prodigiously successful first company Just the Job. She also gets to work with advertising agencies like Saatchi

& Saatchi. I'm sure you've all seen the one for Wilberforce with William Byron Stevenson. Raise your hand if you haven't seen that advert, girls."

Unsurprisingly, nobody raises their hand although there are audible giggles from the back. Rebecca feels herself starting to panic. These girls are on the cusp of puberty, or there already. Is this going to be an exercise in crowd control?

"Don't delay, it's a Wilberforce day!" Mr Colverton's rendition is the worst Rebecca has heard, by some margin. "I hope Miss Ferguson will tell us about the making of that advert, because I for one as a Leeds supporter would find that fascinating."

He looks across to the small table where Rebecca is seated.

"I certainly can do," Rebecca says. The story of the Wilberforce advert isn't in her speech and she's slightly miffed that she'll now have to improvise.

"And as well as living in her luxurious house and running her own exciting business, a little birdie tells me that Miss Ferguson will be getting married next year."

That little birdie is almost certainly her secretary Debbie. Sally wouldn't talk about her forthcoming wedding quite so freely.

"But one thing I can tell you, girls, is this wonderful lifestyle didn't fall into Miss Ferguson's lap. It wasn't presented to her in a grotto by her fairy godmother!" He waits rather too obviously for laughter – none is forthcoming. "No, girls, Miss Ferguson got where she has by dint of sheer hard work and persistence. It's not easy for ladies in this day and age to take control of their destiny. But that's what Miss Ferguson has achieved. And in just one minute, when I've finished rambling on..." – another short pause, uncrowned by laughter – "she will tell you exactly how she did it. So please join me in giving Miss Rebecca Ferguson a very warm welcome indeed."

There are eighty girls in the hall and the applause is resounding. Rebecca rises to her feet and steps towards the lectern, passing a grinning Mr Colverton going the other way.

"Good afternoon, everybody. And thank you very, very much, Mr Colverton. I almost don't know how to begin after that. I could start by saying that just because I'm wealthy and successful, it doesn't mean I'm not a normal person and that real life doesn't happen to me too. Three days before I visited your school to see your annual play, which was extremely good by the way, my car broke down in a small country lane near Laxton. It was after midnight and I was terrified, especially when I met some very odd people also up at that time. I went in search of a public telephone to call my fiancé. When I found one, it didn't work, of course. Why on earth I expected a public telephone to work at that time of night, I really can't explain!" This does get a few laughs.

"The point I'm making, is that a great job and a high standard of living are fantastic, and definitely worth striving for. But they won't insulate you from the trials and tribulations of everyday life. I still don't have a fairy godmother, Mr Colverton, much as I'd like one!"

Rebecca gets home at six pm and runs herself a bath, relieved to find that Larry is out. She pours herself a glass of wine and drinks it whilst soaking. The next tribulation she must deal with will be the following day. She's received a phone call at work from Simon confirming what she had anticipated. She instinctively goes into planning mode, but then catches herself doing so. Instead, she concentrates on the feeling of just lying there, and how relaxed she is starting to feel drinking the wine. It is a much-needed indulgence and by the time she gets out of the bath she is almost herself again.

CHAPTER FIFTY-NINE

7 OCTOBER 1980

The next morning, Rebecca asks Debbie to check Brian is in his office. "He's there, all right," Debbie confirms. Brian is situated in the basement of the building, and Rebecca is halfway there before she stops and decides to deal with the matter the other way round. She returns to her desk and calls William Clayton. He arrives within minutes.

"Thanks for dropping everything at short notice, William. I'm not sure how much you know about Brian's personal life." William looks uncomfortable and she continues without further hesitation. "Either way, I'm only going to talk about the work position. I want you to take over as head brewer – from today. You can help recruit for the job you're currently doing."

"What about Brian?" William asks.

"Brian is leaving Keighley Beers."

"It's not fair to kick a man when he's down."

"It's best we avoid the detail and just stick with the work situation. Which is that I'm offering you a promotion, if you want it?"

William glances down. "Yes, of course I want it."

"I'm pleased. Debbie will type up your new contract. I'm

not sure exactly what we're paying Brian, but you'll get the same."

William nods, satisfied with that part of the arrangement.

"Have you seen Mr Sheridan today? I ought to let him know what's happening."

She decides at the last minute to take Roland with her, just in case. She hasn't set foot in Brian's room for at least two years and, when they go in, she immediately notices the acrid smell, as well as its total disorder. The smell is explained by what Brian is up to. He is on his knees in a dark corner of the room talking in low tones.

"That's it, this big one is yours if you want it. That's my girl."

He clearly hasn't heard their entrance and Rebecca coughs to attract his attention.

"If you could tear yourself apart from your friend for just one moment, Brian."

He rises slowly and turns around, a cluster of green beans in one hand. She cannot help looking past him into the cage, where the hamster is standing, it's tiny paws pressing against the bars to steady itself.

"What do you two want?" Brian asks suspiciously. He's wearing short sleeves despite the room's chilliness. The arm which had worn the plaster cast is pale and withered in comparison to the other.

"We need to speak with you. I suggest we sit down."

He does so behind his desk which is covered with unwashed crockery and cups. Roland pulls up two other chairs and Rebecca begins straight away.

"You're finished here, Brian. I'm not in the business of employing wife batterers. I learned from a police contact that you're not going to be prosecuted this time round. Personally, I think it's a shame you won't be behind bars like your hamster friend. Please clear your things and be out of here within one hour."

Brian nods. "I can do it quicker if I get help."

"Ask William. He's used to doing pretty much everything in this department."

A flicker of anger appears in Brian's eyes, then he smiles sardonically. "This is all fine by me, Rebecca. I have other plans."

"Perfect," Rebecca says.

"And you'll receive your company pension in the normal way," Roland says.

This hadn't been discussed, but now it's been said, Rebecca thinks she'll let it go. "And I'll write you a reference if you want," she continues. "Although don't expect anything other than complete honesty."

"I won't be needing a reference. Not for what I'm going to do."

Back in her office, Roland says he thought the exchange went surprisingly well.

"Thanks for deciding his pension arrangements," Rebecca says.

"Sorry, I thought that was standard. Anyway, he'll need it to support his little friend. Who'd have thought he's been keeping pets in there?"

"I don't like rodents, but that one was cute," Rebecca says.

CHAPTER SIXTY

8 OCTOBER 1980

Rebecca has an appointment in Nottingham, to meet a Mr Parfitt about a beer festival that she is sponsoring. While she's there she plans to visit the castle which she has never done before. There is one other item on her to-do list for the day, the idea for which came to her when she was addressing the girls at Ingram Road Primary School. A phone call has already ascertained the hall of residence she needs to visit. She plans to get there early, an aunt with some distressing news.

She drives into the campus via the west entrance just before eight am and finds the correct car park. A porter shows her into the office of Dr Victoria van der Bilt, who's already working at her desk. She tells Rebecca that as the founding warden of the hall, she is less than keen on relatives turning up unannounced first thing in the morning. Rebecca quickly decides she fully deserves her scary name.

"But if it's important family news, perhaps I also need to know?" she asks Rebecca.

"It's confidential at this stage."

"In that case, there's no sense in delaying," Dr Van der Bilt says.

They head down a corridor and up some stairs, the warden walking purposively ahead, stopping outside room 118.

"At this time in the morning, he's almost certainly in there." She leaves Rebecca standing outside the door.

Rebecca knocks and there's a muffled call from inside. She knocks again, more loudly.

"Who is it?"

"Can you let me in please? It's urgent."

The door is unlocked and opened and the occupant peers at her blearily.

"Can I come in please?" Rebecca says.

He is still computing what's going on as she marches past him, yanking the curtains open. He's wearing boxer shorts, and as soon as he recognises her, he groans and sits on his bed.

"It's you."

"How's university life?" Rebecca asks cheerfully. "Maths and philosophy, wasn't it?"

"It's all right."

She looks around the room, the walls bare, except for a single poster stuck up with Blu Tack. "I see you're a Frank Sinatra fan."

"Dennis 'Sinatra' Moss? He's this geezer who sings in *The Happy Return*. He's meant to keep the students away, but they've started hiring him for events on campus. People nick the posters, it's a joke really."

"So, you're continuing where you left off in my car. Stealing things."

"I'm sorry about that," Duncan says. "I was desperate. I know it was wrong. I don't normally behave like that."

She looks again at the picture of Sinatra.

"It's only a sodding poster."

"I could have stopped you getting into this university. You

could have been in court, prison even, had I pursued it. You realise that, don't you? I could have ruined you for life."

"So why didn't you?"

She remembers his capacity to ask annoying questions.

"I felt like a fool for even letting you in my car. Just imagine what the police would have said."

He nods, appreciating her honesty. "I can make an instant coffee if you like. My roommate keeps our milk on the window ledge."

He gestures beyond the small corridor and bathroom to what Rebecca realises is a second connected bedroom.

"I didn't come here to have a coffee with you," Rebecca says. "You can get dressed. We're going for a walk. Take your service till card."

He pulls the clothes he was wearing the night before over his boxer shorts and T-shirt and there is a waft of stale cigarettes. Outside, the campus is still deserted. They walk along curving roads and reach the student banks near to the main union building within minutes. Rebecca instructs him to withdraw fifteen pounds.

"I think I had eleven on me that night. But then there was the expense of replacing my purse. It wasn't dear, but I don't see why you shouldn't pay for that too."

On the way back to the hall he asks why she's bothered about it. Since the night he met her, he's discovered who she is.

"My family talked about you. I know you could easily afford to lose that money."

"That isn't the point, Duncan."

"My dad said you're a millionaire. He was amazed you were driving such a crappy car."

"So, you told them everything? Did you mention you propositioned me and then stole my money?"

"They had the abbreviated version," Duncan says. "But I

still don't understand why you've come all this way to find me."

"For a start, I have meetings in Nottingham today. But it's a matter of principle. My father was framed for stealing money. It was more than you took from me, but the point is he didn't do it. And it cost him his job and ultimately his life."

"What do you mean?"

"I mean, the biggest thing you've had to deal with is finding your dad's dirty magazines. I found my father hanging from a beam in our garage, and I was much younger than you. Had someone taken the time to put things right at his work, he'd still be alive today. And I have to live with that fact."

Back at the car park, Rebecca points to the Datsun. "I got rid of that crappy car you mentioned. I won't be breaking down in country lanes again."

Following her meeting about the beer festival in Nottingham and a tour round the castle, Rebecca returns to her office. She knows Cherry is likely to pick up the phone as she works from home, but the relief on hearing her voice is so overwhelming that Rebecca finds herself fighting back tears.

"I'm so sorry, Cherry. You must think I've completely lost the plot."

"Of course I don't. And I miss you."

Rebecca tells her about the receipt going missing from her purse and asks if Cherry has any memory of her purchasing the drinks in the Space Needle.

"Not really," Cherry says. "Maybe you're getting it out of perspective. Do you really think he's been through your handbag? Isn't it more likely you never put the receipt in there?"

"I really don't know, that's the problem."

"But I understand why you might be feeling a little paranoid, right now. I'd be frantic in your position."

"Thanks," Rebecca says. "Although I'm not sure that's terribly reassuring."

CHAPTER SIXTY-ONE

9-11 OCTOBER 1980

They're kissing in front of the stained-glass windows on the stairs on their way up. There's a tearing urgency which she doesn't recognise from their three interrupted years together.

"Is this where you seduce all the men you bring to this hotel?" He glides his mouth across her face to nibble at her earlobe.

"Always," she says. "Though I've usually shed my clothes at this point."

"In reception?"

"Exactly, whilst checking in."

They're kissing again in the corridor outside their room, before she can even unlock the door. For decency's sake she has to pull his hand out of her knickers.

He's inside her within seconds of entering the room, Rebecca uncomfortably pressed against an ornate wooden cabinet, a still life oil painting hanging above the bed behind him. Burning candle, bottle of wine and citrus fruits slide in and out of focus as he thrusts into her. The sheer intensity is making her legs feel wobbly – this might be the best sex she's ever had.

"Jesus Christ, Simon," she says afterwards. "I asked you along to keep me company, not to savage me like a wild boar."

"Sorry. It's been a long time coming."

"If only the same could be said of you."

"Don't worry, there's plenty more where that came from."

"I'm here to work, remember?" Rebecca says. "Make a cup of tea and we'll unpack our bags."

They drink it sitting up on the bed. It's eleven thirty and her meeting at the distillery is not until after lunch. He confesses he was frustrated by her insistence on travelling separately, only meeting in a café near their hotel. He's used to being careful but that did seem over the top. She says she's spending more time planning what she does these days than actually doing anything.

She tells him it is Larry's fortieth birthday that day. In the last few weeks, he seemed to be having a bit of a crisis, leaning uncharacteristically on her for support. Curiously, he hadn't seemed bothered she was going away on the actual day itself. He was planning to stay overnight with his brother, who he doesn't even like. But he'd insisted that they celebrate at the weekend with a romantic night away.

"Where are you taking him?" Simon asks.

"Paris. We're flying first class. And I've splashed out on the hotel. I don't want him feeling short-changed."

"How are you bearing up generally?"

"It's hard to explain because it's so strange. Imagine having to think carefully about everything you say and do, whilst pretending to the person you live with, that life is normal. But not completely normal. Because I'm meant to be in the throes of romantic love. Really looking forward to spending the rest of my life with him."

"That's the problem, isn't it? You might be spending the rest of your life with him!"

"I'm not finding your humour particularly helpful."

"It wasn't a joke. No one's making you do this. I told you a month ago it was a bad idea."

"No, you told me it was the only way to make sure he faces justice."

"True, but I also said you were mad. Anyway, what about Larry? Have you noticed anything different about his behaviour?"

"He's going full steam ahead with the wedding plans. The arrangements are taking up all his time as far as I can tell. He's very meticulous."

"Isn't he consulting you?"

"I'm just letting him get on with it. If it keeps him out of trouble."

"I don't suppose you're too bothered which flowers he's ordering for the reception."

"I pretend to be tremendously interested. I might be a better actor than I thought."

That evening, after supper in the hotel, they go back to their room. They open a bottle of whisky she was given at her meeting that day, and she tells him what's causing her sleepless nights. The receipt from Seattle.

"Christ, Rebecca! He may already be onto you. Your life is in even more danger now."

"I knew I could rely on you not to dress it up."

"You can't stay in the same house any longer. This has gone beyond reckless. It's utter stupidity."

"But I don't know for sure if he even found it, or if it's just my imagination. I don't even know what I did with the receipt."

"But if he has it, God knows what he'll do to you."

They look at each other. Rebecca shrugs. "I'm carrying on."

"I understand you want to see justice done. And as a policeman I respect that. But now has to be the time to stop."

"Can I still count on your support?"

He pauses. "Of course."

His words are still going through her mind the following night. *'Beyond reckless... utter stupidity.'* And this from a hard-bitten copper. If he thinks this, what's she doing sitting in her living room with Larry, watching *The Nine O'Clock News*? Perhaps he watched the evening news with Sarah before pinning her to the bed the following morning, forcing her face into the pillow until she could breathe no more. Others too, like Pamela, have tried to make her see sense. But Simon had been practically the only person on her side. She feels more isolated than ever.

The big story that evening is the Conservative party conference. Margaret Thatcher has talked about "an autumn of understanding" being followed by "a winter of common sense". There is no indication that she'll be buckling under pressure. The report continues with an extract of her closing speech.

"To those waiting with bated breath for that favourite media catchphrase, the 'U' turn, I have only one thing to say. 'You turn if you want to'." There are approving laughs, a round of applause, and smiles from Heseltine and Howe. Thatcher stands resolutely at the podium, poised to deliver the punchline: "'The lady's not for turning'."

"My word." Larry laughs. "You have some woman leading your country right now. What would you do?"

"I wouldn't turn either," Rebecca replies.

"I thought you might say that," he says.

The following morning, he's filled with bustle and enthusiasm for their forthcoming trip. He says that now he's passed forty, he's perfectly reconciled to it. He unwraps his birthday present at breakfast, and, like an over-enthusiastic schoolboy, immediately announces he will take it to Paris.

She'd read about the Sharp Pocket Computer back in August. Thinking it was perfect for Larry, she splashed out one hundred and twenty-five pounds. Rather than giving it to him straight away, she saved it for his birthday.

"I can't believe I can programme one thousand four hundred and twenty-four steps through BASIC on this," he says, looking at the box.

She's now doubtful whether she should have given him anything that enhances his thinking capabilities. But at least he likes it.

"You can take over the world now, Larry."

He is fiddling with his new gadget throughout the drive to the airport. As they step into the aeroplane, he tells her that, like John Lennon, he has entered a period of domestic harmony and peace. He turns and kisses her as they taxi towards the runway.

"Paris here we come," he whispers into the same ear that Simon nibbled in Glasgow just two days earlier.

"I can't wait," she replies.

CHAPTER SIXTY-TWO

1 NOVEMBER 1980

They have cross words even though Rebecca has told herself she should let it go. When they got into bed the night before, Larry mentioned he'd be spending time with a friend the following day. Rebecca said nothing then but brings the subject up at breakfast. Who is this friend and why isn't it appropriate to introduce her? It is the weekend after all. She hasn't met one of his friends. She hasn't even met his brother Kirk.

Larry smiles, as if surprised she even cares about this stuff. Of course he'd have no objection to her meeting any of these people. He'd love her to, but today isn't the best day. Saul recently separated from his wife and needs to discharge some feelings. He's only in the UK a short time, and today is their one chance to meet. And as for Kirk, Larry confesses, he's ashamed to even be related to "the arch-philistine". Not so ashamed to prevent him staying with Kirk on his birthday, Rebecca points out. Larry says he was desperate. She was away on business, if she remembers.

These reasonable explanations should have been the cue for Rebecca to drop the subject, but for some reason she ploughs on. She tells Larry that he is secretive and selfish. Worse still, she accuses him of not having real feelings for her, of simply being out for what he can get from the relationship. Even as she says the words, she realises she's virtually paraphrased what Joan told her in Seattle.

If that's how you read the situation, that's fine, Larry tells her. He could of course mention the many caring things he's done for her since they met, but he is short of time. So why doesn't she think about that while he's gone from the house? She'll have several hours, and she might even be surprised by what she remembers. When he saw off the very strange journalist would be a good place to start.

When he goes out, he leaves a letter addressed to him with a Washington postmark lying on the living-room sideboard. The sideboard containing the serviette holder he proposed marriage with back in February. How everything has changed since then. He must have left it out with the intention she read it. Her first thought is that someone has tipped him off about her trip to Seattle and this is his way of telling her he knows. But why would he do that? He is way too clever to reveal something in anger that might be counterproductive to his long-term plans.

She waits fifteen minutes after he's gone before carefully removing the letter from its envelope. A handwritten note attached to the letter says it's being sent via Larry's brother in England, as Larry's solicitor is refusing to cooperate. Rebecca recalls Mark asking her for Larry's address. She had been clear that she couldn't tell him and that the Postlethwaites must never let on she had visited Seattle.

The letter is short. It refers to the judge's recent decision regarding Larry's inheritance as a beneficiary from Sarah's will. It's not completely clear to Rebecca, but this latest decision appears to have reversed an earlier judgement that had gone against Larry. The letter doesn't mention the family's theories about Sarah's death, but there is a needling tone, and it says they will keep fighting until they've clawed back every last dollar Larry inherited. It is signed Mark Postlethwaite, but clearly represents the family's views. It certainly doesn't show them in a good light and Rebecca wonders if that's why Larry left it out. If he suspects she knows the Postlethwaites' theories about Sarah's death, this letter could cast doubts on their motives, showing them to be small-minded and money-grabbing.

Trying to work out why Larry left the letter out is difficult enough. But there is worse to come. Rebecca has been thinking recently about the diary she kept as a teenager. She remembers an entry from after her father's funeral in July 1961. For years she'd kept these words in her head, a clarion call to herself to stay strong in tough times. She now feels the need to read that message from her younger self. She surely still has the diary. It must be in the attic in the boxes of exercise books, birthday cards, letters, exam certificates and other childhood memorabilia.

She gets out the stepladder, leaning it against the landing wall. Climbing several rungs, she pushes the hatch through inside. Standing on the top rung, she's able to pull her weight into the dark space above, although her shoulder muscles strain as she does so. It's freezing inside, and she fumbles before finding the light switch. Although not a hoarder by nature, she's always surprised by how much is up here.

She and Larry had put a few of his boxes to one side. She looks at them and instinctively knows he's returned since they did so. Is it because they're so tidily grouped? Or something else?

There is no proper floor but the lighting is good, so she carefully makes her way along the boards towards Larry's belongings. He'd said when he moved in that he would rationalise his things. If anything, he has added to what was there.

Her eye is drawn to a black square plastic record box resting on some sealed cardboard cartons. It looks new – at the very least she doesn't remember seeing it before. Something about its position suggests it has been placed for easy convenience.

She opens the catch. Rather than LPs, she finds maps, photographs, notebooks and odd bits of paper. She pulls out some black and white pictures of women snipped from newspapers. She recognises the faces and names. Marcella Claxton, Emily Jackson, Patricia Atkinson, Wilma McCann. All victims of the Yorkshire Ripper. Her heart almost breaking free from her ribcage, Rebecca picks up the box and moves to a space where she can sit and sift its contents. The maps would appear to be where the murders were committed, a separate one for each, some photocopies, some Ordinance Survey – there are even handwritten X's and the women's names added in Larry's writing. Here is a photo of a playground stuck next to a headshot marked Jayne MacDonald. Both must have been taken by him and developed in Boots. There are similar photos in a pouch.

The Yorkshire Ripper is a subject Larry claims to find distasteful. Whilst always showing concern that Rebecca never walks alone at night, she also recalls him saying, "You Brits have a prurient interest in this stuff." They'd even joked about Brian Sheridan being the Ripper. And yet, Larry has been conducting his own secret tour of the murder sites, compiling a grisly dossier. Didn't he tell her he was researching local history when they first met?

There is an extra twist. She pulls out a small red notebook which is definitely familiar. It's the one he removed from a shoulder bag the day they met. She opens it and there are handwritten details about Irene Richardson, including her address and age when she was murdered in February 1978 in Roundhay Park. And there on the next page, in amongst these details of murder victims, Rebecca's own name and telephone number appear. They are neatly written, and she recalls Archie calling out her number, proud to know it off by heart. Larry must have been visiting Roundhay Park that day because Irene Richardson had perished there a year and a half earlier. Another stop on his tour. Rebecca's mind jumps to their trip to Morecambe and the time she spent waiting while Larry surveyed the stomach-turning exhibits in the waxworks museum. She cannot bear to look at the box's contents a minute longer. She replaces everything, sealing the catch.

CHAPTER SIXTY-THREE

5 NOVEMBER 1980

The following Wednesday, Rebecca, Larry and other members of the Ferguson family are back in Roundhay Park eagerly awaiting the start of the firework display. Larry has been saying for some time he wants to experience an archetypal British bonfire night.

"I've never done the whole thing," he told Rebecca. "I mentioned going last year but you went out with Roland instead. I want to hold one of those sparklers, I want to feel it in my hand, and to eat a piping hot sausage roll on a cold night."

Feeling a little squeamish about going alone with him to Roundhay Park, Rebecca invited Roland and Nicola to accompany them, as well as Eileen and the twins. It is indeed a cold evening, just as Larry had wanted, and they've already bought hot drinks and toffee apples for the kids, to keep them going.

They are at the back of the crowd, having arrived late, and are chatting amongst themselves. Roland suddenly leans towards Rebecca and whispers in her ear, "Do you remember what a funk I was in last year? Nicola had just chucked me. And now she's standing next to me holding my hand."

Exactly on cue, Lindsay says, "Maybe you and Nicola will get married, as well as Rebecca and Uncle Larry."

There is a pause and Nicola giggles nervously.

"Perhaps you could start by painting a lovely picture of them," Rebecca says. "Just like the one you were doing of us earlier."

Eileen and the twins had arrived at Rebecca's house an hour before they'd been expected. Rebecca found Lindsay some paper and watercolours and she started a picture of Larry and Rebecca eating their dinner. Rebecca said how glamorous Lindsay had made her look, whilst inwardly shuddering at this depiction of apparent domestic harmony.

"She's a great little artist," Larry says. "I'm keeping that picture. It'll be worth a fortune one day."

"And if Aunty Becky gets murdered by the Yorkshire Ripper, you'll have something to remember her by," Archie pipes up.

"Archie! That's a horrible thing to say." It's rare for Eileen to reprimand her son.

"Well, she's almost been murdered once," Archie says. "Larry called in the middle of the night and woke me up about it."

"He's right," Larry says. "All women need to take care right now. Stay close to your menfolk and we'll all have less to worry about."

Eileen agrees, even though she doesn't have a boyfriend right now. Nicola says, "Roland never lets me walk anywhere alone."

Rebecca is finding the conversation slightly surreal. It's the first time she's been out with Larry since being certain that he too is a murderer.

"When are they going to catch him anyway?" Archie asks. "They're taking their blooming time, aren't they?"

Before anyone can agree, there is an angry explosion of lights in the sky followed by a volley of ear-splitting cracks and bangs. The fireworks are finally beginning.

CHAPTER SIXTY-FOUR

24 NOVEMBER-1 DECEMBER 1980

Rebecca's making notes following a telephone call when the door of her office opens. Looking up from her desk, and seeing it's only Debbie, she returns her attention to the page.

"I'm sorry," Debbie says.

"What is it now?" Rebecca asks in a jokey fashion, before noticing the purple blotches under Debbie's eyes and her tear-stained cheeks. "What's the matter?" she asks, this time more gently.

"I don't think I can do this anymore. I'm really sorry."

"Do what anymore, Debbie?"

"I'm going to have to resign. I'm so sorry."

"Resign? You mean you've got another job? – well, that's great–"

"There's no other job," Debbie interrupts. "It's the journey. I can't do the journey anymore. I don't want to let you down. But I can't." The last three words emerge as a squeak, as if someone squeezed her throat while she was saying them.

"Sit down a moment," Rebecca says, rising from her seat and

pulling a chair across for her most junior member of staff. "And you might want to slow down. I'm not fully understanding you."

Debbie sits and begins crying silently, kneading her palms into her eyes. Standing awkwardly, Rebecca places a hand on her shoulder. "Why don't you want to do the journey?"

"It's just – this last one. In Headingley. I used to live in Headingley."

"Which last one?" Rebecca asks. "What d'you mean, Debbie?"

What Debbie has been trying to tell her, and which she now explains a little more coherently, is that the murder of a student has been reported that day. Debbie heard it on the radio. Initially, the police told a roomful of deeply sceptical journalists that there was nothing to connect Jacqueline Hill's death to the Ripper, but later corrected their mistake after the autopsy showed evidence of the use of a ball-pein hammer.

"I have to take two buses each way, with a walk at both ends," Debbie says. "I think it's best if I stay at home for a bit. I'm just so worried it's – I'm so worried it will happen..."

"Well, it's not going to happen to you," Rebecca finishes the sentence for her. "Because we'll arrange for a minicab to pick you up. And take you home."

"A minicab?" Debbie still looks worried.

"Yes, we'll use the company we know. All their drivers are lovely. And I'll pay for that personally, every morning and every night, until this madman is caught." Then realising the extravagance of her promise, she adds, "Perhaps you can ring them and ask for their very best price. And make it sound like you're shopping around."

The news of this latest murder increases Rebecca's anxiety about her own situation, and she spends several days trying to get hold of Simon, calling him at work and leaving messages. He doesn't return her calls but when they eventually speak at four o'clock on a Monday afternoon, he tells her about a new crack team that's been assembled.

"Well, it's because the prime minister got so angry about the Jacqueline Hill murder and threatened to take over the investigation herself."

"She couldn't do a worse job than they're doing," Rebecca says.

"That's what Thatcher said too. So they pulled out all the stops and gathered this team of hardened pros under this bloke called Lawrence Byford. And they're taking a long hard look at the evidence. They've already decided the letters and tapes from Mr Wearside are a load of cobblers."

"You mean a hoax?"

"Yes! – a hoax, Rebecca. Though you'd have to have been as thick as two short planks to have believed it in the first place. And something else they've noticed is that all the detectives working on this are suffering from mental exhaustion. Morale is at an all-time low."

"I appreciate you're all tired, Simon. And under a bit of pressure. But I need to speak to you."

"A bit of pressure! Christ almighty, Rebecca – you don't know the half of it."

"I get it, but I'm under the cosh too. I need to move ahead now. Put my plan into action?"

"What plan?"

"You know, gather my team, set up the recorders? And have that all-important conversation with Larry. I don't think I can wait any longer."

"You'll have to. All our leave has been cancelled after the Hill murder. We're on our knees here, Rebecca. I don't even have time for this conversation to be honest."

"Yes and meanwhile I'm living with a murderer."

"That's your choice. These women being attacked with hammers and screwdrivers don't have the luxury of deciding."

Rebecca has the distinct feeling she's standing with a noose around her neck. With the platform beneath her wobbling.

"But you promised you'd get the equipment together. You said you'd rig it up throughout my house."

"And I will if you give me a sodding chance! You don't seem to understand – there's a massive spotlight on what we're doing right now. Didn't you see the rumpus in today's *Daily Mail*?"

"I don't read the *Daily Mail*."

"It doesn't matter! The whole fucking world is watching our every move. There's no way I can get the equipment together for at least a month. I'll need to pull in some serious favours anyway."

"All right, all right – I understand."

"And to be honest, the best time to borrow it without being noticed will be between Christmas and the new year."

"I get it, Simon. I'm just not sure I can hold on any longer. I'm convinced Larry suspects something. He keeps looking at me in this funny way."

"Then stop being a hero and move out. Go back to that hotel in Glasgow. You can afford it. Unless you want to be the next murder we're investigating."

CHAPTER SIXTY-FIVE

1 DECEMBER 1980

As soon as the conversation with Simon finishes, Rebecca writes a letter to Lawrence Byford. She says she has heard about the work of his team, and it's her opinion that the regular detectives working on the Ripper case need to be given leave and replaced by others from different areas in the country. She knows one detective who's showing signs of severe strain and exhaustion. She says she hopes he'll follow the advice of a leading member of Leeds' business community.

She stops the car in Keighley on her way home and posts the letter. She can't face the thought of dealing with Larry tonight. She just wants the evening to pass without incident, so she can get up and go to work again the next day. But he's in the hall as she walks through the door, clearly angry.

"Do you not remember anything? Our agreement this morning?"

"Agreement?"

"What planet are you occupying right now, Rebecca?"

"What have I forgotten? – just tell me."

"We're meant to be collecting the invitations!"

"Oh." She's relieved it's something so innocuous. "Can't we go tomorrow night?"

He sighs, exasperated. "You know I wanted to get them sent out last week. We've delayed long enough. I could have picked them up myself, but I thought it would be a nice thing to do together – a joyous thing, but you obviously don't agree."

"I'm sorry, Larry. I've got so much going on at work right now."

"Clearly. If we leave now, we'll get there just before it closes."

She moves the Datsun out of the drive, so they can travel in his car.

"I've been meaning to ask," he says, pulling out of Lidgett Park Road. "You were having a conversation about me on bonfire night. I heard my name once or twice. What was all that about?"

"What conversation was this?"

"Sorry, I was being vague. It was with the twins. On the way home after the fireworks."

Rebecca thinks back and remembers Archie and Lindsay pulling her to one side as they approached the outskirts of Roundhay Park. There were streams of people leaving and Lindsay had whispered into her ear that they wanted a secret conversation.

"And it has to be now?" Rebecca had said, wondering what it was all about.

"Yes, now."

They'd hung behind the others and Lindsay said that she and Archie were both in agreement about this.

"In agreement about what?" Rebecca asked.

"That Larry is no fun anymore," Lindsay said. "We used to like him, but now he's so serious all the time. And really moody too!"

"So, what do you want me to do about that?" Rebecca asked.

"Not marry him, of course!" Archie said.

Larry is waiting at a red light and turns to face Rebecca, raising his eyebrows.

"Lindsay and Archie don't think you're much fun anymore, Larry. And frankly, after the fuss you're making about these invitations, I tend to agree."

CHAPTER SIXTY-SIX

3 DECEMBER 1980

When Rebecca arrives at the comfortable, utilitarian house in Chapeltown, they explain that Polly has just read an essay aloud. They continue to discuss it sitting around the wooden kitchen table while Sandra prepares dinner. Because it's Sandra cooking, Rebecca is assured she can expect a vegan feast. In the meantime, she is given a huge glass of white wine to keep her going.

"Have you warned her?" Beth asks Pamela, then smiles at Rebecca.

"Warned her about what?" Pamela laughs.

"That once we get into one of our debates, there's no stopping us."

"It's fine – really," Rebecca says, looking at the first of the photocopied sheets Polly has slid across the table. The essay is called Compulsory Heterosexuality and Lesbian Existence. "I'm bound to learn something," she adds.

Rebecca had received a call at work from Pamela who told her she'd been living with three other women for six weeks. Polly is doing a PhD in literary theory, Sandra is a teacher at the same school as Pamela, and Beth is a poet who doesn't have any money. Pamela told Rebecca they take it in turns to cook evening meals and don't go out unless all four are together. They're always happy to have friends over for dinner or to stay for longer, but guests are occasionally disappointed that their hosts do little other than read and talk. They don't have a television set and tend to avoid mainstream culture. Rebecca had been intrigued by these details. It didn't seem to be a lifestyle Pamela would naturally gravitate towards. Rebecca was desperate to get away from Larry when they spoke, and fortunately Pamela invited her over the same evening.

"Because of my PhD, I'm particularly interested in language," Polly tells Rebecca. "In the essay, you'll find Adrienne Rich creates her own terminology. She doesn't like the word 'lesbian' for example. She says it has patriarchal associations – clinical even."

"What does she prefer?" Rebecca asks.

"She likes 'lesbian experience' and 'lesbian continuum'," Polly says.

"It gets complicated," Beth says, "because you don't have to identify as a lesbian to be part of the lesbian continuum."

"That is confusing," Rebecca agrees.

"It's a different approach," Polly says. "I've been thinking about this essay for a week or so now. And I'm beginning to understand the lesbian continuum as a state of being that has more to do with sharing joy than erotic experiences."

"Or like an omnipotent female energy," Sandra adds, carelessly tossing a handful of sliced onions into a sizzling pan.

"And what about compulsory heterosexuality?" Rebecca asks. "What's that about?"

"We might have to go gently here," Beth says. "Pam says you're getting married."

"Theoretically," Rebecca says and leaves it at that. There are understanding smiles around the table.

THE COMPANY SHE KEEPS

"Okay," Polly says. "Adrienne Rich is saying that society assumes women are innately sexually oriented only towards men. And that all kinds of male power are harnessed to support this assumption, and to deny the existence of lesbian experience. And let's be clear, we're talking about the full gamut of options being deployed: from violence and subjugation to cultural imperialism and exclusion."

Rebecca can feel her brain straining to process the terminology – the wine is not assisting. She finds herself wondering who in the house is sleeping with who. Pamela hasn't mentioned having a new partner since Sally, but Rebecca knows she can be secretive. Maybe they all share one bed and there's a nightly free-for-all. Polly is extremely tall and exudes intellectual prowess. Beth with her flame-red hair might have stepped out of a Pre-Raphaelite painting, and Sandra, although not a conventional beauty, has a compelling personal magnetism. Rebecca could see Pamela falling in love with any one of them or even all three. A part of Rebecca now regrets not taking the opportunity to experience something physical with Cherry while she was in America. Their night away in Mount Rainier National Park would have been the perfect time for discreet experimentation. Cherry had respectfully made clear that she'd happily have taken things a stage further had Rebecca been willing. But Rebecca had pulled back. She'd kept her at arm's length, certainly not out of any loyalty to Larry. Why was that?

A Siamese cat glides in and jumps on Polly's lap. She tickles its neck and it lifts its head so she can stroke under its chin.

"This is Sophia," Polly says to Rebecca. "She may look all soppy and romantic, but don't be fooled by appearances. She has been known to terrorise our guests!"

"Thanks for the warning," Rebecca says, laughing.

The women start talking about how Beth once met Adrienne Rich.

"What an incredible person. So straightforward and honest," Beth says. "Such integrity. I had dinner with her a couple of times afterwards too. She was very encouraging to me as a poet."

"Sylvia Plath mentions her in her diaries," Polly says. "Something about a woman with shining black hair, honest, forthright, even a little opinionated."

"That's rich coming from Plath," Sandra says, and they all laugh.

"And you know W H Auden picked out Adrienne Rich's poems for an award and wrote the introduction to her first book," Beth says. "She's simply an amazing poet."

She begins reciting one of the poems off by heart: something about an old man with a clenched fist of blue and white, and bodies of sick children, but Sandra leans over Rebecca's shoulder and says rather too loudly in her ear, "Adrienne Rich's husband killed himself – Beth won't mention that."

Rebecca, distracted from the poem which she'd like to have heard but intrigued too by the suicide connection, turns in her seat and mouths, "Really?" and Sandra nods. Then into Rebecca's ear again, "Left New York in a rented car and was found a few days later..." She holds two firearm fingers to her right temple.

Beth finishes reciting the lines to appreciative applause from Pamela and Polly, and Rebecca asks, "How did you meet Adrienne Rich?"

"I was in New York and was involved in this programme connecting poets and prisoners," Beth says. "Adrienne arrived at the Bedford Hills Correctional Facility at the same time as me, and she was using a cane to steady herself. She's not an old woman, but she suffers from arthritis. It was freezing that day, and I thought about taking her arm to help her up this icy hill. But you know what? I didn't have the nerve to do it."

Sandra has sat down at the table, eager to hear the story. "Why didn't you help, Beth?"

"I guess I thought she was going to be this real virago. But she's anything but scary though. I'd never laughed with anyone so much before I met Adrienne."

"And how did the prisoners like her?" Rebecca asks, now fascinated by this poet who she'd never heard of before that evening.

Beth nods her head and smiles at Rebecca. "Her poems were both ferocious and eloquent. They took the audience by surprise. The women were still asking questions about her book as they were led back to their cells."

"I'm not surprised," Sandra says. "I first read her work in an anthology of gay verse – I can't remember its title, and there's a good reason for that." She laughs loudly.

The others look at Sandra expectantly. "Well?" Pamela says. "Spill the beans."

"I was at college and I didn't want my roommate knowing I was gay. I thought it would freak her out. So I ripped the cover off the poetry book."

Laughter erupts around the table and Rebecca is amazed to see this gathering of scholarly feminists descend into a clucking and fluttering flock of chickens, arms flapping in imitation of wings. She joins in, enjoying their easy camaraderie; she's been missing this.

CHAPTER SIXTY-SEVEN

3-4 DECEMBER 1980

W hen the dishes arrive they live up to all expectations. A lentil and vegetable bake, spicy potato wedges, thinly sliced carrots with a coriander sauce, and salted kale cooked to perfection. Neither Larry nor Rebecca have been inclined to prepare anything elaborate lately and Rebecca announces she hasn't eaten so well in ages.

The food is accompanied by a second bottle of wine which Rebecca brought. The women are fascinated by Rebecca's career, her success within a deeply patriarchal world, although Polly points out that it's useful for those successfully exploiting women's labour to be able to point to "the decoy of the upwardly mobile token woman" as Adrienne Rich refers to it.

After the meal, Pamela and Rebecca take coffee up to her room.

"I really like your new friends," Rebecca says. "I didn't know what to expect but I've honestly found them to be a breath of fresh air."

"They like you too," Pamela says. "And Sandra, whose family own this house, said that if you ever want a break from your enforced heterosexuality and fancy moving in with a bunch of leftie lesbians, you'd be more than welcome."

"That's kind," Rebecca says.

"There's another bedroom with just books in it. Sandra says we can find space for them elsewhere."

"You don't know what a tempting offer that is."

Rebecca tells Pamela about the tense trip she made to Paris with Larry, which felt as if she was walking on thin ice the whole time. And also of her worries that Simon may let her down with the plan to entrap Larry.

"Meanwhile, relations between me and Larry are deteriorating all the time."

"Look," Pamela says. "Don't go back to your home. Why not abandon this crazy odyssey? – it can't end in anything but disaster. Move in with us. You could do so starting from tonight."

"You're right," Rebecca says. "I don't know what I've been thinking."

They make a bed up for Rebecca on the couch, and Polly, Beth and Sandra, who have been told that Rebecca has a few relationship issues, agree to clear the spare room first thing in the morning. Rebecca explains it will just be for a while, until she gets her act together. She telephones Larry to say she's staying over with her friend as she's too drunk to drive. He offers to collect her, but Rebecca tells him not to bother. It's late and Pamela will lend her clothes for work the next day.

The following morning Rebecca doesn't head straight to work, stopping instead at her solicitor's firm in Keighley. She has known Ted Beaumont forever, he was the family's lawyer when she grew up, and he's taken care of all her legal business since then. He recently advised her about her will.

Rebecca asks how he is and he tells her pretty good. He and his wife cannot wait to buy a property in Spain and enjoy the warmer climate in their twilight years. Ted has been completely bald since Rebecca can remember, but his skin and complexion make him look like a much younger man.

"That sounds fantastic," Rebecca tells him. "But I can't believe you're retirement age."

"I went to school with your father, if you remember?" Ted says.

"Yes, I remember." Ted mentions this connection every time she sees him, and it occasionally leads to an interesting memory or anecdote she hasn't heard before.

"A terrible thing that was. Everyone who'd met Frasier knew he wouldn't have stolen that money."

Rebecca nods. She doesn't feel inclined to rake over this particular injustice right now.

"I'm actually here to talk about my will, following on from our last conversation," she says. "I want to add an extra clause, in case anything happens to me before my wedding. I know it's not strictly necessary."

"Let's hope it won't be," Ted says.

When she'd first asked Ted about what would happen in the event she predeceased Larry before their wedding, he had assumed she was considering making an allowance in her will for him if that unlikely scenario came to pass.

He's now surprised to learn the opposite is the case. She is so concerned that Larry should receive nothing if she dies before they marry that she wants a specific clause to that effect.

"It's not for me to ask why," Ted says. "But I'd appreciate some comfort at least that you've thought this through."

Rebecca assures him that she has. He expresses reservations about a marriage starting on such rocky foundations but agrees to draft a suitable clause and send it to her for review.

"I know every woman is worried about the Ripper right now," he says. "I've got young girls in this office who make all their journeys together – they never go back from work alone. My secretary told me that she breathes a sigh of relief every time she walks through her front door still alive."

"I know," Rebecca agrees. "I pay for a minicab for my secretary to take her home and bring her to work. Well, two minicabs, since Sally cottoned on to the arrangement."

"And that's why you're doing this? Because you think you might be murdered by the Ripper before your wedding?"

"The reason I'm doing this is because Larry has plenty of his own money. My family need it more than he does."

Now that he has begun talking about the Yorkshire Ripper, Ted is not keen to be deflected. He cannot believe they don't know who the killer is. Surely somebody somewhere must have reported something significant.

By the time Rebecca gets to work, she has already changed her mind about moving in with Pamela and her friends. It is only one month more now until she will be able to put her plan into action. She can surely last out until then. She could arrange another work trip in the meantime. Who knows, she might even persuade Simon to join her. She telephones Pamela's house and speaks with Beth. It was an incredibly kind offer for them to make that room available for her, Rebecca says, but she's decided that she cannot take them up on it, for the time being.

CHAPTER SIXTY-EIGHT

9-19 DECEMBER 1980

Rebecca has a problem with her autochange cassette player. Her Barry Manilow album is lying mangled inside it and she's frightened to even use the second player for other music. Larry promised to fix it, but that was a week ago and he's clearly forgotten or become distracted by other concerns, such as his computer record of spending on their wedding, or the separate list of invitation responses. It is because of her broken music player that Rebecca is listening to Radio 4 on the morning the UK wakes up to the news of John Lennon's death in New York. Eyewitnesses are talking about how, after the murder, the gunman calmly waited outside the Dakota Building until police came and took him away.

Larry calls her at work as soon as she arrives. "Did you hear? They killed John Lennon!" He sounds muffled, strange – almost as if he's been shot himself.

"Yes, it's unbelievable." Rebecca had never been a fan of The Beatles, put off for some reason by their puerile sense of humour, preferring instead American bands like The Byrds and The Doors. Even so, she's saddened by Lennon's violent death. It is further proof that the world is going mad.

"The gunman was smirking," Larry manages to say. "He was reading *Catcher in the Rye* when they arrested him, for crying out loud." There is a guttural groan, reminding Rebecca of Walter's description of Larry telephoning after Sarah died.

"I'm really sorry, Larry – I'm meant to be meeting William Clayton now."

There are the sounds of Larry gasping and crying, then he mutters something about *Catcher in the* fucking *Rye* and hangs up.

Larry seems to be affected by this event in a way that Rebecca would never have thought possible. The first thing he says when she returns home that evening is, "Ronald Reagan says it's a tragedy, but he won't support gun control when he becomes president."

Over the next couple of weeks, he goes out only to buy copies of the daily newspapers, as well as a flotilla of tacky fan magazines about Lennon. He then returns to bed where he spends all day reading them. It's as if his new personal mission is to discover every known fact about the killing, about Lennon's most recent recordings, and all that led up to both.

"Me and John Lennon were born on the same day and part of me died with him," Rebecca hears Larry telling Ken Tobias one morning, as he returns home with yet more newspapers. "I worked out there were just minutes between our births. It feels like an omen when something like this happens."

Rebecca had never realised that Larry was even a Beatles fan, in fact he'd turned the radio off recently when 'Hey Jude' came on, saying he found it irritating. She's mildly entertained by his inconsistency, although also alarmed that he continues to find people more interesting in death than in life. She does, however, derive some reassurance from Larry's distracted behaviour. She was worried that she wouldn't survive another month sharing the same house, but December is marching briskly forwards, and his onset of depression allows her developing plan to become more solid by the day. If she can quietly continue without arousing his suspicion, everything will surely be okay.

CHAPTER SIXTY-NINE

20 DECEMBER 1980

It's a Saturday and just after lunch, Eileen and the twins drop by unannounced at Rebecca's house. They've been to the park and as soon as Rebecca opens the door, Lindsay and Archie shoot past her to use the toilets. Rebecca is perplexed by this unexpected visit. She has something urgent that afternoon. After a few minutes discussing what's happening on Christmas Day and whether it's still possible to get everyone together, Rebecca has to absent herself in order to drive to Pontefract.

She's told Larry she needs a new challenge. She is tiring of the beer industry and fancies moving into hotels. For this reason, she has set up a meeting with a local hotel to discuss a jointly funded project.

Rebecca has met business associates at Wentbridge House before, always enjoying the acres of gardens and grounds surrounding the hotel. She also feels reassured by the old-fashioned and slightly pernickety world view of its staff.

Rebecca has instructed everyone to arrive there separately. They will be shown to the meeting room booked in the name of Keighley Beers. It's a room she has used before, and she has chosen it because people cannot see the occupants from the gardens outside. She is leaving nothing to chance.

Rebecca is first to arrive and waits in a state of agitation until Roland is shown into the room.

"While I've got you alone, Ro," Rebecca says, "I'm wondering if you'd mind hosting the family on Christmas Day."

Roland sips from the coffee he's just poured and bites into a digestive. "Go on," he says, his face giving away nothing.

"I don't want to be alone with Larry. And also, Eileen has made it very clear she's on the lookout for a family arrangement to attend. Preferably one with someone else doing the cooking!"

Roland laughs and says Nicola had been saying it would be nice to see his family this Christmas, and that might as well be Christmas Day itself. "She's decided not to trek over to Cornwall this year. She'd prefer to spend a few days with me."

"That's a good sign," Rebecca says.

"I'm sure I could twist her arm to cook the turkey, stuffing and roast potatoes."

Pamela, Simon and Sally have now arrived and are helping themselves to drinks. Rebecca thanks them for coming and they sit at the small table on one side of the room.

Simon immediately confirms he now has all the necessary equipment. "I won't bore you with the details but suffice to say I've got hold of several covert listening devices with RP audio masking. They were developed by a Dutch company for the CIA and the Yorkshire police force obtained a job lot when the Yanks were upgrading. And the microphones are tiny – smaller than Opal Fruits."

Just as Simon is saying that the battery-powered devices are extremely difficult to detect, a male member of the hotel staff knocks at the door and asks if everything is to their satisfaction.

"It's all perfect," Rebecca tells him.

Instead of disappearing, the man enters the room and starts

to clear away empty cups before noticing the conversation has stopped around him. "Don't mind me," he says.

"Could you possibly clear those away later?" Rebecca asks. The man apologises and quickly departs. Roland and Sally start laughing.

"Goodness only knows what he thinks we're planning," Pamela says.

"Anyway," Rebecca says. "Had you finished, Simon?"

"I was just saying I'll need around three hours with an electrician to set up the equipment. The guy I have in mind is completely trustworthy."

"That all sounds great, Simon. So the first outing I need to arrange for Larry will be for when you and the electrician come in. We'll speak separately about that. What we all need to talk about today is the plan for New Year's Day. In the morning I'm going to whisk Larry out for a brisk walk. I'm thinking of that as outing number two for Larry. And while we're out, you guys will let yourselves into the house with the key Simon will still have from when he visited with the electrician. I suggest you all arrive at eleven o'clock."

She tells them they'll hide in a small room at the top of the house. Technically, it's a spare bedroom for guests, and Rebecca and Larry rarely step inside it. The room has a long fitted wardrobe which Rebecca has cleared completely. Although it won't be comfortable, they'll sit inside this wardrobe; she'll leave foldaway chairs there. And with the small speaker Simon will have rigged up, they'll hear any conversations Rebecca and Larry are having, no matter where they are in the house.

"And you'll confront Larry?" Roland says.

"That's the plan. I haven't quite worked out how I'll do that. Hopefully I'll get him to admit to killing Sarah without him becoming violent. And then Simon will come downstairs and arrest him. Sounds simple enough, doesn't it?"

"What could possibly go wrong?" Simon asks.

There is another twenty minutes of discussion and questions before Rebecca thanks them for their time and support. "It means so much to me that you're doing this," she says. "I can't tell you how relieved I am that I won't be alone with Larry when we have that conversation."

Roland hugs his sister for a long moment. "We'll be seeing you first on Christmas Day."

CHAPTER SEVENTY

20-26 DECEMBER 1980

Buoyed by her success in getting Roland to host the entire family on Christmas Day, Rebecca rings Ken Tobias's doorbell when she returns home. She needs a favour from him in order to set up the first outing for Larry.

"Come in!" Ken says. "I feel like we haven't seen each other in ages. That must explain why your new car's looking so dirty these days."

Rebecca laughs and steps into the hallway. "I won't keep you long. Larry said you guys are relaxing at home over the festive period. I thought you might like to pop over for drinks tonight. Get things off to a flying start?"

"What a lovely idea," Ken says. "We don't have a babysitter though. Why don't you guys stop by us instead? How about eight thirty?"

"Perfect. I didn't intend to invite us over just now."

"No worries," Ken says. "We always have fun with you guys. Although I've been worried that Larry seems down in the dumps."

"He's been feeling low ever since John Lennon died."

"So I gathered."

"I've been trying to find ways of getting him out of the house to be honest. I was thinking if only we could go out with you and Jill one day. But he wouldn't want me to ask – he'd feel like a charity case."

"Perhaps I should suggest it?" Ken says. "We've been thinking about spending a day walking in the Moors, so maybe we could all do that?"

"That would be perfect." Rebecca is surprised by how much of a master manipulator she's become. "I'm sure you're the one person Larry likes enough to say yes to such a suggestion."

Ken nods. "We can do Boxing Day. I'll bring it up when you come over."

True to his word, Ken slips it into the conversation later that evening. He doesn't do so immediately, but like a consummate professional, he first lets the wine he's selected work its magic. Then, when everyone is relaxed, he casually lobs in the suggestion of a Boxing Day walk in the Moors followed by a leisurely pub lunch.

The next morning Rebecca heads to a phone box and reaches Simon at work. She tells him that he and the electrician will have plenty of time to set up the equipment. And that will be on Boxing Day morning. The day comes around soon enough. Rebecca and Larry set off in Ken's car with Ken and Jill's young son sitting on her lap in the back. Larry amuses everyone with the story of their Christmas Day, which included a rather awkward family dynamic.

"It was the first time we'd seen Alison and her husband since Rebecca stopped supporting their business venture. And Ahmet was particularly frosty towards us."

"Uh-oh," Jill says.

"Let's just say you could have cut the atmosphere with a knife," Larry explains, laughing. "And that was after we'd cut the turkey."

294

"Don't you just love Christmas?" Ken asks. "It's the perfect opportunity to air those festering family grievances."

"I tried to keep things convivial," Rebecca says, "by talking about our forthcoming wedding. But that was also ridiculous as Larry's made all the arrangements, so every question I got asked I had to deflect to him."

"Rebecca's been kind of busy at work," Larry says.

Throughout this conversation in the car, Rebecca's mind is on what will be happening at that moment with Simon and the electrician in her home. Despite emphasising the importance of the house appearing untouched when they return, she's terrified they'll leave telltale signs of their visit; brick dust from drilling, small pieces of plastic cable or something catastrophically obvious like a cardboard box. If only Simon was as fastidious as Larry, but she's noticed there's something slightly haphazard about the way he tackles almost everything.

They park at Hutton-le-Hole on the south side of the Moors. Rebecca is concerned when Jill says they won't be able to go far, as Joseph hates walking, but it turns out they have his buggy for when he tires. They decide on a circular walk connecting the Hutton-le-Hole to the other moorland village of Lastingham. Larry has done some research and says if they return across the Spaunton escarpment they can expect lovely sweeping views.

Rebecca wonders whether the walk will last long enough and whether they'll arrive home too early. What if Simon and the electrician are still finishing the job when they return, or if there have been unexpected difficulties? Her fears are partly allayed as when they reach Lastingham's St Mary's church, it has an eleventh-century crypt and Larry gets into a detailed conversation with a local about its history.

In the event, it is five o'clock when Rebecca and Larry

return home, and to Rebecca's great relief the house appears exactly as they had left it.

"That was some walk," Larry says. "I didn't realise the Moors are so beautiful. Although I was a little disturbed by what Jill was saying about the bodies of those small children still buried there somewhere."

"Horrible, isn't it?" Rebecca says, thinking that Larry would not have been in the least disturbed by this information. In fact, he would have found it thrilling.

While he is having a shower, Rebecca takes the opportunity to check the cupboard in the top room and finds the listening equipment neatly stored under a pile of sheets. It is just as she agreed in advance with Simon.

Everything is now set up. She has done all she can possibly do to prepare for what is coming. She just needs to get through the weekend and then spend two days at work before New Year's Eve. She's promised Larry she'll take the day off so they can get ready to celebrate in style.

CHAPTER SEVENTY-ONE

31 DECEMBER 1980

Rebecca is very aware that, if everything goes to plan, tonight will be the last she ever spends with Larry. Curiously, she is keen to look her best. Inspired by a fashion spread in the newspaper, they go shopping together, eating a simple sandwich lunch in a bakery. Their trip ends in Debenhams which, now she's in her mid-thirties, Rebecca regards as her favourite ladieswear shop. She buys a knee-length maroon woollen skirt with matching jacket and a blouse. The shop assistant says that wearing them together Rebecca looks drop-dead gorgeous.

Early in the afternoon, Rebecca, who hadn't wanted to make too big a thing about their New Year's Eve meal, suggests going out to eat. They might still be able to find a good restaurant that isn't completely booked. And she's willing to pay extra if necessary to reserve a table.

"No worries," Larry says. He spent the whole day yesterday cooking while she was at work. He promises an Uncle Sam-themed banquet. "You'll be begging for mercy by the end of it! This will not be an occasion for anyone worried about their waistline."

"That's so nice of you. And I didn't even notice."

"I hid the dishes in the freezer, or in the messy corner of the kitchen."

"An Uncle Sam-themed banquet? Intriguing."

"There's more to it than that," he explains. "It's also an homage to the great breakfast cereal."

"Really?"

Larry laughs. "I kid you not. I'll explain when I serve it up."

The evening gets off to a strange start. Having spent another hour in the kitchen perfecting his creations, Larry insists that Rebecca take a seat on the sofa. He stands in front of the disused fireplace, facing her.

"Listen, I know you don't want to spend the night talking about John Lennon. And I don't either because I want this New Year's Eve to be especially memorable. We're getting married in just over two weeks, after all."

A chill passes directly from Rebecca's neck to her lower spine. She shifts in her seat.

"So, I'll get this over and done with," Larry continues. "Lennon was a great man, a visionary, and his death hit me hard. But I'm pulling through now, thanks to your help. You've been incredibly patient."

He turns and places a disc on the turntable and the familiar chords of 'Imagine' fill the room. Larry joins Rebecca on the sofa, cupping her hand between his fleshier palms. They listen in silence. When Lennon sings about having no possessions, Larry turns towards Rebecca and kisses her on the nose.

It seems the evening will be all right after all, with Larry back to his best form. He makes two gin and tonics. He demolishes his in seconds, but she takes hers through to the dining room while she waits for the food. Bringing the dishes out one by one, he announces each with a smile and modest bow.

"Ground beef shape-ups!" These are individual meat pies in pastry boats served with Tabasco sauce.

"Moist and crispy chicken!"

"That smells divine," she says.

"Bisquick and zucchini pie," he says, holding two more dishes. "And potato chips with onion dip."

To accompany it all, he's bought an extremely acceptable Californian red.

Rebecca surveys the table. "This looks incredible."

"So, let's tuck in."

And the challenge for her is to discover the connections to breakfast cereals as they plough their way through the feast. She's soon totally into the game, laughing as she makes her guesses.

"I'm betting the chicken batter has Rice Krispies in it."

"Yes!" Larry shouts.

Suddenly remembering her own peculiar situation, Rebecca again wonders if she's drawn the wrong conclusions. Will she make an utter fool of herself tomorrow?

By the time Larry brings out the sweets, Rebecca's stomach is groaning in protest.

"Hot buttered Cheerios!" he announces.

"Well, that's rather obvious. I don't get a point for that, I suppose?"

"Afraid not."

A little later she says, "The banana breeze definitely contains Corn Flakes!"

Larry squeals with delight, meaning she's guessed another one correctly. Even now as it flits through her mind that he's a murderer, she's sure that trapped within his fractured soul is a loving little boy who can't wait to get out. A little boy who's gone to such trouble making so many dishes.

"This is my personal favourite," he says, bringing in yet another pudding. "Purple poke cake with blackberry Jell-O!"

"Larry! There's no way we can get through even a quarter of this."

"Tomorrow's another day," he says.

"I know this sounds ignorant," she says. "But isn't Jell-O actually jelly?"

"Not at all." He holds up a forefinger and leans forward in his chair as if he's about to deliver an important lecture. "Jell-O's a dessert, fruit flavoured; it jiggles when you touch it. Some folks eat it plain, and some top it with whipped cream. Jelly is a spread for bagels, toast or crackers. We'd usually eat it with peanut butter or cream cheese."

"So what you're saying is that jelly is jam?"

"No, no, no!" Larry waves his arms windscreen-wiper-style in front of his chest. "Jelly is made from the juice of fruit while jam is made from crushed fruit."

"So how do you make jelly?"

"Also by crushing fruit, but you strain out everything but the juice. And you boil that with sugar and pectin."

"Isn't that how you make jam?"

"No!" Larry says with emphasis, as if she's just blasphemed in his local church. "With jam the crushed fruit is left in, often with the seeds. So jelly is smooth and spreads evenly while jam tends to be lumpier."

"I'm so glad I asked." Rebecca smiles, and Larry shrugs as if to say he was only answering her question. "The point is, I love American food," Rebecca continues. "In fact, there's only one thing better. And that's American place names. Los Angeles, Las Vegas, San Diego, San Francisco – they're all so fabulous."

"Connecticut, Colorado – I see where you're coming from."

"So much more interesting than Blackpool, Grimsby and Stoke. Who thought up our names anyway?"

"You think American names are that much better?"

"There's no comparison."

"Oklahoma," he says, beginning a game.

"Oldham."

"Sacramento."

"Skegness!"

Larry laughs. "Albuquerque."

"Acton."

"Hidalgo County."

"Hull!" Rebecca shrieks.

"Wyoming."

"West Bromwich."

By now, they are helpless with laughter.

"You win," Larry says. "Or should I say Uncle Sam wins?"

Rebecca remembers when they gave Brian a lift home, having saved him from being arrested at the racetrack. How they'd become almost hysterical when he walked into his house without thanking them.

"And Seattle?" Larry says. "My good old hometown. How about that as a name?"

"Not quite as impressive," Rebecca says.

"You'd like it there. I'll take you one day."

"That would be nice."

"The Space Needle! We'd go there, we'd have a couple of liqueurs in the lounge, and then take in the view."

Rebecca feels a lurch in her stomach, as if she's in rapid freefall.

"Yes, that would be nice," she says, conscious of her lame repetition. She's now desperately trying to wrench herself from her stupefaction. There was danger in the way he said "Seattle" and in the words "Space Needle" – and wasn't that what she bought Cherry there, two liqueurs? He must have found the receipt, and now he's toying with her like a wild cat pawing its prey before savaging it.

"We've time for coffee," Larry says.

"Time before what?"

"Before we watch television. I checked earlier and there are some decent things on."

She looks at her watch. It's nine fifteen pm. "Okay," she says.

CHAPTER SEVENTY-TWO

31 DECEMBER 1980

He disappears into the kitchen and Rebecca slaps the side of her own face hard, twice. What was she doing allowing him to lull her into such a relaxed state? She must be on her guard. There are strong indications that things are going badly awry. If he's planning to take her to Seattle one day, does that mean alive or in an urn? And as convincingly as he talks about the future, it's significant they've never discussed their honeymoon other than him saying he'd sort it out and that it will be a lovely surprise when they get there.

He brings in a pot of coffee, strong and bitter. She's grateful for the injection of caffeine. He's leafing through the newspaper and stops at an advert for recruiting policemen.

"Who'd be one of Yorkshire's finest at a time like this?"

"A policeman?"

"The whole world is fascinated by your local force's ineptitude. How can they have not caught the Ripper by now? They have so much information if they could only pull it together."

"I didn't know you were interested in him." Rebecca feels dread surfacing once again.

"But you did know! Because you went through my newspaper clippings in the loft."

"That was an accident – I just had a quick look." She can hear the panic rising in her voice.

"It's okay, it's no bother," he says pleasantly. "That's it." He's found the television page. "So, Barry Took is selecting this year's TV highlights. That's at ten. And then there's a variety show. Why don't we head due north first?" He arches his eyebrows suggestively.

"I'm a little bit full right now," Rebecca says.

"Nonsense." Larry rises to his feet. "You've had plenty of time to digest. And you owe me this one after everything I've done."

Before she knows it, he's leading her firmly upstairs by the hand; then he opens the bedroom door and ushering her in first, pushes her onto the bed with a jolt.

"Larry, I'm not sure I'm in the mood."

"Of course you are."

He's already on top of her, they are fully clothed and her face is pressed into the pillow. Larry roughly pushes up her skirt so that it's bunched around her waist and is grabbing at her crotch through her knickers.

"I'm really not sure about this, Larry," Rebecca says.

"Well, I'm damn sure about it."

There is lightness in his voice, but he's now yanked her knickers right down and is trying to enter her from behind; she is nowhere near ready.

"Stop, Larry – this is not what I want."

"But it's what I want."

She is struggling desperately, kicking upwards and backwards at him, trying to free herself in any way she can, but he's pinning her to the bed, using an elbow and forearm to rest his body weight on her back. Her ribcage feels like it's being crushed while he forces himself inside her. She could swear he's done this before, and she thinks of Sarah.

"Stop it, Larry! – now!"

"Enjoy. This might be our last time ever!"

She registers this, of course, as he groans noisily, humping her painfully from behind. He's managed to get one arm underneath her now and with his hand flattening her left breast he's jerking her backwards towards him. And just as suddenly he withdraws his arm and pulls his penis out of her. But he's still using his body weight to keep her forcibly on the bed, one hand now planted between her shoulder blades. And then she feels the sticky warmth of his sperm spraying on to her buttocks, cooling rapidly as it dribbles down her legs and between her thighs.

She feels thoroughly soiled, used, desecrated. But still she knows that she must remain strong. There is worse to come. Of that much she's sure.

"Get in the shower."

He pulls her up from the bed and she kicks her knickers off from her ankles so at least she can walk. He shoves her into the bathroom with a look of such menace and aggression that she barely recognises him.

"Undress."

He stands at the door staring at her while she takes off the skirt and blouse she bought earlier that day. Humiliated by her nakedness, she climbs into the shower. He is tugging off his own clothes now, and she realises he's going to join her in the cubicle. She remembers how they once made love in this very spot on the day they became engaged. Thoughts race round her brain so fast she can't even speak. Did her razors run out last week, or is there one left? He pulls the shower nozzle off its catch and hoses her all over with freezing cold water, as if she were a dog or a horse, paying particular care to direct the stream at her undercarriage and buttocks.

Having finished this, he attends to himself, complaining about the temperature of her stupid shower. And now he's out, throwing a towel in the general direction of the cubicle before returning, towelling himself, and lobbing her a fresh pair of knickers.

"Now get dressed again."

She thinks about making a run for it and glances over his shoulder at the bedroom door.

"It's locked," he says. "So don't even consider it."

Feeling more terrified than she can ever remember, she puts the same skirt and blouse back on. And then notices he's holding a kitchen knife.

"Come back into the bedroom. Stand facing the wardrobe with your hands clasped behind your back."

"Larry, have you completely lost your senses? First, you rape me on my own bed and now you're threatening me with a knife."

"There'll be plenty of time to talk later. I'll answer any questions you have, I promise."

"I want to talk now."

"I asked you to stand facing the wardrobe with your hands clasped behind your back."

She picks up her vintage hand-painted lamp, raises it above her shoulder and lunges at his head. He ducks out the way and the upper section of the porcelain smashes on the wooden bed-frame.

He's immediately standing upright again, this time the knife is pointing towards her.

"I'm not going to ask again. Stand facing the wardrobe with your hands clasped behind your back."

She can see no other option, so does as he asks.

"What are you going to do now?"

She's fully expecting him to cut her throat; no doubt he has a plan to make it look like suicide. She hasn't prepared for this, for her death. All her focus has been spent avoiding it. She feels rope being wound tightly around her wrists. After tying them together, he binds her legs with more rope. He unlocks and opens the bedroom door and, wedging his hands beneath her armpits from behind, drags her backwards down the stairs, her Achilles tendons recording each step with a painful bump. At the foot of the stairs, he scoops her up like a roll of old carpet, and carries her through to the lounge, breathing heavily all the while. He dumps her on the sofa. She lies there facing into the room, her blood pumping loudly in both ears. What next?

CHAPTER SEVENTY-THREE

31 DECEMBER 1980

Larry looks down at her as she lies on the sofa. He suddenly smiles.

"Okay," he says.

He switches on the television and there's Barry Took, in his thick square glasses and grey suit, talking about another year of fabulous entertainment being over. Or perhaps not so fabulous, at least not according to Martha Graves of Crick, Northamptonshire.

"I love Barry Took," Larry says. "A voice of reason in a thoroughly illogical world."

"You said you'd answer any questions I have."

"Fire away."

"Can you at least turn the television off?"

He does so. "I'm definitely watching some later. Whatever you say."

"What is going on, Larry? What the fuck is going on?"

He gets out of his armchair and pushes it from behind, so he's positioned nearer to her. As if he wants to afford their little chat the seriousness it deserves.

He sits down again and sighs. "What is going on, Rebecca, is that you've made some very serious mistakes."

She waits. There's no sense in prompting him now.

"Starting with your trip abroad which was reasonable enough, if it were essential for business. But to pretend you were still in Europe when you were flying to Seattle to visit Sarah's family, twice! I found that disappointing."

"How do you know this?" Her jaw is so tense she can barely get the words out.

"Easy. Joan's husband is an old friend of mine. From college. Hell of a nice guy. Vaughan? You might remember him being at the Postlethwaites. He mentioned you had an attractive friend – Cherry, wasn't it? Vaughan thought you were sleeping with her. 'Shame on you', I said, 'for casting aspersions on my fiancée!'."

She stares at him in silence.

"Anyway. So he contacted me soon after you returned. And he was over here last month, but I told you his name was Saul in case you got suspicious. Joan isn't aware we're still in touch. But I knew, of course, you'd been to Seattle even before Vaughan called."

"The receipt."

"I wondered if you'd twigged!" He's leaning down so his eyes are on a level with hers. "It was one of those things, wasn't it? You couldn't say anything to me – I couldn't say anything to you. It's so much better now it's all in the open." His tone changes. "You were digging around, Rebecca. You had no right."

She is silent for a moment. "You're right, Larry – I'm sorry. It was wrong of me; I delved into something that had nothing to do with me – and as you say, I had no right."

"I'm glad you're starting to see it my way. Any other questions?"

"What are you going to do to me?"

"I'm going to kill you. Tonight. I'm not sure exactly what time."

"You can't do it here. It would be obvious it was you."

"Please, Rebecca. You're talking to an old pro. Allow me a little more credit."

"My friends will guess you killed me. They won't believe it was suicide. They know I'd never do that."

"Who said anything about suicide? I've come up with something so much better."

"Well, even so, Simon's a detective, you know."

"Ah, Simon, he's not so smart. He probably thinks he got away with sleeping with you in October in that hotel. I couldn't be arsed following you, by the way, but I did watch him board a train to Glasgow. Whereas you decided to fly."

So he knows pretty much everything. Clever as she thought she'd been, she hasn't got a single thing past him.

She rolls backwards slightly, trying to shift into a more comfortable position. Larry rises and places a cushion beneath her head.

"Is that better?" She nods. "I'm not such a terrible guy. I still care about you, despite everything you've done."

"You won't inherit anything. I've changed my will to make sure."

"We'll see about that. I have a good lawyer too."

"How did you kill Sarah?"

"I suffocated her. Anyway, don't you want to know what's in store for you? It's way more inventive."

"I'm sure you'll tell me either way."

"Okay, so we'll have an argument tonight. And you'll storm off in my car, because it's blocking yours. I've already parked mine where we're heading. I did it yesterday. You didn't notice it wasn't in the drive."

"So you'll make it look like a car crash."

"Not so fast. My plan's much neater. Any ideas? Think about it – really think about it. This could be more fun than the breakfast cereal game!"

"I've no idea," she says flatly.

"Okay, so if you're not playing ball, let me ask you a different question. Have you discussed Seattle with your friends? The purpose of your trip? Your suspicions. It's kind of important to me."

Rebecca hesitates, unsure how to answer.

"And I'll know if you're lying," Larry continues. "So just come out with it."

"In all honesty, I haven't, Larry. Because I was never sure about it."

"That's good. But why didn't you discuss it with them?"

"I always had doubts. And I didn't want to appear foolish."

"Doubts? What doubts?"

"The mother began talking about Sarah's murder as soon as I stepped inside the door. It felt odd. And when I went back, I found the whole family so strange I couldn't ever trust what they were saying."

Larry laughs. "It's nice to know it wasn't just me that found them weird. I suspected you might think that too. But you talked about it with Cherry, obviously, because she accompanied you, second time."

"Yes, that's true. And I rang her from here to talk more about it. She's the only one, though. And she wasn't convinced either. 'That family's as mad as a box of frogs' – those were her words."

"Nevertheless, I'll have to deal with her."

Rebecca's head is suddenly awash with images of her beautiful friend, making a cocktail in the reservation, serving her pasta in her kitchen. And then, startled, by the sudden appearance of Larry in her bedroom.

"No, you can't do anything to her. They'll catch you for sure in Seattle, because you're already known to them. You'll spend the rest of your life in prison. The best thing would be to let me go now. And we can just part. No questions asked."

Larry laughs, rocking back in his chair as if it's the funniest thing he's heard in ages.

"All right, I lied – I have discussed it with my friends here," Rebecca says. "They know all about it."

"Oh no, too late, you can't fool me with that now."

"I have. Simon, Pamela, my brother Roland–"

"You're bluffing, Rebecca."

"It's true, you can check–"

There is the sharp trill of the doorbell. Larry freezes for a moment, then looks at Rebecca. "Expecting anyone?"

CHAPTER SEVENTY-FOUR

31 DECEMBER 1980

Rebecca shakes her head. Maybe it's Simon, maybe he's had a sixth sense that something is not right. And is popping over to check she's okay! But he has his own key, so why would he ring the bell?

"I asked if you're expecting anyone!"

"I'm not, no."

Larry leaves the room, returning half a minute later. "Open wide." He places an Indian rubber ball inside Rebecca's mouth. It's sufficiently large for her to have to strain her jaws to accommodate it.

"I found it in the dresser." Larry is now tying a silk scarf over her mouth. The doorbell rings again. "My word, so impatient."

The ball is a relic from Rebecca's childhood. She used to bounce it against the wall of their home in Armley. Sometimes, the twins play with it. Now, with her mouth filling with saliva and the ball setting off her gag reflex, she wishes they'd lost the bloody thing.

Satisfied the scarf is secure, Larry goes to the front door.

From her prostrate position on the sofa, she hears Ken Tobias's jovial tones.

"Hey! I have a few people over and as luck would have it our bottle opener just broke."

"Isn't that just the way?" Larry laughs. "I'm sure we've something you guys could borrow. Wait there a moment."

Rebecca hears him rummaging in the kitchen drawer. This is an opportunity to act. She tries to call out, to make any kind of noise, but the ball and gag make it impossible. She attempts to roll towards the edge of the sofa, wondering if she can disguise her landing on the parquet floor. However, with both her hands and feet bound, moving is far from easy. She is straining her stomach muscles to get anywhere at all.

"This is a spare so there's no need to return it for a few days," Larry is saying from the door.

"Perfect. Thanks so much," Ken says. "How's Rebecca?"

"She picked up a bit of a cold. When we were out walking. Better you don't say hello."

"Shame," Ken says. "I thought you might both pop over later and meet our friends."

Rebecca is at the edge of the sofa and a final push sees her rolling over it and onto the floor with a thud. Her elbow in spasm, the momentum keeps her rolling into a small table, knocking Larry's gin and tonic glass off in the process. It smashes into tiny pieces.

"Jesus, what's she doing in there?" Ken laughs.

Larry is laughing too. "She's been showing me her old things. Boxes of stuff from her childhood."

"A trip down memory lane?"

"You got it. It sounds like she might have just dropped some ancient artefact. Anyway, I won't detain you, Ken."

By repeatedly drawing her knees into her chest, Rebecca

has changed direction and is rolling towards the door of the lounge.

"So, we won't see you later?" Ken says.

"I'm pretty sure Rebecca won't be up to it. But I might pop over if she hits the sack before me."

"Sounds good," Ken says.

Rebecca is at the threshold of the living room, desperately attempting to get through the opening by bunching her body together and straightening it. Her stomach muscles are screaming in pain.

"So maybe catch you later," Larry says.

"I hope so, buddy," Ken says. "And thanks again for the opener."

The front door closes and Larry bustles back to find Rebecca wedged in the doorway of the lounge.

"Not so fast, old friend. We haven't finished watching television yet."

He picks her up and returns her to the sofa, this time sitting her up. He unties her gag and removes the rubber ball from her mouth.

"Ken! Help!" Rebecca screams as loudly as she can. Larry slaps her face, much harder than she'd done to herself earlier when he was getting the coffees. "Once more and the ball goes back in!" he says.

He sweeps up the glass, tutting as he does so, then switches the television on again. Leonard Sachs is introducing *The Good Old Days* which Larry is delighted to learn is coming from Leeds City Varieties.

"We could have gone," he says, as if they've missed out on a great opportunity. "I love how they're all dressed like Victorians, don't you?"

Danny La Rue breezes onto the stage in a massive scarlet dress with fur trimmings. He sings 'When I Take My Morning

Promenade' and 'Oh! What a Beauty'. Larry joins in with the second song.

"The grand dame of drag," he muses, looking again at his newspaper.

Next up is comedian Duggie Brown.

"Are you having a nice time?" Duggie asks. The audience shouts "Yes!" and Larry murmurs, "We certainly are." "I'll soon put a stop to that," Duggie says.

"Oh no you won't!" Larry says.

Duggie Brown continues with a joke. "This little old spinster was all by herself on Christmas Eve."

The audience goes, "Ahhhh."

"Not Ahhhh!" Duggie says. "Shame!"

Rebecca is amazed to hear Larry shouting "Shame!" along with the audience.

"Thank you," Duggie says. "So she's sat there in her attic, by the fire with her cat." Larry chuckles expectantly. "And out of the fire jumps a spark, and the spark was a fairy, a real-life fairy. And she was surprised, this old lady."

This gets more laughter and Larry turns to Rebecca. "You have great comedians in Yorkshire. I wish we'd gone to this."

"She'd never seen a fairy before," Duggie continues. "'I'm your fairy godmother. I've brought you three wishes'. And the old lady said, 'I was about to make a cup of tea'."

"That's a good thought," Larry says. "I'll make tea in a minute."

"And the fairy said, 'What would you like for your first wish?' And the old lady said, 'Well, I wish I was younger'. And the fairy goes PING. And she was a beautiful-looking girl, twenty-two years old. And the fairy said, 'You've got two wishes left'. And the lady said, 'I wish I had more money'. And the fairy goes PING, and the place is so full of money, you couldn't budge. And she said, 'You've still got one wish left'. And the lady said, 'My cat's been with me a long time, I wish he was a handsome, strapping prince'. And the fairy goes PING, and the cat was a handsome prince. And the prince got hold of this lady, and he put his arms round her and cuddled her, and he said, 'I bet you wish you'd never taken me to the vet!'."

There is laughter, applause and cheering. Larry joins in, repeating the punchline as best he can through his laughter.

"Anyone made a New Year's resolution?" Duggie says. "I've made one. I've given up gambling, I've given up smoking, and I've given up women. It's been the longest twenty minutes of my life."

"Could we please turn this off, Larry?" Rebecca says. "Just do what you're going to do to me."

"Aren't you enjoying it?"

"It's unnecessary to make me suffer like this."

"I was thinking of heading next door," Larry says. "You could watch *The Old Grey Whistle Test* or Kenny Everett while I'm gone. What's it to be?"

"Just kill me. However you're going to do it."

"I haven't told you, have I? You'll curse yourself for not having worked it out. You're going to be the Yorkshire Ripper's latest victim! Not exactly, but that's what the world will think. I've made friends with a guy the police use. He takes photos of the crime scenes. He's shown me some – horrible! But I have inside knowledge. I'm going to take you somewhere he might lie in wait, kill you and leave your body just like one of his. It will be absolutely authentic. I won't go into the details, they're too disturbing. But the pathologist won't think twice before deciding you're number fourteen."

"Then carry on, Larry." She feels devoid of fighting spirit and just wants it over and done with.

He nods and raises the ball between his finger and thumb when she says she has one last question.

"Did you ever love me, Larry? I'm curious. Or was I always just a means to an end?"

Larry nods his head slowly. "Fair question, I don't blame you for asking it. I think I did love you. As much as I've loved anybody, that is."

And with that he replaces the ball in her mouth and ties the scarf around her face once again. He goes outside to open the boot of her car and then returns.

"Look," he smiles, lifting up one foot, "I bought new boots – his size. Too big for me, but they sometimes find his footprints – so I thought, why not?"

He makes sure that her ropes are still firmly tied, picks her up and carries her through the front door, checking each way before placing her carefully inside the boot. He leans inside and whispers, "I'll untie you when we get there. But I'll have to hit you from behind with a hammer. It's the way he operates, I'm afraid." And with that the boot comes down and she is in darkness.

CHAPTER SEVENTY-FIVE

31 DECEMBER 1980

I t is freezing cold in the boot, and yet Larry doesn't start driving straight away. Rebecca lies on her back wondering what's happening. She wriggles around but the ropes are expertly tied. Minutes tick away and she guesses he was seen by a neighbour and is rethinking his plan. She imagines him pacing up and down inside her living room, going through every possible remaining option, meticulous to the last. Twenty minutes have now gone by, half an hour maybe. Is she going to spend the whole night lying in the boot? She'll freeze to death if she does. Maybe that's his plan and the Yorkshire Ripper story was simply to put her off the scent.

She hears Larry calling, "Goodnight." And then the voice of Ken, "Happy New Year." And seconds later, the sound of her own front door closing. So he did go round to Ken and Jill's house after all. They're his alibi.

Five minutes later and again she hears footsteps and a key in the lock. The door opens and the car sags as Larry climbs into the driver's seat. He puts on some loud music, a live Beach Boys album he loves, and the revving of the engine signals the journey is finally underway. At the beginning, there are a series of turns, stops and starts. Rebecca has no idea where they're going or how long it will take, but Larry has soon joined a main road and is travelling at pace. She continues wriggling in the hope she can loosen her binding. She's shifted her position and is now lying over what she assumes is the spare wheel, as there's something digging uncomfortably into her shoulder. A sharp piece of metal perhaps? A sharp piece of metal! Manoeuvring as best she can, she tries to achieve a position where her bound wrists lie directly over it. Wedging her feet in one corner of the boot, she drags herself forwards by exerting her thigh muscles. She can feel the metal with her hands now through the protective cover. Gripping the cover with her tied hands and applying some force, she manages to get the jagged edge to pierce the material and stick proudly through it. Pulling again with her thighs, she's now in the perfect position. But can she possibly sever the rope by rubbing it against the metal? It's not the thickest, the diameter of a skipping rope possibly. If she works at it steadily and the journey is long enough, there may be hope.

They have been travelling for about ten minutes and there is no indication that Larry has turned off the main road. If only she knew which road they were on she might be able to work out where they're heading. She continues to rub at the rope. Her thigh muscles doing the heavy work are approaching a point of exhaustion.

A few more minutes of steadily chafing the rope and there's a snap, exactly what she was hoping for. The binding is severed and her hands are free. Clearly, whenever they arrive where they're headed, she needs Larry to think she's still secured. She undoes the scarf around her mouth, removes the rubber ball, then reties it.

She can roll over more easily now but what she really needs is to get under the cover she's lying on. When she bought the car, the dealer referred to the spare wheel and jack underneath, should "hubby or boyfriend" ever need to change the wheel for her. She feels along the edge of the boot and finds a line of clips that are easily released. But pulling the covering from under her is a different proposition. Positioning herself at one end of the boot, she wriggles violently, sliding the cover beneath her as she does so. It is now possible to roll the rest of the cover away. Lying on her front, she finds the wheel and explores its shape. How on earth does it come out? In its centre there's a knob which, with a little effort, can be turned. It's on a screw thread and a minute more of turning and it comes off in her hand. Leaning on her elbows, she tries to pull the wheel out of its container.

The car swerves quite dramatically, and Rebecca is rolled over as a consequence. Making her way back to the boot's centre, she realises Larry is driving more slowly. They must be approaching their destination. She pulls desperately at the wheel and this time manages to drag it up and off the pin holding it in place. Each stage of the process leaves her more exhausted, but she must continue. There may only be minutes, or even seconds, before he stops the car and opens the boot. She pushes the wheel to one side, and now finds the jack. Compact, metal and reassuringly heavy, she slides it with ease from its holder. Luckily the Beach Boys cassette is still playing, surely masking any sounds she's making. She wonders if the car just performed a U-turn. Perhaps Larry went the wrong way and she has an extra minute or two. She spends a few more moments untying her legs, and then quickly spreads the cover out across the boot and lies back leaving the rope visibly around her legs.

Larry parks the car and climbs out the driver's side. From inside, Rebecca can hear him whistling 'Do You Wanna Dance?' as he walks around to the back. He opens the boot.

"Okay. I hope the journey wasn't too uncomfortable? We're

in Studley Park by the way. Exactly the sort of spot where our friend might attack a random female."

He thinks she still has the ball in her mouth beneath the scarf, so she cannot answer.

"I'm now going to untie your arms and legs. And I'll take the scarf from your face. At this point you can of course run away. But I will pursue you. And I will be faster than you. You may prefer to just walk slowly in front of me, and I'll let you get ahead before catching up. And when I'm about three steps behind, I'll leap forwards and hit you several times with my ball-pein hammer. And that will be that. You won't feel anything afterwards. My use of the screwdriver later will be academic as far as you're concerned. So what you do next is your decision. But I'm guessing you'll want this over and done with."

He checks her one last time, lying tied and bound, her hands behind her back just as he'd left her.

"Happy New Year, by the way," Larry says, bending into the boot.

"And the same to you," Rebecca says, dealing a stunning blow with the car jack to the side of his head. He lets out a rasping, throaty groan, and sitting up she wields the jack again, this time catching him with an upwards movement to his mouth and chin. He totters visibly in front of her and she climbs quickly from the boot and onto the pavement. Somehow, he's managed to regain his equilibrium and pull the screwdriver from his pocket; he's waving it wildly, making lacerating contact with her left ear. A charge of pure electric agony forks out from her wound. Weakened and with blood flowing freely down the side of her face, Rebecca runs along the road towards the park with Larry staggering after her.

Turning, she thinks she sees the glint of the hammer in his hand. He must surely be weakened too by the blows he's received. She has no idea of the extent of his injuries, all she knows is he's gaining ground, his puffing and blowing getting increasingly louder.

She swerves into the park, darker still and more uneven than the road. She may be able to hide there, catch him unawares. There are trees and she darts behind one. She hears displaced leaves and the noise of a foot in a puddle as he tramples past her.

He stops, not far ahead. There's a click and the beam of a torch stretches in front of him. He is scanning the park ahead, searching for her. She waits, trying to contain the noise of her breathing. He's ten yards ahead at best. He's now turning in an arc – the torch held in front of him. She scrambles around the tree but he picks her out easily with the beam.

She sets off again, desperately trying to increase the distance between them. But the ground is marshy and wet and she stumbles, her weaker left ankle letting her down once again. She hears him hawking and spitting behind her, he must almost be within striking distance. And his hammer is indeed raised as she turns once again, and this time with both arms she wheels the car jack into his face with a satisfying smack. This at least has the effect of stopping him in his tracks, but more than that, he wobbles on his feet and drops the hammer as he sinks in front of her like a stricken ship, his head making squelching contact with the ground. He lies on his back gasping, the rod of light from his torch extending upwards into the sky.

She bends over and pulls the torch from his hand and surveys his battered face. Only one eye is open and it meets hers, but he is too weak now to move or speak. "Why, Larry?" she asks. His single eye continues to stare at her. She lowers the beam. The screwdriver is pointing out of his coat pocket. She withdraws it and, kneeling over him, unbuttons his coat. Then, raising her arm as high as she can, she stabs the screwdriver in and out of his chest in a frenzy.

CHAPTER SEVENTY-SIX

1-2 JANUARY 1981

Exactly on eleven, Simon opens Rebecca's front door and enters the hallway, followed by Pamela, Sally and Roland. There are beads of blood on the wooden floor and light coming from the living room. Simon motions for the others to remain where they are. He walks warily towards the living room.

Rebecca is on the sofa, motionless, the side of her head caked in dried blood. There is blood too on her shoulder and on her blouse. Simon walks towards the sofa, his eyes fixed on Rebecca, not leaving her for a millisecond.

She raises her head slightly and in a voice devoid of expression says, "I forgot you lot were coming."

"Christ, Rebecca – I thought you were dead!" He sinks to his knees and kisses her repeatedly on the forehead.

"Please – the pain is slightly more bearable if I keep my head still."

"But how long have you been here?"

"Last night some time. I collapsed when I got back."

He surveys her more closely. "Your ear is practically hanging off. Where is he? I'll kill the fucking bastard!"

"You're too late for that," Rebecca says.

Hearing voices, the others have trooped into the lounge.

"Oh my God, Becky," Pamela says, staring in disbelief.

"Fucking hell!" Sally says.

"Sally, don't you think you should clean her up?" Roland mumbles.

"I'll give it a go, but she needs to go to hospital." Sally disappears and returns a minute later with a bowl and flannel.

"You do look a right state, Becks," Simon says.

"At least I've stopped bleeding," she murmurs.

Sally bends down to start dabbing at the side of Rebecca's face.

"Wait!" Simon says. "This is a crime scene, for God's sake. Where's Larry anyway?"

"I killed him," Rebecca replies simply, as if confirming she's taken the rubbish out that morning.

"You're going to have to tell us exactly what happened," Pamela says.

Ironically, Rebecca feels slightly stronger for having eaten some of the left-over purple poke cake. They brought it to her on the sofa and she was unwilling to touch it at first, vacillating only when she saw everyone else tucking in so enthusiastically. She has responded to a barrage of questions: Where did it happen? – Studley Park; How did she get home? – She drove herself back, somehow; Why didn't she go to the police? – She couldn't face it, she just wanted to be alone; Why didn't she call an ambulance? – She was sure she was going to, she can't remember now.

"So he wanted to make it look like a Ripper killing?" Pamela says. "I hate to admit it, but that is very clever."

Sally looks at Pamela, almost imperceptibly shaking her head.

"I guess he was an evil twisted genius," Pamela continues.

"It's all very well singing his praises, but he's lying dead in a wood and we should probably do something about that," Simon says.

"What are you suggesting?" Roland asks.

Simon looks at him levelly. "I'm suggesting we need to put this matter in the hands of the police. It's already several hours since Rebecca killed him."

"But you are the police," Roland says.

"I know that, but we need to take Rebecca to a station." Rebecca winces in pain. "Or hospital, and then a police station."

"You don't want to get involved, do you?" Roland says. "That whole surveillance equipment thing was not by the books at all."

"I don't give a toss about that," Simon says.

"Oh, so your boss knew about it, did he?"

"Of course he didn't."

"Well, you're looking at the end of your career then," Roland says.

"I don't care about that. I care about doing the right thing for Rebecca."

"Guys, calm down," Sally says. "There's a dead body in Studley Park and you're arguing about Simon's career prospects."

"I don't give a fucking shit about my career prospects! But I do care about Rebecca going to prison."

"Who said anything about prison?" Rebecca says, waking up slightly. "It was self-defence."

"Of course it was," Simon agrees. "But it doesn't look great that you headed home afterwards. And then all of us sitting around eating his purple sodding poke cake instead of reporting his death. Some unsuspecting walker has probably tripped over him by now."

"But Rebecca's badly injured," Pamela says. "She hasn't been in a state to report anything."

"That's her trump card," Simon says. "And why you haven't reported this earlier, Becks, because you collapsed at home – in fact, you were unconscious for hours."

"Exactly," Pamela says. "That's what you need to say!"

"You obviously still don't know me," Rebecca says. "I'm not making anything up. In fact, you couldn't make up what I'm going to tell them."

Rebecca has spent Friday morning in hospital having surgery to her ear. She's now at the police station on Lidgett Lane, preparing for an interview about the events of New Year's Eve. She is going through everything in detail with the solicitor she has been recommended by Simon. He's perfectly pleasant, younger than her though, but his response to the end of her story is surprising.

"What I'm saying, Miss Ferguson, is when this comes to trial, it may not play well that you unbuttoned Mr Appleby's coat before stabbing him eighteen times with his screwdriver. Is it just possible you've misremembered something? Maybe his coat had become loose during the chase, for example? It might have been flapping open, temptingly perhaps, when he fell to the ground. And after all you'd been through, who'd blame you for what you did?"

"It certainly wasn't flapping open. Because the screwdriver was in the top pocket. I wouldn't have seen it otherwise. What I said to Sergeant Clarke is the truth. I stabbed Larry Appleby to death. It was a deliberate action, something I did on the spur of the moment. But it was a result of provocation, extreme provocation."

The solicitor sighs and unscrews the lid from his fountain pen. "Let's go through this once more. I'm particularly keen to understand his intention to make you look like a victim of the Ripper."

CHAPTER SEVENTY-SEVEN

4-5 JANUARY 1981

I t seems time has finally been called on the Yorkshire Ripper claiming any further victims, as on Sunday reports of his arrest begin to circulate. Debbie sees an item on television about him being caught in Sheffield with a prostitute in his car. The police became interested because the car was carrying false number plates. When Debbie hears the reporter's words, "And we understand the suspect is safely in custody", she finds herself crying uncontrollably. Later, despite it being dark, she walks to the off-licence and buys a bottle of Martini. "They've caught him," she says to the young man working in the shop. "They've caught the Yorkshire Ripper! How amazing is that?"

The man nods and rings the sale up on his till. "I heard that too," he says. "Will that be everything?"

The following morning, Debbie tells the minicab driver she will no longer be needing their services for the drop-offs and pick-ups from work. And they won't need to collect Sally either. She thinks how pleased Rebecca will be that she's cancelled the contract so promptly.

When Debbie arrives, Roland gets everyone together to make an announcement. They all think he's about to say something regarding the arrest of the Ripper, and Dave even asks if he should get some fizz and glasses, but Roland is looking shaken. He tells them Rebecca was injured over the new year and will be off work for a while. He cannot give any details, as her injury is the subject of a police enquiry. Also, he would like them to know that Rebecca is not staying at home and is uncontactable. For the time being, he will be in charge. So any business-related questions should be directed to him.

CHAPTER SEVENTY-EIGHT

5 JANUARY 1981

R ebecca is actually staying with Pamela and her friends in Chapeltown, although they've hardly seen her since she arrived late on Saturday night, having been charged with murder that morning. She is lying low in the room they cleared for her, seemingly not keen to come out.

Sandra has taken food to her a few times, and Rebecca has at least eaten some of that. But when they've invited her to join them downstairs she has declined. That Monday they consider telling her the big news, and that the culprit they've arrested is appearing in court that day. But they decide that, bearing in mind Larry's fascination with the Ripper (which Pamela explained to them), it would be insensitive. However, later that evening, Beth answers the door to Simon. He's tracked Rebecca's whereabouts through Roland. Simon introduces himself as a good friend of Rebecca and asks to see her.

"You have a guest," Beth calls from outside Rebecca's door.

"It's me," Simon adds, and enters the room.

He finds her sitting on her bed, her back against a wall. Her face is grave and she doesn't appear to be occupied. She looks up at him and smiles sadly.

"Thank you, Simon," she murmurs, without saying what she's thanking him for.

He moves towards her slowly. Puts his hand gently on her shoulder for a moment.

"At least you've been given bail, eh?"

She nods.

"I've been worried about you," he continues. "You might have told me where you were staying."

"I wanted to be somewhere quiet. And I couldn't face being at home with all Larry's things."

"I'm not surprised." He moves across to stand by the window.

"I've been asleep most of the time since I got here."

He nods. "Your friends seem nice. Good people. And you won't believe this, it *was* the guy I interviewed with Andrew Laptew. You remember, don't you? Apparently, it took him ages to crack. Eighteen hours. But I said, didn't I, there was something weird about him – well, both of them – when we went to his house? I knew it. We both did. And when I heard they'd arrested a Peter Sutcliffe, I felt this thunderbolt in my chest. I got in my car, dashed up to the police station, opened my locker door and found my notebooks. And there was his name. It was in the notebook, Becky. I'd underlined it."

Rebecca has remained silent throughout the story. She now says, "Simon, I have no idea what you're talking about."

"Sorry, I've been gabbling on like a lunatic. You do know they've arrested the Ripper, don't you?"

"I didn't," Rebecca says. "Debbie will be relieved."

"The whole country's relieved. And the top brass are delighted. Tickled pink. They're taking credit for the whole thing."

"I'm pleased for Debbie."

"Look, I'm not expecting you to be interested in this. Not

332

with everything you're dealing with. But they're not happy about that surveillance trap. I've been called to a meeting. I can take a trade union rep."

Rebecca widens her eyes and sighs. "I am interested, Simon. And I'm sorry. You'll let me know what happens, won't you?"

On his way out, Simon is offered a cup of tea by Sandra. Beth comes in and makes herself a herbal drink. The three sit at the kitchen table.

"You got him in the end," Sandra says.

"Thank God," Simon replies. "Apologies it took so long."

The two women smile politely.

Simon considers telling them about his visit to Peter Sutcliffe, and how their report not being read probably cost another three women's lives. He decides against it as he doesn't want to appear defensive. Or like he's seeking to blame others. Instead, he tells them of the strange discovery the officers made when they asked Sutcliffe to remove his clothes. "You'll never guess what he was wearing."

Again, the two women attempt to shape their expressions into something that will pass for interest, but neither speaks.

"To be honest," Simon continues, "the strip search should have happened earlier. As soon as he became a prime suspect in a murder investigation. But, from what I've heard, they messed it up. It was only much later they asked him to remove the clothes he'd been wearing since he was arrested. Apparently he was hesitant."

Simon looks up at Sandra and Beth, unsure what they're thinking.

"So he takes off his trousers and the reason for his hesitancy becomes clear. Underneath, he's wearing a V-neck sweater, his legs inside the long sleeves. With the sweater pulled up over his buttocks, and the V-neck at the front exposing his genitals. Why was he wearing that, they asked him, and Sutcliffe described them as leg warmers. However, apart from exposing his private parts, this item had reinforced padding sown into the areas where his knees would be. Well, as you can imagine, he'd have been much more comfortable when he was kneeling over his victims, and the easy access to his – you know – his privates, meant he'd have been able to masturbate as those poor women lay dying. Or after they died. And that tells us everything we ever needed to know about that sick bastard's motives and his state of mind during the attacks."

There is a long pause. Eventually Beth says, "I fear that you're overestimating our interest in this topic."

And with that Simon thanks them for the lovely tea and hurriedly disappears.

CHAPTER SEVENTY-NINE

14 APRIL 1981

It is a lovely spring day, not that you would know this in the small room that has been allocated for Rebecca to have a last-minute conference with Jeremy Tate QC, her barrister. Mr Tate, a buff man in his fifties, has asked to see Rebecca, as the prosecuting barrister has indicated a willingness to reduce the charge of murder to manslaughter, providing Rebecca pleads guilty to the lesser charge. Mr Tate's advice this morning is that she should do so. Rebecca is adamant she will do no such thing. She killed Larry in self-defence and she's certainly not pleading guilty to manslaughter, or murder for that matter. She has never heard anything so ridiculous in her life.

"In that case," Mr Tate says, "a lot is going to rest on whether we're allowed to adduce evidence that Larry killed his first wife in Seattle. And because he was never tried for that, this is an interesting point." He explains that there will likely be several hours of detailed legal submissions and arguments behind closed doors, all before the jury is sworn in.

Rebecca has been back in her own house since late January. But in the intervening time it's as if she's been living as a human camera, aware only of the sounds and images passing in front of her, and of her body as she navigates the three-dimensional world around her. Many years ago, she'd dealt with her father's funeral in the same way, filtering any feelings that might disturb her equanimity. But this time the living but not living has lasted longer. She's felt little about anything, or anyone – and to an extent that includes Simon, who she's seen regularly since he was suspended from the force and his wife instigated divorce proceedings. She's not been going into work herself either, instead existing on a day-to-day basis, doing little more than is necessary to survive.

Speaking of human cameras, she has a sense of appearing in the film of her own life as she's taken from the cells and through the myriad of passageways that lead to the courtroom in which her case will be heard. Mr Tate has told her to expect a packed gallery, including, as might have been predicted, many of the feminists who've adopted her case as a cause célèbre. Rebecca tries to imagine what it will be like walking out in front of the press, the spectators, the court officials, the lawyers, the jurors and the judge. She doesn't have long now before she finds out. And, heading towards her in the corridor is another defendant, also being led to his trial. He looks dapper in his blue suit and open-necked shirt, and, with some consternation, she realises his face is a familiar one from the newspapers. But at least she feels something as she approaches Peter Sutcliffe in the bowels of the Old Bailey, and as they pass he meets her eye and smiles urbanely, even flirtatiously, as if to say, "Fancy the two of us meeting in a place like this". Rebecca does not respond; he is already just one more moving image she records on the way to her trial.

EPILOGUE
6 SEPTEMBER 1981

Following the calamitous start to the year, Rebecca sold the Datsun 280C as it had painful associations for her. She hasn't felt like getting behind the wheel since, so Roland is driving her down to London in advance of her first term. They've been chatting about his holiday in Greece with Nicola when he suddenly changes the subject.

"You're more like your old self today," he says. "It's only just occurred to me."

"Yes, I feel so much stronger than immediately after the trial."

"And deciding to do this one-year course, that's probably been good for you too."

"I agree. The idea of becoming a lawyer, doing something completely different, has given me a fresh sense of purpose."

"While I'm stuck with Keighley Beers," Roland responds with a laugh.

"I'm really grateful you're holding the fort in my absence."

"I've often wondered why you didn't study law in the first place," Roland says, indicating to turn off the motorway. "I mean you've always been that way inclined."

"I honestly never thought about it until recently."

"Was it the trial that inspired you in the end?"

"Well, my barrister noticed how interested I was in the legal arguments. He told me that if I didn't get sent down for murder, I'd make an excellent lawyer."

"I'll bet he doesn't say that to many clients."

"I certainly hope not."

Roland is parking at the service station. He turns to Rebecca as he switches off the engine. "And I'm curious about how he assessed your chances. Was he expecting a not guilty verdict?"

"I've no idea what he was expecting. He didn't give much away at all. But I thought I'd be acquitted because there were eight women on the jury and they'd be more likely to believe that Larry intended to kill me. I got a letter from one of them afterwards saying how delighted she was by the outcome, although I suspect she was looking for a job."

The Blue Boar café has spongy seats, white tables and suspended light fittings that look like UFOs. Over coffee and BLT sandwiches, which they both agree are top-notch, Roland admits that he's been thinking a lot about their father. "It was twenty years in July since he died. I'm not sure if you clocked that anniversary with everything else that's been going on?"

"I realised on the day. I still remember that afternoon vividly, you know."

"It's more of a blur to me, but I'm not surprised that you do."

"I sometimes think the best lesson he taught us was the difference between right and wrong."

"That's why he would have approved of your career change. And he would have been so proud of you."

"Proud of me," Rebecca says. "That's nice – but proud of me for what?"

"Proud of you for everything you've achieved. Everything you've done."

"Everything?"

Roland pauses for a moment. "Yes, absolutely everything," he says.

Rebecca has been staring into her coffee, but now looks up at her brother and gives a half smile as she considers how to respond.

THE END

ALSO BY JAMES WOOLF

Indefensible

ACKNOWLEDGEMENTS

I first started writing this novel in March 2017. For a long time it was called *Three Steps Behind* and each chapter began with a document evoking the period (newspaper articles, handwritten notes, adverts, diary entries, a *Private Eye* cover, etc.). In those days Larry was called Steve, Mervyn was called Gregory and there were lengthy documentary sections about Peter Sutcliffe. A version some 14,000 words longer than the copy you are holding was submitted by a literary agent to publishers in late 2018, but didn't land at this time. I would like to thank the following people who helped me with this novel during its lengthy gestation period.

My many readers including; my partner Philippa (who also came up with the title for the book), my writing buddy Hannah Persaud who read the first outline and then commented on each chapter when it was first written; our good friend Jessica Hall for her early encouragement; members of the Law Society Writing Group who fed back on the novel including Silva Gashi, Nick Denys, Simon Bunn, Bipasa Chowdhury, Paul Wilson and Lorraine Mullings; other work colleagues Michael Lonergan and Grace Toller.

Fiona Quinton, Karen Child and June Wilson for supplying information on what it was like growing up in Yorkshire in the 1970s, and to June Wilson again for her comments on the manuscript in progress.

The Leeds Library for their efficiency and helpfulness in providing access to their microfiche collection of *Yorkshire*

Evening Posts from the relevant period. My experience in accessing these records was far more pleasant than Rebecca's in Seattle.

Alan Simkins, who advertised a collection of copies of *Beer Magazine* in December 2016 dating back to 2008. I accepted the magazines without any particular interest in the subject as I thought it could take me down an interesting avenue for my writing, which proved to be the case as I decided to make Rebecca the owner of a brewery.

Ben Davies for reading the text and providing his expertise on 1970s cars.

My brother Simon for advice on marketing and the drinks industry.

James Badenoch KC and Robert Seabrook KC for an informal last-minute discussion on the possible outcomes of the murder trial referred to in the epilogue, given the specific circumstances in Studley Park. I was reassured that assuming that the defence being run was self-defence, a simple acquittal with no attempts by the judge or prosecution to construct a manslaughter charge would have been entirely possible. A big thank you to Clark Chesis for facilitating this conversation.

And finally, to the fantastic team at Bloodhound Books, including Betsy Reavley, Shirley Khan, Tara Lyons, Hannah Deuce and Patricia Dixon.

A NOTE FROM THE PUBLISHER

Thank you for reading this book. If you enjoyed it please do consider leaving a review on Amazon to help others find it too.

We hate typos. All of our books have been rigorously edited and proofread, but sometimes mistakes do slip through. If you have spotted a typo, please do let us know and we can get it amended within hours.

info@bloodhoundbooks.com

Made in United States
North Haven, CT
02 July 2024

54316408R00209